UNDER THE POMEGRANATE TREE

LESLIE MOÏSE

PEARLSONG PRESS
NASHVILLE, TN

Pearlsong Press
P.O. Box 58065
Nashville, TN 37205
www.pearlsong.com | www.pearlsongpress.com

Trade paperback ISBN: 978-1-59719-097-8
Ebook ISBN: 978-1-59719-098-5

ALSO BY LESLIE MOÏSE
Love is the Thread: A Knitting Friendship | *Judith
Linked by the Joy of Words*

Library of Congress Cataloging-in-Publication Data

Names: Moïse, Leslie, 1960—author.
Title: Under the pomegranate tree / Leslie Moïse.
Description: Nashville, TN : Pearlsong Press, [2021] | Summary: "In the
    ancient Middle East, a sheltered young woman fleeing her rich and
    powerful father's plans for her marriage is thrust into a violent world
    in which her only tools—or weapons—are her knowledge of plants and
    healing"—Provided by publisher.
Identifiers: LCCN 2021029276 (print) | LCCN 2021029277 (ebook)
    | ISBN 9781597190978 (trade paperback) | ISBN 9781597190985
    (ebook)
Subjects: LCGFT: Novels.
Classification: LCC PS3613.O4 U53 2021 (print) | LCC PS3613.O4
    (ebook) |
    DDC 813/.6—dc23
LC record available at https://lccn.loc.gov/2021029276
LC ebook record available at https://lccn.loc.gov/2021029277

To my sister, Nancy

Author's Note

THIS WORK IN NO WAY COMMENTS on African American enslavement, or contemporary experiences of enslaved people. The novel's setting predates Islam by millennia; it is not a commentary on Middle Eastern culture, or contemporary paganism.

CHAPTER ONE

MY FATHER'S PERSONAL SLAVE, BEN, crept along the path toward me. Even though the season had yet to turn from spring to summer, sweat slicked him above the loincloth. He peered from side to side as if some beast might pounce on him here in the enclosed garden behind the stronghold. "Your father requests your presence." Ben kept to the shadows, like sunlight wasn't for the likes of him.

My father? Why? My fingers clenched on the lavender stems with their sticky juice. Father often stalked past me in the halls of the stronghold, one of the mightiest in all of Ammon, as if I were invisible. Had he seen me in the garden with Aunt Kupo earlier, while we tended the plants—a job my father would consider a slave's task? Aunt Kupo had gone inside to rest, while I remained here by myself. Had someone seen me dirtying myself—as they'd see it—and reported to father? The lavender felt like live coals in my hands.

Ben's rounded shoulders drooped. "Miss Sarai. Your father says come."

"Sarah." I corrected to the less formal version of my name. "Do you know what he wants?"

Ben bent almost double, as if intent on folding himself out of my sight. "Your lord father waits." His throat worked.

All the saliva in my mouth dried. I let the lavender fall, then wiped my palms on the embroidered skirts of my robe. Had all the moisture in my body gone to my hands? "Very well." I wiped them again, tucked the knife into my bag, and heaved the wide strap over my shoulder. I'd rather face father without any burden hanging off me, but if he wanted me right away, he wanted me right away. "Lead on." I gestured toward father's wing of the citadel, and the slave trotted off.

As we crossed the garden, already hot under the sun, my stomach shriveled like a seed inside me. I paused at the shadow cast by the sandstone stronghold to draw a deep, unsteady breath. By the time I entered the building he had scuttled so far ahead of me I might as well be unattended. As I entered the vast room where father conducted his business, Ben ducked back into the hall, face averted.

Only diffused light slanted in from outside. Eyes shut, Father sat in an elaborately carved chair made of stone from his own quarry, one of the richest providers of stone in the whole land of Ammon. I stood before him for a long time, but he never opened them. His nose looked especially hooked, his lids extra thick and heavy. *Does he even know I'm here?* Surely Ben had announced my approach. At last I scuffled my feet.

Father's eyes flew open. His brows arrowed down toward his nose. "You're here at last. You kept me waiting long enough." He hitched himself upright in the chair. It took him a couple of tries, he was so big. Not softly padded like Aunt Kupo and I were, but thick-bodied. Hard. "I've selected a husband for you, one who brings more wealth and honor to our family."

Marriage? Money? "I don't want to marry." My voice sounded as fragile as a flower petal. I took a breath, tried to firm it. After all, there was precedent in our own family. "I want to stay single, like Aunt Kupo."

"Ridiculous." Father huffed out a breath. I felt its heat on my cheek.

I couldn't help wincing. *Wealth. Honor.* My marriage only meant that for him.

Father pinned me with a glare that would have melted stone. "I have spoken. You will marry before your sixteenth birthday." He flicked a hand laden with silver rings toward the doorway. "Now be gone."

"I want to stay single, Father." I felt even shorter under his scowl, but made myself go on. "Aunt Kupo never married."

He didn't flicker an eyelash, but he seemed even bigger because of his stillness. I swallowed with difficulty, and crept back a step, like the slaves often did, before I caught myself. Would his hand whip out and clutch me by my robes, or would he leap to his feet and shake me? Strike me?

At last he banged one fist on his thigh. I nearly skittered out of my sandals. "What have your wishes to do with it? And my sister did not wed because she proved too obstinate for any man. You are biddable. You will do as I say." He flicked that hand once more. "Be grateful I have told you my plans. Now. Be gone." He stretched his legs out before him. "I will sleep through the heat of the day." Father closed his eyes as if I had already left. As if I had never been there.

My marriage. Already arranged. He didn't see the flinty set of my jaw, though my stomach squeezed into my throat. But he must've heard silence when he expected retreating footsteps.

Eyes still shut, he chopped a hand through the air. "I said be gone."

This time I didn't back away. "I have no desire for a husband." Could he even hear me?

His eyes slitted open. "I have spoken. You wish to feel my wrath?

9

I will not say 'be gone' another time." His voice gritted like sand on stone, his hands clamped on his knees as he braced to stand.

In spite of the hot room, my fingers and toes, my cheeks, went cold. How often had I heard my mother, Calominra, cry out as he beat her? The shuffle of my sandals as I retreated both relieved and shamed me. In the safety of the passage, out of father's sight, I curled in on myself even as my fists knotted.

Father thinks he can arrange my life to suit himself. Well, he could, couldn't he? Already he and some unknown man had decided the future without my knowledge or consent.

As my knees turned to fog and I sagged against the sandstone wall for support, the warm scent of horse washed around me. Uncle Achior had gone out to ride at dawn. Now he strode around the corner, glimpsed me in mid-step and smiled, then hesitated. "Sarai? What's wrong?"

How I longed to collapse against him and sob out my trouble. But wouldn't he agree with father's decision? Be pleased at my impending marriage? *My impending doom.*

"Nothing." I stiffened my knees, straightened away from the wall. But I couldn't quite steady the wobble in my chin. "Father just told me I'm to be married soon."

The delicious smell of horses, of freedom, grew stronger as my uncle folded me in his arms. "What wonderful news. No wonder you are overcome with joy."

I knew it.

"Who's the lucky man?" He stepped back.

Only my clamped teeth held back my wail. "I don't know."

"Your father didn't tell you?" When I shook my head, Uncle Achior stepped back. "Well, that's something for you to look forward to, isn't it? Now I must get out of these clothes. They're covered in horse hair." The odor of his stallion faded as he marched away to his rooms. In spite of my misery, I sniffed the air until it smelled only of the scented oils my father used on his hair. I hurried away.

SOBS GAGGED ME as I stumbled to Aunt Kupo's rooms. *I mustn't cry.* What if a member of the household saw me and reported to my father? The door to Aunt Kupo's room stood open, as always, should anyone from Uncle Achior to the lowest scullion need healing. I slammed it behind me. On her bed, Aunt Kupo snorted and propped herself up onto one elbow, blinking. "Who's there—what do you need—oh, Sarah." She frowned. "What's wrong?"

Every muscle in my body squeezed tighter. Fighting not to howl, I told her what had happened. "What can I do?"

"I'm not surprised your father has such plans. You are of marriageable age now."

"I told you years ago, I want to stay single, like you."

Her expression, always still and knowing, took on a tinge of pity. "You were a child when you said that. I shouldn't have let you believe the world works that way."

My mouth dried like desert sands. *Not Aunt Kupo too.*

She twisted her lips. "You will be able to use the skills I have given you in your own household, care for your slaves. Heal your children of their ailments—"

"No." My body felt so tight it could have bent a spear tip. "I will never marry. I want to care for everyone the way you do." And I couldn't do that with a husband wanting me to respond to his beck and call every moment of the day.

"You truly want independence?" One look at my face gave her my answer. "I see." She stretched out on her back to stare at the ceiling.

My voice wavered. "Aunt Kupo?"

"I'm thinking, Sarah. You have already seen what use it is to object."

"When my suitor comes, I could just refuse him. Isn't that what you did?"

Aunt Kupo hiked herself up in the bed. Gray hair fuzzed around her face like a plant gone to seed. "If you refuse your suitor flat out it will only make your father angrier. More determined. He'll ignore you and push the marriage through."

My belly knotted around my backbone.

Aunt Kupo's gnarled fingers curled and uncurled. "Once married, you'd be in a position to help others. Have money of your own."

"But it wouldn't be my money, would it? If mother wants anything, she has to ask my father to buy it. She wears her best robes, has the slaves carefully dress her hair. Orders father's favorite dishes for dinner. Then asks him for what she wants." *She begs like a pauper on the streets, only better dressed.*

Aunt Kupo nodded. Neither of us said that father sometimes refused mother's requests. We both had heard the shouting.

"I want money of my own."

My aunt squirmed deeper into the bedclothes. "Perhaps you can tell your father—"

"No one tells my father anything. I don't want to marry at all." The decision made so long ago seemed as much part of me as my skin or bones.

She lifted one hand. "Perhaps your betrothed won't be so bad. Perhaps he'll be young. Handsome." Aunt Kupo peered at me as if to gauge my reaction.

"What difference will that make? He'll just make more demands on me."

Her lips pursed. "True. And on your body, from what I've heard from married women." She dropped back against the pillows for a moment, then straightened. "If your father hasn't already made all the arrangements, we have time to make plans."

If.

My aunt shifted once more in the bed and clambered out. "Now, what did you do in the garden after I left…"

A FEW DAYS LATER I was in the garden, gathering plants. Not to study. After seven years of learning from Aunt Kupo, I knew everything about the herbs and trees within these walls. A rufous-tailed lark lit in the pomegranate tree nearby, fluted a snatch of song, then flew away. I stooped over a bunch of basil, my cutting knife ready in one hand.

Between the plants, I saw robes flickering toward me. I straightened away from the basil, the hand with the knife held against my thigh, out of sight. Then the person moved into the courtyard and I released my held breath. Not my father, just my cousin Tamar, sedate in her favorite saffron-colored robe. I suspected she preferred it because when she stood with strong sunlight behind her, everyone could see the shape of her body through the cloth. As a fine lady, she'd deny the idea with widened eyes. And discreetly curved lips.

Her dainty sandals came to a stop beside me. For years, Tamar had limited her conversation with me to what had to be spoken, nothing more. She passed me in the corridors of the house with only a small nod, as if all the hours we'd spent playing together and sharing secrets never existed.

Now a faint flush colored her cheekbones. Tamar actually appeared eager to speak to me. "Have you heard the news?" She didn't wait for my response, just hurried on. That at least had not changed. My cousin still spewed words so fast they tumbled out on top of each other. "No, you can't have. You'd act more excited. Guess—no, how can you? Such wonderful, exciting news. Your father has set a date for your wedding."

My lips tingled. Tamar forgot herself long enough to hop in place, skirts of her robe floating around her legs. "I can't wait to hear what foods will be served at the feast after the ritual, can you?" She gave another hop of excitement. "And what performers will entertain us."

Performers. Food. Set the date. I stiffened further. "I don't want to marry."

She laughed as if I'd said the funniest thing she ever heard. "Don't be silly. All girls marry. It's what women are made for."

As small girls I'd been the one who led, while she, the pretty one, tagged after. But now she sounded so sure, so certain she said what was right and I must obey. Not just my father, but everyone in our country. Well, all the men. The weight of her certainty squeezed the air from my chest. I planted my feet in the dirt. "Aunt Kupo never wed."

"Oh, Aunt Kupo." Tamar sniffed, a sound perilously close to a snort. "My mother said it was the shame of the family how nobody wanted to marry Kupo. But marriage is what a woman is for, to serve her husband all her days and bear him children." Her face looked dreamy, curved lips parted as if she were about to take a bite of something delicious. "My mother married at thirteen, a year younger than I am. And you're a whole year older than me."

To steady myself, I focused on the rosemary at my feet. As my cousin talked, I'd backed across the garden path. My fingers felt clammy on the smooth wooden handle of my hidden knife.

Don't argue anymore. Arguments gained me nothing, not with Tamar, certainly not with my father. My cousin believed with all her being that marriage was a woman's only possible fate. And my father knew I existed so he could dispose of me at the greatest gain to himself.

No, talk only wasted my breath. I needed another way. But what?

"**Father has set a date** for my wedding." Horror shook the words from my lips as I stumbled through the door of Aunt Kupo's room.

Aunt Kupo glanced up at me from beneath wispy eyebrows, then bent again over the roots spread to dry on her windowsill. "When?"

"I don't—don't know." Why hadn't I asked Tamar?

"Worry never saved anyone from trouble. Action does."

"What action?" Aunt Kupo had met her betrothed many times, so my mother once whispered to me, and managed to offend him. She'd behaved so badly he not only refused to marry her, but word of her obstinacy spread, so no other men bid for her hand. But from Tamar's news, I might not meet my betrothed until the day of the wedding. I couldn't imitate my aunt's behavior.

Aunt Kupo's lower lip pushed out. "If you're set on remaining single, Sarah, we must think of something. Come up with a plan."

We. My shoulders loosened. I wasn't in this alone. In spite of my father's arrangements for me.

A FEW MORNINGS LATER, when we were out in the garden gathering plants, Aunt Kupo spoke as she bent over the lemon balm. "You will have to disappear."

I straightened from the acacia I was clipping. "Disappear?"

She glanced over her shoulder as if to make sure we were unheard. "If a girl isn't here, she can't marry."

"Disappear?" *How? Where?*

Aunt Kupo shuffled a step away from me, leaning on her stick. "Maybe you'll solve that part of the puzzle on your own." She tottered a bit farther away. I frowned after her. Was it my imagination, or did she move more unsteadily than she used to? Then I seemed to hear what she had said fully.

"How can I solve a problem so big?" I couldn't turn away from her eyes, which gazed at me steadily and told me the answer. I'd think of something. I had no choice.

"They will be hunting for a girl, so you cannot look like a girl."

I pricked my finger on an acacia thorn. "What?"

"When you run away. You need to look like someone else. Disguise yourself."

"When who hunts for me?"

Her wispy eyebrows rose to her hairline. "Your father's men, Sarah. Maybe your betrothed too, depending on who he is." My aunt put both hands on my shoulders. I'd stepped closer to her without realizing it. "Your marriage means money to your father. Of course he'll try to bring you back." She grunted a little as she stooped to gather lemon balm leaves.

I glanced down at my rounded body. "But I look like a girl. How can I disguise myself as something else?"

Aunt Kupo grinned up at me. "Keep your mind open. So will I."

I **THOUGHT OF DOZENS** of disguises every time my father entertained another man. All of them were so old, with graying hair and wrinkled skin. *Surely Father wouldn't choose so decrepit a man for me?*

At first I thought of running away disguised as a servant girl. That might be a good way to conceal myself—they seemed invisible enough. But I watched them soft-footing their way around the house as I never had before, and realized none of them could walk out of the gates without causing an uproar. That furor would end in capture before they made it to the edge of my father's property. An unknown serving girl wandering through the house? Impossible.

How about a boy? I considered that less than a single heartbeat. Same problem, not to mention I'd have to wear nothing but a tattered rag that could too easily reveal my femaleness. A few years back I could have managed it, but not anymore.

Now I stood at the edge of the garden, near the boundary of the stable yard, and looked around me. Father always forbade me to visit the horses. I smelled their warm scent. Tantalizing. So close. Maybe I couldn't think of a disguise to outsmart father's plans for me, but I could visit his horses. See Uncle Achior's war charger, Desert. Did I dare?

I hitched my robe to my knees and ran. At the stable entrance, I paused to close my eyes and breathe in the compelling odor. Many elements combined to make that smell. Warm horseflesh, hay, manure.

Not dander, though. The stable workers groomed the horses every day, polished them like gold or precious jewels. Anyone whose charge developed dandruff would be beaten. Or worse.

Tiptoeing as I rarely did outside the temple, I approached the stall nearest the entrance and saw Desert, Uncle Achior's mount. The gray stallion snorted as I gazed at him through the bars. Maybe he knew I wasn't supposed to be here, though his eyes looked soft, large and kind. Interested. Maybe I smelled different from his usual companions. The slaves who cared for him probably stank of sweat as well as the usual stable odors. A female must smell different from the scents of men in leather armor, the smoke and stench of battle. And I smelled different from all of them, with the perfume of lavender, basil, rosemary and plant juice clinging to me, like they did to Aunt Kupo.

I stared at Desert's long legs and powerful haunches. If only I could swing up onto that muscular body and canter away from my father's house, away from my unseen, unknown bridegroom, more swiftly than I could ever move by myself. I crept to the stall beyond Desert's. My father's favorite steed, another gray stallion, named Singer. He stood with his haunches turned toward me. His long tail, more silver than Desert's black-streaked one, lazily switched at flies. And I knew how I'd disguise myself.

I grinned as I thought of my flawed plans to try to emulate a slave. But this idea—if I could manage it—wouldn't raise any difficulties. I'd be invisible to most people. Aunt Kupo herself had shown me that.

I skipped in place, then looked at Singer's head, his ears pinned back, his velvety lips crinkled to bare his teeth. He lashed out to kick the wall, and I winced and drew a shaky breath.

First I needed to find the courage to approach Singer. And that was only step one.

CHAPTER TWO

EARS FLAT TO HIS HEAD, Singer lunged at me as I sidled up to his stall. I dodged back, as frightened as a sacrifice chosen for Bael, even though the door stood solidly between us. When Singer snorted and turned his back, I straightened, trembling. After a moment's thought, I went to the garden for some apples. When I returned and offered one, Singer faced me again, ears flickering.

Would he lunge at me again? He snorted, softer this time. He took a cautious step toward me, and then another. His muzzle hovered over the fruit.

"No one's ever given you apples before, have they, boy?" My father had never given me a soft moment. Why would he give one to a horse, even his favorite?

Singer's ears quivered at my lowered voice. His eyes looked bigger, softer. Curious. He blew a great puff of breath that feathered over my face.

ON MY NEXT VISIT to the stables, Singer nickered as soon as I set foot inside. One hoof banged against his door. Eager for apples. As he took the last bite, ears pricked, I dared to pat his neck.

He sighed, turned his back. With longing, I admired his flowing, smooth tail. It was just what I wanted, but…I focused on his powerful hind legs and flinty hooves.

"You're a faithful visitor." A light male voice spoke behind me. I wheeled as an old man, bent-backed and knobby at the joints, paced out of the shadows. He wore simple garments, fabric knotted around his lower body. "What do you here, miss?"

Someone has watched me. Has he told Father? "I love horses."

"I am Nahash, who feeds and cares for my master's horses." He kept his eyes low, but a corner of his mouth tugged up. "I love horses, too."

He's named for one of the most violent kings ever to rule Ammon? Had his mother called him that, or had my father given him the name as a sour joke?

Nahash shook his grizzled head. "You're not supposed to give a horse treats."

I'm not supposed to be here at all. He knows what I'm doing. Perhaps Nahash was well named after all. Here in the stable, I stood in his kingdom.

"You'll train him to nip." He sounded so calm. Not accusing me, just telling me. A faint smile still played about his mouth.

"But—" If I didn't feed Singer apples, how could I ever sneak into his stall? "My visits to the stable please me so much. If Father learns I come here, he'll make me stop."

Nahash lowered his eyes again.

Will he make me leave to save himself a beating if Father finds out? "I want something to remember Singer by."

He frowned and glanced around the spotless aisle. "I don't understand. You want some hay—"

"No, I want some of his mane and tail hairs, but I'm afraid he'll kick me."

His long body tipped toward me. "You have good cause to be afraid. Shall I get the hairs for you? It won't take a moment."

Nahash looped a jumble of straps and rope over one bare shoulder and entered Singer's stall without hesitation. So fearless. Expertly he dropped the jumble over the stallion's head. They sorted themselves into order behind Singer's ears, around his nose, on either side of his face.

I hitched myself onto the door to watch as he tied Singer to a sturdy post. He stroked the stallion's silky gray shoulder. "Nahash, I want a thick bunch of hair." I indicated how much I meant with both hands.

Nahash studied me a moment, then nodded, and made his way along the stallion's body to his tail. He kept one palm on Singer's haunches.

"Why do you touch Singer all the time? Won't he bite or kick you?"

The groom chuckled. "Not at all. Because I'm touching him, Singer knows where I am and won't be surprised when I pull the hairs from his tail."

"Pull the hairs?" I'd pictured him cutting them.

Nahash gathered the long hairs in one hand, then combed through them with the other.

Singer's head drooped, ears lax, as if he enjoyed the sensation. Some hairs came out with the stable man's fingers, but the stallion knew nothing about it. And the method left no short, sticking-out hairs as a knife would have done. By the time he finished grooming the stallion's tail, Nahash had collected more hair than I'd thought possible. Not enough, but a start.

I grinned at him as he worked his way back to Singer's head in the same way, stroking the stallion's side at all times. "I could never have gotten so much."

He flicked a glance at me. "Indeed not."

It would never have occurred to me to tie the stallion up, to touch him. "Thank you."

I FOUGHT NOT to race back to the house. I'd pictured creeping into the stallion's stall and his hooves hammering me into a limp, bloody lump. Now, thanks to Nahash, I remained uninjured, and had a start on my disguise.

Aunt Kupo stooped over some rosemary with a knife in her hand, ready to cut off a few slips. I ran across to her. Quickly I told her my idea, and how Nahash had helped me. Then I showed her the bunch of hair.

"Your Father will hear of it by sundown." Her lips pursed. "So much for your secret."

"Nahash fears my father as much as I do."

"Hmmm. True." She tucked her stubby knife into the pouch she wore at her wide hips, then nodded. "You did well not to tell Nahash why you want the horse hair. A high born woman would never explain."

My brows pulled together. *But I did give him an explanation.*

"It comes in handy at times. Just give an order, and a slave must obey. No one wonders what you're up to if you're authoritative." She straightened, winced, and pressed a hand to the small of her back, the rosemary poking between her fingers.

THE NEXT DAY, though I lingered as long as I dared, too many slaves criss-crossed the space between house and stables for me to risk visiting again. At last I returned to the coolness of my room, where I twitched onto my bed. I didn't know any words bad enough to express my feelings. *Curse it. Curse it.*

But the following day I found my path clear and raced into the stable. Nahash's bent figure swept the aisle clear of dust.

I stumbled. "Oh. Good day to you, Nahash."

His eyes widened. "Good day to you, my lady Sarai." He shifted a bit, then stood a little taller. I nearly had to bend backward to keep my eyes on his face.

I wiggled my shoulders, and turned back to Singer. The stallion leaned so hard against his stall door the wood creaked. I stroked my palm under his heavy fall of mane, ready to dodge if necessary.

How could I do as Aunt Kupo said and give an order to Nahash? I took a deep breath. "I want more horse hair." My statement sounded too loud. What reason could I give? "I'm making a braid of Singer's hair as a keepsake, and don't have enough. Will you help me?"

Nahash didn't change expression by so much as the flicker of an eyelid. "Nothing easier, miss. I can collect the hairs every time I brush him." Then he frowned. "Would you like hair from the other horses as well?"

I almost laughed aloud. "No, just—" Wait a moment. Uncle Achior's stallion was gray, too. "All gray hair will look prettier than a mix. Could you get some from Desert?"

Nahash's eyes crinkled. "As you will it."

This time I couldn't bring myself to watch as Nahash gathered what I needed. I swiveled to stare out into the sunlight. I'd remember Nahash with gratitude every time I touched the hairs.

A FEW DAYS LATER I stood in the garden under a pomegranate tree, resting after I gathered some roots. I wiped my forehead—digging roots was sweaty work—when Nahash approached the invisible line between stable and courtyard. I waved him toward me. He shook his head.

Of course. My father would never allow anyone not of his family to entered the courtyard, unless he sent them on an errand. I crossed to him instead.

When I was within a pace or so, he held out both hands. In them was a bunch of horse hair as big around as the pomegranate's trunk. "Here you are, Miss Sarai."

I clamped my mouth to hold in my squeal. So much horse hair, more hair than I'd dared imagine. I tipped back my head to see Nahash's face. "How did you get so much?"

"I combed Singer's mane and tail every day since you last came to the stable." He lowered his voice even more. "I hid the hair in my rolled-up sleeping mat."

From the way he kept his gaze off my face, he knew as well as I did Father's reaction if he caught Nahash essentially stealing—even horse hair—from his master.

"I never imagined you'd gather so much. Thank you." My hands shook as I reached out for the hair. The knowledge that I'd stolen from my father, that he had provided the idea for and means of my escape, thrilled me to my core. It took all my will not to run from the stables, my treasure stuffed down the front of my robes. The horse hair prickled. When I reached my own room, I slammed the door behind me and took out the treasure to gloat.

Hair. Beautiful, long gray hair.

"Why did you bring that wad of filthy hair to your room?"

I reared back to find my cousin Tamar sitting on my bed. "What're you doing here?"

Her lips moved into a pout. "To bring you the good news. I heard two of the slave women talking about the fine dinner your father ordered for tomorrow night."

"So?"

Tamar bounced off the bed, pink robes eddying. "Your bridegroom comes to meet you for the first time tomorrow. You'll get to see him for the first time." She closed her eyes and hugged herself. "You'll get to speak to him, hear his voice—"

The pulse hammered in my fingertips. While she had her eyes shut I dropped the horse hair on the floor and kicked it under my bed. "Oh."

"That's all you have to say?" My cousin stared at me. "You're about to experience one of the biggest moments in a woman's life."

"I'm just—stunned at the news." Truth.

Tamar sank back onto my bed to study me. "You don't even seem excited."

When I'd dashed into the room with my bundle of horse hair, excitement had sizzled in every fiber of my body. Could I imitate that feeling now? I tried to hop in place, but my feet felt like blocks of stone from Father's quarry.

My cousin looked me up and down, her dainty nose wrinkled. "You acted happier about your filthy bundle of hair." She peered around the room. "What're you going to do with it, anyway?"

The tale I'd told Nahash rolled off my tongue. "Make a decoration."

"Why?" Her nose screwed up even more.

"I love horses." Also true, though my cousin knew nothing of my fascination. Quick, I needed a reason she might believe. "Uncle Achior loves Desert. If my betrothed also loves horses, I thought he'd appreciate it."

The lie sounded flat in my ears, but Tamar nodded. "How thoughtful." She stood. "I hope he adores horses, then. Foul, smelly creatures. Though I suppose they're of some use for soldiers and so on." The last words drifted back to me as she trailed away down the hall.

I collapsed on my bed, trembling. *Tomorrow. Tomorrow night.* Tomorrow my—I could barely stand to think the word—bridegroom and I would meet face to face.

I dropped to the floor and retrieved my precious horse hair. How to create what I wanted with it? I did something I'd never done before, took up my hand mirror and held it before my face as I tried to arrange the horse hair.

Sunlight glared in the sky by the time I tossed the mirror and horse hair aside. I bit back a scream. No matter how I wrapped the hair, my own dark hair peeped through. The gray hair looked like horse hair wound around my head.

Tomorrow night. Tomorrow night. No matter how I tried not to think about it, to focus on my problem with the horsehair, the dinner with my betrothed crowded my mind. I drew back one foot to kick the nearest heap of fabric for my bridal clothes, and stooped to finger some plain stuff, suitable for a wife overseeing the cleaning of floors, perhaps. Yes.

It took me quite a while to find my needle and some dark thread, longer still for me to stitch a piece of the material so it fitted my skull like a cap. For the first time in my life, I blessed my mother's insistence that I learn to sew as I stitched the thick coil of long gray hairs in place.

There. At last, I tucked my own hair under the cap, studied my reflection in the polished copper mirror. The wig didn't look quite natural. I finger combed it so it framed my face. No, not quite right either. As if they had a will of their own, my fingers parted the hair into three sections and braided it as I used to braid Tamar's hair, long ago when we were children. Then I wound the braid into a coronet around my head and considered it. "Yes."

CHAPTER THREE

HALFWAY OUT THE DOOR TO MY ROOM, the wig shifted. With a gasp, I dodged back and shut the door, knees wobbly. In my eagerness to show Aunt Kupo my creation, I'd nearly ruined everything. What if someone had seen me with the wig?

With unsteady hands, I tugged it off. Maybe stitching the braids into place would stop my hands trembling before I went to my aunt—But the bone needle kept slipping out of my grasp. Finally I hid the wig under my bed, then hurried to Aunt Kupo's room.

My secret bubbled out as soon as I saw her. "The first part of my disguise is ready."

"What?" Aunt Kupo's shoulders rose to her ears as I described my wig. She leaned closer. "Well done, Sarah. But it might be a good idea to have two disguises. That way you can wear a different one each day, to make it more difficult for pursuers to track you."

My stomach wrapped around my spine. In the thrill of gaining the horse hair and creating the wig, I'd forgotten why I needed them. Soon, I'd be leaving Aunt Kupo forever. And someone would follow me. Track me. Try to force me back to my father's control.

When I stood up, the floor seemed unsubstantial. I wobbled to face the door, and Aunt Kupo scrambled off her bed to grasp my hand.

"Don't you want to hear my idea for a disguise?"

My lips felt stiff. "Later, Aunt Kupo." I tottered back to my room.

AFTER BREAKFAST NEXT DAY, I returned to my room to continue work on my disguise. Just as I poked my needle into the cloth, my door swung open. *Curse it.* With difficulty, I made myself keep still. No one would guess why I wanted this robe.

Two women crept through the door and bobbed to me. The elder of the two elbowed the girl at her side. The girl reddened. "Your father sent us to you, Miss Sarai."

"Why?" My hands curled into the cloth nested in my lap, and the needle stabbed my finger. Yelping, I sucked the wound.

The older woman, dark hair streaked with gray, stepped into the room. "To cleanse and perfume you, dress your hair, and dress you. You must honor this house when you meet your bridegroom tonight." With a small sound of distress, she took my disguise from me and examined my pricked finger.

"But—none of my robes—that is to say—I haven't finished my new robes."

The girl giggled. "Don't worry, Miss Sarai, your father had us make the robe for tonight."

Oh. "Where is it?"

The older woman clucked. "Worry not, you'll see it soon enough. We've too much to do first."

"Too much to do?" Dinner wouldn't happen until sunset.

The girl dimpled at me. "You'll see." In spite of her ragged robes and work-roughened hands, she sounded as merry as Tamar.

The older woman edged back a step. "Stand up, Miss Sarai, and put down your sewing. You'll not have time to touch it again today."

SUNSET'S ORANGE RAYS slanted through the windows as I advanced down the passage to the dining room. My jeweled sandals weighed me down. Already the space between my big toes and their neighbors ached from the thin straps, and I'd only worn them from the moment before I left my room. The two women had bathed me and washed my hair. Rubbed perfumed oils into my skin and scalp. Brushed and brushed and brushed my drying hair until I wanted to scream that if they kept this up, I'd be bald.

At last they'd produced a robe crusted with jeweled embroidery. Not even my mother Calominra had such an elaborate gown. The thing was so stiff, for the first time in my life I was glad I had someone to help me dress. Unlike my usual simple robes, I couldn't have wrestled into this thing on my own.

Now I paused at the entrance to the dining room. The jeweled collar at my throat choked me. Earrings the size of my thumb dragged at my lobes.

Father sat at the head of the long table, lamb and roast fowl and vegetables heaped on the golden plate before him. My mother, Calominra, perched on the chair to his left, and a man with thinning gray hair hunched in the chair opposite her. Where was my potential bridegroom? Ah—this man must be his father, come to negotiate for him.

As I hesitated on the threshold, my father turned his head. Scowled. "At last. Here's my daughter, Sarai. Sarai, your betrothed, Hasheem." Father helped himself to more lamb.

That old man, my betrothed?

Candlelight sparkled on the jewels at my mother's throat, wrists and fingers as she leaned toward my ancient bridegroom. He looked old enough to be Aunt Kupo's father. I stayed in the doorway as if my feet had sprouted roots and grown deep into the floor.

Wrinkles seamed his face under skin blotched with age. His hands appeared stringy as they lifted meat to his mouth. Candlelight flickered in his dark eyes as he stared at me. "So this is Sarai."

"Indeed." My father bit off the word, and waved one hand at the chair beside the old man. "Come in, daughter, that your betrothed might see you better."

Aha. This supper was so the old man could decide if I looked young and juicy enough to suit him. What was his name? Hasheem? The idea of myself wed to this ancient creature sent my stomach into my throat.

Hasheem's mouth crimped as I scuffed into, the room, my feet pinched by my jeweled shoes. "She's not as handsome as my first three wives. But her hips are better suited for producing sons."

Father took another bite. "Yes, she's sturdy."

He might as well be speaking of a horse for sale. *No, some creature of less value than a horse.*

Father snapped his fingers. "Be seated, daughter."

As I hitched myself into the chair at Hasheem's side, I choked on a shout. *So you don't think I'm as handsome as your earlier wives? But you'll condescend to marry me for the sons I might give you.* I clamped my lips so the words wouldn't escape. What would my father do if I spoke like that to a man? The memory of my mother's screams as he beat her gave me all answer I needed. I could easily rid myself of Hasheem with a few unmaidenly remarks. But my wails of agony and the meaty sound of Father's fist on my body would follow Hasheem as he slammed out of the citadel.

"More lamb?" Father didn't offer the platter himself, of course. A girl, better dressed than her usual tattered rags, scurried to hold it out to Hasheem before my father stopped speaking.

What to do, what to do? Show myself awkward? Spill food on myself? On the floor? The meal dragged on as I fought to think of a failure of manners bad enough for the old man to reject me, but innocent enough father wouldn't punish me for it.

No use. If I lost this chance for his prestige and honor, he'd punish me.

Then I realized the dish before me held rice pudding. Dessert. The endless meal was nearly at an end, and I hadn't found a safe way to disgrace myself.

Hasheem shook his head. "It looks delicious, but I never touch sweets before bedtime. My thanks for sharing such a fine meal with me." Partway to the door, he paused. "Good evening, Sarai."

He left without even glancing at me, taking away any chance I had of getting him to end our betrothal.

I CREPT ALONG the passage toward Aunt Kupo's room, eyes stretched wide to see as much as I could in the dark. My robes whispered against my legs, my bare feet making no sound on the stone. Edging to my aunt's door, I tapped it with my fingernails. No one would hear such a small sound so late at night, but I couldn't risk Father—not after I'd pleaded a headache and left the dining room.

Feet shuffled closer on the other side of the door, and it opened a tiny bit. "Who's there? Who disturbs me so late at night—Sarah." The door swung wide. Aunt Kupo caught my sleeve and dragged me inside. "Well?"

"He's old enough to be your father. His family builds temples."

Her wrinkled hand found mine, drew me deeper into her room. "A suitable son-in-law for a quarry owner."

"Yes." The single syllable almost choked me.

"How sad my brother won't gain such a valuable ally."

A wild laugh rose in me. I clapped my hands over my mouth.

She hugged me close. "You must leave soon."

"As soon as my disguise is ready. I haven't even started sewing a suitable robe." I leaned my head on her shoulder.

"No time for that. You can wear an old robe of mine, one I keep for working with plants." She tilted my chin up to smile into my eyes. "Yes?"

"Yes." I sobbed out the word as my head sank to her shoulder.

Chapter Four

BEFORE THE SUN ROSE THE NEXT MORNING, I crept back to her room. "Aunt Kupo?" I whispered her name five times before she stirred.

"Wha—what're you—" She yawned hugely. "—doing here?"

I want to be with you, gathering plants together. While I can. Why couldn't I think of a thing in season? "Let's work in the garden together."

Aunt Kupo thrust her legs out of the covers. "You go ahead. I'll meet you in a moment."

Out in the fresh, soft air, I found a basil plant close to the walkway. It could stand trimming. As I stooped over it Aunt Kupo joined me, and rested one hand over mine on the handle of the knife.

Together we trimmed leaves from the basil. As the sun rose we moved away from each other, busy over the plants. With sunlight flooding the courtyard from one wall to the next, I called to her where she stooped over a clump of lavender. "Aunt Kupo, do you—"

My father stomped into the courtyard. "What's all this noise?

Can't a man sleep peacefully in his own house?"

My mouth stayed open, but no sound came out. My bowels froze.

He looked me up and down, mouth crimped. "What do you here at this hour?"

"We're—" *Working together.* No, he wouldn't like that answer at all.

"Silence. Go to your room, and stay there like a proper maiden until I call you." He swiveled, sandals grating like a knife on rough wood. "You." He chopped with the blade of one hand, glaring at Aunt Kupo. "I told you never to distract Sarai with your nonsense. I told you years ago not to do this. She will be a wife and mother, as is a woman's lot. A normal woman. She will have no time to waste on leaves and roots and such. Grubbing in the dirt."

Hopeless to protest. I protested anyway. "Aunt Kupo makes medicines that keep your household well. I'll do the same when I have a household of my own—"

He whipped toward me, robes flaring. "Silence." Then he took a hard step toward Aunt Kupo. "You will leave my daughter alone." He shoved her with both hands.

My aunt fell on the stony path.

"Aunt Kupo—" I rushed to help her as her cane rattled to the ground.

Father brushed me aside, stumbled over the fallen walking stick. With a grunt, he snatched it up and struck Aunt Kupo across the back of her legs. Her mouth bunched, every year of her life on her face.

"Father, no—" I lurched forward. As if I could stop him. As if anyone could.

He shifted the stick and smashed the knobbed end of the cane against her legs, her body, the arms she folded over her head. Her wails tore through me.

"Stop. Stop." It came out in a strangled whisper. If I made too much sound, he'd turn on me. Back flattened against a pomegranate, I flinched at every thud of wood on Aunt Kupo's curled body.

Who would help us? Not my mother, who'd probably not even glance up from her jewels at the sound of someone in pain. For the first time, I felt the softness of my body. I knew my vulnerability, the vulnerability of anyone who wasn't tall, muscular. A man. Even Nahash would be better able to defend himself, and he was a slave.

Aunt Kupo's screams faded into mews. She shrank against the earth, as if that might save her. While she wept, Father stood over her a long moment, then let the cane fall as if he couldn't be bothered to hold it any longer. "Our father should've beaten you when you were young. Every day, until you learned obedience." He swung on one heel and stomped away.

I crouched against the pomegranate. Leaves caught my hair. It took all my will to step out into the open. I ran the last few steps, as if that might make up for my hiding earlier.

Aunt Kupo rolled toward me with a groan and peered up into my face. Tears smudged her dusty cheeks. "Help—me—up—cannot—stand. By—myself."

As gently as possible, I eased her to her feet. When she stood more or less upright, my shoulder propped under her arm, I edged toward the passage to her room. Every moment I glanced the way Father had gone to make sure he wasn't coming back.

We tottered as fast as we could. *Faster. Faster.* Before he swooped down on us and hurt her worse. Hurt me. At last we reached the shelter of her room and my aunt collapsed on the bed. Trembling, she dragged the bedclothes over herself. She grimaced toward the door. "Best—close that."

The only latch was on the outside. I pivoted to search the room for something to prop against the panel to keep it shut.

Aunt Kupo crooked a finger at me. "Don't. Bother. Nothing in here. Could stop. Him. Only make him. Angrier." She snuggled under the blankets. "Ginger tea."

I nodded. "That should ease the pain." *Some of it.*

She spoke as if her aches came from ordinary causes. I turned hot all over. Father had beaten her for her knowledge. For loving me.

Silently I fetched what was needed from her trunk. I nested a small pot of water in the corner brazier to heat. When it hissed and bubbled, I poured it into the cup of shredded ginger and supported her while she sipped.

"I'll leave tonight," I whispered, even as I glanced at the closed door.

Aunt Kupo peered at me over the steaming cup. One of her hands fumbled out of the bedclothes to cover mine. "That would be best."

This is our goodbye. "Aunt Kupo—" *Will I ever see her again?*

She let go of my hand, reached into the breast of her robes. "You'll need this." She dropped coins into my palm.

"But you use this to buy herbs that don't grow in Father's garden—"

She hugged me close. "Daughter of my heart, I'd rather know you're safe." Shaking, she eased back. "Good luck to you." We embraced.

Tears choked me so I couldn't even say goodbye. As if letting go tore the skin from my arms, I released her and stepped back. Silently, we looked into each other's eyes. At last she nodded toward the door. I stumbled out, bumping the jamb as I went.

SWEAT POOLED beneath my breasts. My jaw felt mortared together as I eased out of my room. If only I had a sack to hide my disguise in—maybe I'd find a sack tomorrow.

Where would I be tomorrow? On a shuddering breath, I sneaked along the passage. These walls had trapped me my whole life, just like the sacrificial pigeons trapped in crates at the temple. *No matter what the future brings, I'll never be Father's sacrifice.* I edged around the stone table and its two stone chairs. Why risk stubbing my toes, or knocking off the bowl of flowers my mother ordered kept there?

As I crept past the table, a female voice whispered out of the shadows. "Miss?"

Leah, one of my mother's personal slaves, stood just across the passage from me. My body felt like I'd swallowed a candle. "I couldn't sleep, thought I'd walk a bit." *Stop talking, stop talking, stop talking.*

"Very good, miss." But Leah glanced at the bundle in my arms before she lowered her eyes.

It took all my strength to resist the urge to shift the things behind my back. "You may go." I waved my free hand down the corridor, and nearly spoiled the effect by grinning. *I sound like my father.*

She padded away. Her footfalls faded. It took a long time for me to edge toward the front door. When I tried to ease it open, the panel didn't budge.

I'd made a disguise—planned my escape—and couldn't get out of the house? I spun in place. *Where's the key?* On the table? On the floor under my feet? I knew what it looked like, a bulky wooden key my father used to unlock the door every morning—oh.

Trapped. I'm trapped. I glanced over my shoulder. Would the girl come back? What if she woke my father, told him I was wandering the corridors?

Down the hall to the courtyard. No gates led from the courtyard to the street—if only they did. But the night air might give me an idea. I scurried under the pomegranate tree where Aunt Kupo had first taught me about plants. My eyes traced the pattern of branches against the moonlit sky, and I clutched my bundle close.

When I was four, the big leaves had caught the sun, so shiny and bright over my head. Longing to touch them, I'd tried to climb the tree. Soon the bark chafed my legs and hands. Weeping by the tree's roots, I'd allowed Tamar to lure me into a game of ball.

Now I crossed to an orange tree close to the garden wall. *I'm not four anymore. I have to do it, so I will.* Disguise stuffed down the front of my robe, I hoisted myself onto a low branch. It swayed under my weight. Leaves rustled as I scrambled for the next highest branch, and the next. Panting, I finally reached a place level with the top of the wall. *Stretch—*

Branches crackled against stone as I hoisted myself over the coping. Would Father hear? Send a slave to investigate, or come rushing out himself? The rough surface scraped my knees. I couldn't see the street—how far down was it? What if someone saw me perched here? I swung to the outer side of the wall and nearly fell. Imagining myself huddled into my robes in the street at dawn, bones broken, I clung to the stones with hands, knees, fingernails, will, then dropped to the rock-hard ground outside Father's garden. *Not so far down after all—*

Disguise a mass of hot cloth and hair against my sweaty chest, I half-expected a shout to rise behind me, for footsteps to thunder in pursuit. Which way should I go? My legs ached to stretch into a run, to tear down the street and leave Father and his plans for me far behind. But if I ran, someone might hear me. See me. Force me back. I kept to house shadows while I hunted for somewhere to change into my disguise.

An alley? I'd never disrobed except in my own room with the door safely shut. The slant of deeper shadow near the corner of the temple? Moloch or the god's priests might see me. At last I reached the marketplace, so different from daytime. Silent. Deserted. The night breeze felt cool, and I shivered at the thought of it on my bare skin. Better don my disguise over my own robes, at least until daylight.

In an empty booth, I squirmed into my disguise. The cloth bunched over my hips and belly, and I had to jerk on the fabric to get it all the way down. Never mind. I'd change to just one layer when it grew warmer. *Where would that be? When?* I tried not to wonder as I pulled on my homemade wig.

Wind whisked across the market. Thankful for the extra layer of cloth between me and the night air, and the horse hair on my scalp, I hesitated in the false shelter the booth gave me. Which way to go? On a deep breath, I ducked out of the booth and just started walking.

Aunt Kupo's favorite merchant in the marketplace came from a distant land. He only showed up in the market once a year. When I'd asked my aunt why, she explained that he had far to travel. "He follows the silk road," she had said.

Now I murmured, "The silk road." There were places far from my father. And there must be settlements closer than wherever the merchant hailed from. Oh, why hadn't I planned where to go? Asked Aunt Kupo for suggestions?

Here at the edge of the only town I'd ever known, I looked at the rough sand in front of my toes. Horses and mules had left a rippled track through the grit, a way I could follow. Long into the night, I trudged along. As the moon sank toward the horizon, I kept glancing over one shoulder. If I stayed on the road, my father's men would find me, but I didn't dare risk getting lost by leaving it. What to do?

Sand sifted over my sandals and rubbed blisters on my feet. I told myself the blisters would be far worse if, like Tamar, I had spent my life indoors. All my years barefoot in the garden while I learned about plants from Aunt Kupo had toughened me. That's what I told myself. But by dawn, I wept with pain. In my imagination I heard the thunder of horses behind me, and the shouts of Father's men.

CHAPTER FIVE

I PUSHED ON UNTIL I THOUGHT I'D BURST. Sweat curdled my double layer of robes, but I didn't dare peel off my disguise, even though no one could see me in the dark. My tongue felt thick and dry. Why hadn't I brought a jug of water with me?

The landscape grayed with dawn and the world regained color and shape. On the horizon before me spread the outlines of a village. Tears trickled down my cheeks. I hobbled on as fast as I could. At the border of the settlement's single street I stopped to toe off my sandals and let the sand stream out of them. Wincing, I shoved my feet back into the shoes, and hobbled to the well at the village center. There, I scooped water in my shaking hands. Drops spattered my robe, but it tasted so fresh when I got it to my mouth. I dunked my fingers below the surface again, wiggling them in the coolness.

As I bent over the well, a woman behind me scolded. "What do you think you're doing? Stop at once. People drink that water."

I jerked around. Father wouldn't send a woman after me, would he? No, I'd never seen her before, broad-faced in plain robes, behind the boards of the first stall in the tiny marketplace. A merchant.

She eyed my robes. "Miss." Her brows rose as she studied my wig. "I didn't think our market drew people from far away."

"Miss." My disguise didn't fool her?

She glanced over my shoulder. "Where are your attendants?"

"I'm—by myself at present." I limped across to her stall. My belly rumbled. Jars of honey. Heaps of olives. Last winter's harvest, from the look of them, but saliva threatened to spill down my chin.

Next she tugged forward a hip-high vessel of chickpeas. What a meal such ingredients would make—My empty belly wrapped around my backbone. I knew nothing about cooking, aside from the preparation of herbs.

She slanted a look at me. "It's all right to touch, dear. My goods are the best in the village. The cheapest, too."

The cheapest? In spite of the warming air, a chill spread through me. How long would the coins Aunt Kupo had given me last? How much would they buy?

"I'll—I'll come back after I see what else the market has to offer." Aunt Kupo had always sought out the freshest and best. It would give me a chance to count my coins, figure how far they'd last.

As I shuffled away, the vendor called after me. "You won't find better anywhere, I promise you that."

Her olives had looked as if she'd polished them all night. I cradled my aching stomach with both hands. "Back in a moment." I retreated to a shaded alleyway to pry off my disguise.

Aunt Kupo's robe, once so neat, was sand-stained and filthy. Horse hair wisped from the braid. Once I'd squirmed free of the robe and removed the wig, I bent to dig out the coins.

From behind me, something scratchy and dark stifled my head. I clawed—it felt like sacking. I screamed, and a fist cuffed the side of my head.

"Be silent." A man shoved me deeper into the alleyway. I stumbled, and he kneed the small of my back. "Move."

He forced me along so swiftly I stumbled again and again. Soon the dirt beneath my feet gave way to the hot hiss of sand. My toes curled, but grit poured over the sandals and scraped my blisters as my abductor dragged me along.

At last we stopped, but when I drew breath to shriek once more, he hit me again. "I told you, keep silent."

"Not that anyone will hear her," said a man with a deeper voice.

My throat turned as sandy as my surroundings. "What do you want of me?" I remembered how Father talked of thieves. "I haven't much money."

Neither man answered. The fabric bunched over my face tightened as they fastened a rope around my neck.

"I'm choking."

From close behind me, another man laughed.

"Remove this at once." I tried to sound like my mother again. If they were Father's men, already come to capture me, perhaps I could intimidate them—

"No." This speaker could give my father lessons in shouting. "If we take it off, you'll see where we go."

Someone shoved me and I fell, knees skidding on sand. I tried to rub them, but someone jerked me to my feet by one shoulder.

"None of that. Move." He prodded me forward. I smelled damp horse hide and heard the thump of hooves. A horse's breath puffed across me.

"What do you want?" I had to cough to clear my throat.

"You'll learn soon enough." A meaty hand slapped my hindquarters.

"She has much to learn."

"And we're her teachers."

CHAPTER SIX

MY STOMACH SEIZED UP WITH COLD. These men didn't come from my father. They would have been too in awe of him to touch me, let alone slap my—body.

Flickers of light reached me through the sack.

How many men surrounded me?

"Where'd you find this one?" The question sounded matter-of-fact, as if I were no more than a chunk of flatbread fetched from the market.

"She made it easy. Went down an alley, so there was no risk of my being seen."

I'd left my disguise in that alley. Would anyone notice it? Notice I'd gone missing? Then my belly sealed tighter. It didn't matter if someone found the wig and robe. No one knew they belonged to me.

"Up you get."

Where? The horse smell grew stronger. If only Uncle Achior would appear. He'd save me.

"He told you to mount up." Someone prodded my rump. Again.

"I don't. Kn-know how. I've never. Ridden."

"Never—oh, for Moloch's sake." Hands gripped the back of my robe to hoist me into the air amid a chorus of grunts. Other hands pushed me face down over the horse. I found myself lying across the saddle. It prodded my middle. "Lie still."

After Singer and Desert's tail hairs helped me escape—after all the times I'd watched Uncle Achior or Father gallop away—after all my years of longing to have a horse plunge across the sands beneath me, my first time riding happened like this? My body heaved with sobs.

A hard hand smacked the back of my head. "I said be still."

Muffled stamps from other horses—how many? Leather creaked. A rider mounted my horse. His knees dug into my thigh and shoulder. The horse leapt forward. The first few strides nearly jolted me out of the saddle. Each step jounced me. The bump at the base of the horse's neck punched into my belly. Falling off sounded more and more appealing.

My eyes burned from kicked-up sand and the musty sack. "I—I need to—wipe my eyes."

"You'll want lots of things before we're done with you. Grow used to it."

Off to one side another man laughed in a way that made me retch even more than the horse's spine. "If we're ever done with you."

In spite of lack of air and the saddle's thuds, my mind felt untethered from my body. *This isn't happening. Impossible this is happening to me—.*

But my insides felt like jam from the saddle's pummeling. In the musty dimness of my sack, I seemed to jolt along for days. I lost count of the number of times I teetered to one side of the horse or the other. A hard hand shoved me straight the moment before I fell.

The first time I'd automatically said, "Thank you." No one answered.

Now tears soaked the sacking over my face. Sand clotted the wet fabric. "Help?" The horses thundered on. "I—can't—breathe."

The horse broke stride. The saddle punched into my guts.

"Dismount, girl," ordered the hard voice.

Shuddering, I drew in the strong odor of the horse's sweaty hide. *So I can breathe after all.* "I don't know how."

He made a disgusted noise and whipped the sack off my head without untying the cord. It nearly pulled my hair out of my scalp. I screeched. Blinked against the sudden daylight.

The men laughed.

"Slide off." The speaker shoved my shoulder.

So his are the knees digging into my thigh and shoulder. The knowledge floated through me. Dream-like. Unreal.

My feet hit the ground and the ache in my belly shot through my head. Nauseated, I stumbled and fell, unable to catch myself with my bound hands.

The man swung off the horse to loom over me, hands on hips, feet planted far apart. His chiseled lips quirked up.

Two men stood behind him. One had thick shoulders, crooked teeth and a beard growing unevenly on his pimpled jaw. The third man didn't stand much taller than I did, with loose hair past his shoulders. He bunched his fists and pushed out his chest, as if trying to seem bigger.

Beyond the men grew a few scrubby trees. A circle of blackened stones to one side marked a fire pit. One low-slung goat-hair tent near the fire pit.

The scrawny man gathered the reins of first one horse, then another. "I'll discard the spare horses."

"Far away, mind. We don't want their owners to find them—or us." The hard-voiced man grasped my wrist and hauled me toward the tent. Over one shoulder he shouted, "Hobble my stallion. Turn him loose on the hill behind camp."

I heard the other two mutter under their breath. Then the man dragging me along shoved me into a room formed by curtains hung from the tent's frame. I fell, sprawled across cushions heaped on top of a finely woven rug. "You will call me Lord Balaam, or 'my Lord.'"

"My name's Sar—"

Balaam shoved me face down on the cushions. "No one cares what you're called." His knee jabbed my back, and he yanked at my robe. Why did he want to remove my clothes? I scrambled to hold the sweat-stiff fabric about me, but with a few rough movements, he had me naked. I rolled into a ball, bent legs hiding my woman parts, hands over my breasts.

Not happening. Not happening. Impossible—

He jerked me onto my back. "No need to be coy. You're what—fourteen? Fifteen? A woman."

"Fifteen." Would he beat me? Even Father left slaves clothed when he beat them.

Balaam peeled my hands away from my breasts and grinned. "You're short, but ample." He hitched his own robes to his waist and fell on me. His fingers dug into my shoulders, held me still.

I struggled to get out from under him. He bore down, forced part of himself between my thighs. *Why has he wedged a hand between my legs? What—how?* I looked down. Something poked out beneath his belly. He started hunching himself, and the thing tore into my softest parts.

I screamed.

He forced himself into the very roots of my body. Every movement ripped me apart.

No. No. No. I'm not here. Not here. Not here.

My screams gagged me. Balaam's thighs thudded against mine, his sweaty chest clung to my breasts. Withdrew. Slammed into my chest again.

I'm in the garden with Aunt Kupo. The fountain is playing. Wind stirs the pomegranate's leaves—

At last he stilled. Lifted himself off my body. I felt the painful slide of something limp from inside me. Sticky blood ran down my thighs. My screams had long ago wrung into sobs.

He grinned and flicked my nose with one finger, stood and adjusted his robe. "Answer at once when any of us call you."

"W-when you call me what?"

"Don't be a fool. When we yell for you to come to us." He jerked his chin. "Now go to Sanipu's room."

My stomach wrapped around my backbone. Which of the other men was Sanipu? *Not again. Not another one.* My body was bleeding, tattered, coated with Balaam's sweat.

He stared at me. "Be gone." He gestured at the room's entrance. When I didn't spring up at once, he cuffed the side of my head. "Don't keep the others waiting."

My blisters from the night before burned at every step. Naked, I hobbled into the large area in the front of the tent. The thick-shouldered man waited there. When I tried to fold over myself, hide myself from his raking eyes, he bared his crooked teeth at me in an expression nothing like a smile.

"Good, you're ready." He waved me toward a drape to my left, which had a trail of mingled jewelry, coins, bones and other food scraps leading under it. "So am I."

The curtain had barely swung shut before he flung his robe aside. The man part of him looked stubbier than Balaam's. Smaller in every way.

Maybe it won't hurt so much?

"I am Sanipu. Lie down and spread your legs."

He wanted me to lie on a rug knobbed with scattered jewelry and debris? "No, please, no—"

Sanipu halted on his stalk towards me. "What did you say to me?" His words fell like stones. "Never contradict me again."

He struck me across the face. Hot blood spilled down my cheek. The male part of him twitched against the thick mat of hair below his belly. With a grunt, he bent over my breasts to pinch and twist my nipples.

I wept from the gritty throb in my cheek. The fiery pain in my breasts, between my legs. *Not here, I'm not here. This can't be happening—*

He laughed, then twisted harder. "Look at me when I'm inside you. You will always look at me." Still laughing, he rested his full weight on me. The scattered jewelry and bones scored my back and buttocks. His foul breath gusted over my face as he forced himself inside me. His—nubbin scraped the bruises and scrapes left by Balaam.

Sanipu slimed kisses across my face. They made me heave as much as what he was doing to me below. By the time he grew still, I felt older than Aunt Kupo. Sanipu got up, flung his robes over one shoulder, and stalked naked into the communal space.

At least he'd not ordered me to go to the third man. Then the drape swished at my back. Toes curled, I turned to find the spindly man hiking up his robe.

"Good, you're already on the floor." Then he glanced at the debris strewn around, and his nose wrinkled. "Follow me." He wheeled out of the room, clicked his fingers when I didn't leap to obey.

I tottered to my feet, every part of me aching. When I wavered into the main room, I glimpsed a curtain to one side just swishing shut.

"Hurry up, girl."

I limped after him. *Again? Another one?*

"On your face." *What?* I peered at the rug. *At least it's clean.*

Unlike the other two, he didn't bother removing his robe. From the edge of my eye, I saw him hitch it up. *Please. Don't—*

He moved astride my body, lowered himself onto me. His long hair fell around my cheeks. "Say my name," he commanded, in feeble imitation of Balaam's tone.

"I—I don't know it."

"Arseen." It came out as a gasping moan.

I said it through teeth ground together. "Arseen." My voice squeaked like a toddler's, and at once he deflated inside me. Why?

He reared off me. "I—I changed—my mind."

"Ar-seen—"

"Stop. Saying. That." Who scuttled away from whom? He yanked his robes down. "Get out."

If I did, would one of the others grab me again?

Arseen twitched aside and kicked me. His aim was off, and the sole of one foot brushed my hip. "I said out."

I crept outside to crouch at the roots of a fig tree. Vomited so hard my spine threatened to jolt through the top of my skull. All I brought up was bile. My stomach cramped with the need to empty itself when it was already empty. Had I ever gone so long without food?

Stiff, filthy fabric wrapped around my head. With eyes dry as sand I peered up at Balaam. *Again? Oh, gods, no. No. No.*

He stood over me again, arms crossed. Sneering. "Go to the small room at the back of the tent. Obey when any of us call for you." He strode inside, robes whirling about his long legs.

Crouched over, I tugged on my reeking robes with small, awkward jerks. Shuffled after him. My feet felt skinless after my trek through the night, my breasts smarted from Sanipu's evil fingers, my woman parts were raw meat. I stumbled around inside until I found the space Balaam must mean. No rugs or cushions, just empty sand. I collapsed, walled by curtains hung from the tent's skeleton. From the look of the cloth, old pieces of the tent's skin formed these curtains.

Tears seeped down my face, slow and hopeless. *Aunt Kupo, help me.*

CHAPTER SEVEN

THE GRIND OF MY EMPTY BELLY WOKE ME. My head felt fuzzy as the wool in my mother's weaving room. For an instant, I didn't understand. Why was sand heaped beneath me, gritty on my face? Why did my body feel so stiff and sore, in such strange places?

Then Balaam yelled outside my section of tent. As much as anything in this encampment could be called mine. "Girl."

When I jolted upright, every bruise and scrape pounded. My mouth felt stringy and dry, as if Arseen's hair filled it.

Sun glared through thin spots in the worn fabric above me. Sweat made my skin sticky—my own and that of the three men. Would I ever bathe again, or would I die filthy?

"Girl." Balaam shouted louder. "Here. Now."

Not again. Not again. Not again. With shaking hands, I smoothed my robes over my legs. As if the cloth could save me from further defilement.

"I'm not saying it again, girl."

Shakily I stood and went out to face them where they waited by the fire pit.

"Time to eat." Father would've envied Balaam's air of command. Eat? *Oh, yes, yes, please.*

Balaam flicked one hand at the fire. "Cook."

Cook? Me? "I—I don't know how."

"Women cook. Everything you need is by the fire." His voice gritted with impatience.

Now I heard the spring bubbling. *Water.* I longed to race over, fling myself face down to drink my fill. I tried to work saliva into my dry mouth. "But the slaves—"

Sanipu snorted. "You're the slave, girl." His thick shoulders vibrated as if he found the idea amusing.

"I meant the slaves in my father's house." I flinched. "They prepared food and served us."

"Your father has slaves?" Balaam looked at the other men. Arseen glanced at my dirty robe, frayed at the hem from sand.

Sanipu smirked. "No matter who her family is, they won't want her back now."

"We've rendered her worthless." Arseen nodded.

You didn't do anything. What would the others think if they knew of his failure?

Balaam shrugged and walked away. "No matter if a houseful waited on you before. You will prepare a meal."

When I didn't move, he tossed over one shoulder, "Now, or get beaten."

I skittered over to study the foodstuffs heaped behind the fire. Chickpeas, mint. A sack of rice. How to render them edible?

"Fetch water." When I only blinked at him, Arseen hefted a bowl and crossed to the spring. "Like this."

"Don't help her." Glaring at me, Sanipu swung one heavy fist toward Arseen, and stomped into the tent.

Sweating swine.

Arseen stepped closer, voice lowered. "You're to prepare meals, so I don't have to."

"Leave her to work." From inside the tent, Sanipu's roar gusted over us.

Arseen flinched. My legs trembled and I collapsed by the heaped foodstuffs. It took all I had not to dive and cram them, raw, down my throat.

Arseen shuffled his feet. "I'll get you started," he muttered. While he filled the bowl at the spring, I crawled after him. Water seeped through my robe as I drank. He returned to the fire pit to shake some chickpeas out of their sack into a pot with the water. I could barely hear him above my own frantic drinking. "Cook the chickpeas—"

With difficulty, I raised up from the water. "How?"

"We're making hummus and bread." He squinted at me.

Hummus. I'd eaten it on a regular basis, but never made it. Now I glanced from firepit to spring, so rudimentary compared to the vast kitchens in Father's house.

"Cook the chickpeas til they're soft, then mash them." He scowled at me. "By all the gods, don't you know anything?"

I couldn't focus on him, because I couldn't stop imagining tangy hummus on my tongue.

After Arseen made the hummus, he mixed bread dough and patted a thin layer of it on the outside of a bowl.

I dared a murmured question. "Shouldn't that be inside the bowl?"

"Shhhh." He darted a glance at the tent. "No, you bake it like this."

As the warm scent of bread filled the air, I nearly wept. They had to feed me soon. They had to. Before I nerved myself to ask Arseen, Balaam strode out of the tent.

"What're you doing, Arseen? Girl, when will our meal be ready?"

Arseen ducked his head. "We're baking the bread now."

Balaam's eyebrows shot into his hairline. "'We?'"

"I'm just showing her how—"

"We captured her because you complained about doing all the work." The leader whipped around and stormed into the tent.

Arseen stared after him. He bunched his robes around his hands, plucked the bowl off the fire and jutted his chin at the tent. "Go to my room."

What's happening?

Arseen grabbed my wrist and hauled me inside, pushed me face down on the rug, hiked my robes to my waist and crammed himself inside me. His fumbling, desperate movements hurt, and beyond the cloth walls, Balaam and Sanipu laughed.

"That's it, ride her hard!"

"We'll wait."

"After all, it won't take long." Both men laughed.

Arseen grew still an instant, then bashed against me frantically. I screamed. He cuffed the side of my head and pumped even harder, but I felt him slip out of my bleeding woman parts. "Shut. Up."

"Do you mean her—or us?" Sanipu snorted.

Arseen flattened me into the rug, scrawny forearms braced by my head. His flesh stuck to mine, glued by sweat. The fibers of the rug scraped my face.

While the other men hooted, Arseen stood and left.

I curled into a tight ball. "How could he?" How could he use me like that after being so helpful?

"It's what men do, you fool." Balaam sounded so loud he might've stood beside me.

I crept to my room and dropped to the sand.

Outside the men ate what Arseen had cooked. Eventually I fell asleep to dream that a huge stone crushed me into a bottomless well of sand. I screamed with no sound.

Sanipu's yell woke me. "Girl, come here."

Disoriented, I blinked at the fabric walls. They billowed as someone kicked the tent. "Get out here."

I scuttled out and nearly crashed into Sanipu in the big room just inside the tent entrance. "There you are. Get out there and clean the dishes."

Clean dishes? How? "Yes, my Lord."

"'Master.' You will call me 'master.'" One side of his mouth curled up. "Speak, girl."

I stared at the ground so he couldn't see my eyes. "M-master."

He grinned and swaggered out.

My hands fisted at my sides. Father roared at slaves, beat them. At least he didn't taunt them, or force his body on the females—or did he? I limped as fast as I could to the makeshift kitchen.

Balaam strode up to stand a handspan away, arms folded. "Get to work."

"In a moment." I didn't dare look at him.

"Now." He punched my shoulder. "And I told you how to address me.'"

What? My teeth clenched. "In a moment—Master."

Balaam punched me again. "My Lord."

As I huddled on the ground, footsteps scraped nearer. "What has she done now?" Sanipu sounded weary, as if I'd failed them a thousand times. Yet when I sneaked a glance at his face, his lips peeled back from his teeth in a sickening smile.

"She called me 'Master' instead of 'My Lord.'" Balaam bent down to smack my ear.

I could barely make out Sanipu. "'Master?'" He kicked my stomach. "That's my title, you stupid girl." He shifted to stand closer to me and kicked me again. My stomach threatened to leap out through my back. My head thudded. Blood trickled from my ear. "Or you'll feel our wrath."

Balaam moved to stand alongside Sanipu. When Sanipu kicked me in the belly once more, Balaam drew back and kicked me as well.

I heaved, spine curled toward the sky, my insides burning. Over the clang in my head, I heard my tormentors laugh.

CHAPTER EIGHT

STILL LAUGHING, BALAAM AND SANIPU left me huddled on the sand. Had Arseen watched, or stayed in the tent unaware? At least he didn't beat me.

If only I could crawl into my small section of tent, huddle around the soreness thumping through my body. But they'd punish me even more if I didn't clean the dishes. Groaning, I hitched myself over to the dirty bowls and platter. The sand abraded my knees and elbows. Moaning, I tried to pull my robe between my legs and the ground. To lift my torso higher.

Now what? Wash the dishes? *No—food.* At last, food within my reach. I scraped my fingers over the men's pathetic leavings and crammed hummus in my mouth. Weeping, I ate the bits of flatbread. How could they have complained about it? I could have eaten so much of it I couldn't move. Not that there was that much of it.

At last I squatted back to study the dishes I had licked shiny. *Wash. Water.* I filled the biggest bowl in the spring, dipped each used dish in the bowl, rubbed the food off with my fingers. I spread the dishes at the edge of the fire circle to dry. Then I crept around the tent and crawled under the back wall to hide in my stuffy little room.

Balaam's firm strides thumped across the tent toward me. "Girl." The curtain at the front of my room shimmied as he burst through. He glanced around, and his mouth turned down. "It's too uncomfortable in here." He clicked his fingers, stalked away. "Follow me."

A chill spread through me. *Again? Not again.*

"Come along, you sluggish creature. I haven't got all day."

By the time I stumbled after him, Balaam was already ducking into his own section of the tent. He clicked his fingers again. "Your reluctance flatters me."

Behind me Sanipu's snigger rolled through the fabric wall. "She longs for my attentions. Don't take long, Balaam. I want a turn."

Another turn at pinching and prodding me? I scurried after Balaam, who skinned out of his robe. He bent toward me, and his finely-cut nostrils pinched. "Take off your robes, girl."

BACK IN MY ROOM, I longed to pull pillows over my aching head. *Aunt Kupo—Aunt Kupo—* If only I could run and cling to her while I wailed out my pain. The stench of my flesh made me gag. When I could bear it no longer, I went to Arseen's room. *At least he hasn't ordered me to call him "master" or "my Lord."*

"Arseen?" No response. *Curse it. Curse everything.* "Arseen."

The curtains parted. Arseen's long hair rumpled down his back. "What?"

Let this be a nightmare. To be back in Father's house, even with an unwanted marriage hanging over me like a sword. "How do I bathe myself? I feel—unclean."

Arseen stared over my shoulder. When I twisted to see what he was looking at, my hands fisted. Balaam, lounging in the shared area close to the entrance. Had he seen me? Heard me?

Arseen stepped closer and spoke low. "Dip a bowl in the spring. Wipe yourself off as best you can with a rag." The drape swished between us.

I gaped at the flap. Arseen seemed afraid? Why?

Balaam chuckled. I scuttled to my barren little "room." With him nearby, I had no wish to cross to the spring and remove my clothing. I'd wash when my tormentors slept for the night, even though it meant being naked in the twilight chill.

After darkness, I crept outside. *They must be asleep by now. They must.* Body reeking, I made my way to the spring. It took several lifetimes for me to dare lift the hem of my robe and drag off the garment. The cool night air smoothed over my body like a balm.

Now I squatted to fill the largest bowl again and dunked in a rag. Oh, the touch of water on my skin. Even cold water in cool air. Little whimpers of pleasure escaped as I scrubbed myself. A skim of grayish water flowed down my legs and over my toes. I hurried to wipe that away as well.

"Girl."

I went rigid. Sanipu. Maybe he was just calling for me in his sleep?

"Girl." He shouted this time.

A tree scraped my naked behind. I'd backed away without realizing. The shadows wouldn't hide me if the men came outside.

"Girl, come when I call you." Sanipu sounded louder.

I peered around me for shelter. Left, right, above my head, where the leafy branches stretched into the night sky. My wet body shivered in the breeze.

A chink of chain, as if Sanipu'd trodden on a fallen necklace on the floor of his room. Robe slung over one shoulder, I leapt onto the tree's lowest branch and climbed. With my robe hampering every move, I climbed with twigs tearing my knees and hands, frantic that the noise revealed my hiding place. At last the tree's familiar scent slowed my hasty climb. How could I feel comforted, trapped up a tree, naked and trembling?

Then I remembered the day when Aunt Kupo and I'd sat beneath one of the pomegranate trees in my father's courtyard. "What do you mean, pom'granate is good for me?" At six years old, I hated the fussiness of eating the thin layer of fruit off each round seed.

Aunt Kupo had laughed. "Pomegranate fruit rewards us for the effort it takes to eat."

Now my arms clutched the branch supporting me. It almost felt as if my beloved aunt enfolded me in her arms. Until—

"Where is she?" Sanipu's bellow seemed to fill the world. He must have gone to my room at the far end of the tent. "Girl. Come here at once, I want you." A moment later, he gave a wordless roar. "She's gone. Balaam. Wake up."

Swearing. Both men. My hold on the branch tightened as Sanipu erupted into the clearing below me. As the smell of his sweat rose around me, I gagged.

"What's happening?" Balaam leapt outside, robe still settling around his legs, sword ready in his hand. "What's amiss?" His hair sprang awry, in spite of his chill demeanor.

A wild desire to laugh pulsed through me.

"The girl's run off. We should've killed her when we had the chance."

Kill. The laughter died in my throat. I shrank against the pomegranate, heart beating so hard the whole trunk seemed to shudder. The bark rasped my sore thighs, my tender breasts.

Arseen joined the others, fully dressed with smooth hair. "Why're you shouting? It's the middle of the night."

"The girl escaped." Balaam's sword swiped the air.

I winced as if the blade already explored my insides. If only I could clothe myself. Would they find my robe in the dark, and know that I hadn't gone far? All I could do was cling to the pomegranate, teeth clenched.

"Can we follow her?" Arseen sounded hesitant.

Sanipu snorted. "At night?"

"In the dark?" Balaam kicked the ground. Sand hissed. "We'll track her at daybreak."

"And make her sorry for what she's done." Sanipu clapped Balaam on the shoulder. "For the rest of her life—which won't be long."

This time, Balaam didn't contradict him. "If the night air doesn't kill her, we will. Best sleep while we can." He returned to the tent. Sanipu followed.

Arseen stood in silence until it became clear they wouldn't return. Then he stooped to feel my washrag. "Be back in the tent before daybreak." He appeared to speak to the open desert, then crossed to the tent.

As if he doesn't want to see me. Why? *Because if he sees me, he'll have to raise the alarm.* I wanted to feel grateful to him. I couldn't.

I crouched in the pomegranate's branches until the bark felt like hot coals raking my bare flesh. Until my arms ached from hugging the trunk. What if Arseen changed his mind and raised the alarm just as I shinnied to the ground?

If I lost my hold and fell, I might strike my head. Come morning, my captors would discover me unconscious, sprawled naked on the ground.

At last I could cling on no longer, and crept out of the tree. For long moments I kept still, pressed against the pomegranate's trunk. Silence. When I finally reached the spring, I dowsed my reeking robe and scrubbed the cloth against itself. After it was as clean as I could make it, I wrung it out. It'd still be damp in the morning, but I couldn't help that.

CHAPTER NINE

"**S**LAVE." **SANIPU'S HARSH VOICE** woke me.
  Curse it, curse it, curse it.

Just before Sanipu lunged into my room, I leapt to my feet. I glimpsed Arseen through the wildly swinging door flap. Balaam marched past him, lips tight.

He slashed the door aside. "Where were you last night?"

I'd thought out my answer while I tried to sleep in my damp robe. "I—going—"

"To escape." Sanipu's broad face creased in triumph. "I told you, Balaam."

"I was going to relieve myself." The words ran together.

"Relieve yourself." Balaam rocked back on one foot and scowled at me. "Where?'

I pointed toward the cluster of undergrowth. "I didn't answer you because—because I—"

"Of course not." Blushing, Arseen touched my shoulder. "Now, we should—"

Sanipu shoved the smaller man so hard Arseen fell face down in the sand. "Now we should take our pleasure with her since she's still here." He rolled Arseen out of his way with one foot and gripped my wrist.

"Don't push me." Arseen rose up on all fours. "You've got the girl for that."

The girl? Girl? I stared at him. How could he say that, after his kindness last night?

"Do not question my authority in front of her." Sanipu raised one fist. "Come with me, girl." He dragged me into his room, one meaty paw clamped around my wrist. The jewels and chains of the fallen necklaces scraped my feet.

I WON'T CRY. *I won't.* But tears seeped down my face the moment I left Sanipu snoring on the floor of his chamber. I felt chilled from the inside out, my sweaty robe heavy against the welts left by his pinching fingers on my breasts and belly. I crawled into my cubicle, all the way to the back wall. As far from the men as possible.

When I raised the bottom of the fabric for fresh air, sand blew over my face. "Curse it." I dropped the cloth wall, then stiffened. I smelled Sanipu. Had he sneaked after me to torment me, force himself on me again?

Cowering, I made myself look. No, I was alone. Why did I still smell him so clearly? Then I realized his scent permeated my robe. I gagged. I needed to bathe again.

THAT NIGHT I carried a bowl of water into the tent after the men retired for the night. What if it spilled? What if my captors caught me? Hunched in a corner to keep the sand floor from getting too wet, I washed as best I could without hurting my torn and bruised parts, then eyed my robe.

After a moment's thought, I eased toward the closed tent entrance, a sliver of light in the depths of the structure's shadows. One of the men coughed, and trembling, I shrank to the heaped rugs that made up the tent floor. At last I risked standing again and made my way outside to the fire pit. Beside the rough circle of stones, I searched the scanty stores of food. With a fistful of dried mint, I scurried back inside to rub the crumbly leaves into my robes until the piercing smell of mint overpowered Sanipu's stench.

NEXT MORNING, I made flatbread for the men's breakfast. As they sat to eat, Balaam scowled. "Flatbread again?"

Arseen's nose wrinkled. "I want more variety in our diet."

Then you should have taken a girl who knew how to cook. "Sorry, master."

Balaam grunted. "After we break our fast, I want you to go in the tent and—"

Again? Would my woman parts never have a chance to heal?

"—and clean. My room needs it, and Sanipu's is worse." Balaam poked Sanipu's ankle with one foot.

"Though not Arseen's. He keeps his things tidy." Sanipu laughed and Balaam joined in.

Head tucked in, Arseen said nothing, but I glimpsed the scarlet flowing under his skin from cheek to ear.

If I tidied now, I'd finish while they ate. But when I hastened toward the tent, Sanipu shouted after me. "Where are you off to in such a hurry, girl?"

I swiveled, tripping on the hem of my robe. "To tidy up."

Sanipu reared back as if I'd slapped him. "To tidy up, Master." He chewed with his mouth open.

I stared at the sand between my feet. "Master." Then I fled to the tent. As the flap shut behind me, Balaam and Sanipu laughed again. I gritted my teeth. Had any of the slaves in Father's house hated us the way I hated these men?

How had Father's slaves tidied? Nothing seemed out of order in Balaam's room. Well, a robe splayed across the carpets. I folded it and added it to a stack of robes in one corner. What else? The scattered cushions. I nudged them together, smoothed a rucked-up corner of a rug beside the heavy chest against one inner tent wall.

Nothing else to do. I scuttled to Sanipu's room. Outside, the men talked over their meal. My stomach burned, my mouth watered. Once I'd lingered over my food like that.

Sanipu's discarded robes littered the floor, layered over each other so I could barely see the carpet. The lumps of scattered jewelry fanned out from the heavy chest against the inner wall. My lip curled. Even my mother put her own jewels away.

Everything reeked of Sanipu's body. Could I rub mint into the carpet? The tent? *There's not enough mint in the world to get rid of his stink.* I hefted the outer wall of the room and tied it so the wind scoured the space, bundled his dirty robes into a pile. As in Balaam's room, I pushed the cushions together and smoothed the rumpled rugs, gathered the jewelry in a heap on top of his treasure chest.

I didn't dare even try to see if the chest would open. *It's locked for certain.* I scooted the tangle of stones and necklaces in the center of the lid, then scurried to Arseen's space.

Cushions piled together, rug smooth, no robes visible. Arseen neither kept them stacked like Balaam's nor dirty and scattered like Sanipu's. But Arseen had worn different robes each time I saw him. Where were they?

My eye caught a small trunk beside the cushions. Did Arseen keep his robes in there? While I hesitated, he entered the room. *Curse it. Curse it.* I'd planned to be out of sight before any of the men caught me.

Arseen paused, stood tall. "Girl—"

"Sarah." Why did I give him my name? Because he kept his room neat, or because the other men bossed him?

His chin jerked. "What did you say?"

"Nothing."

But Arseen took a step toward me. "Your name is Sarah?"

Hands fisted, I didn't answer.

"Sarah." A smile played over his lips. "My cousin's name."

Wind billowed the tent walls. "What's she like?"

"What—none of your affair." Arseen jerked around so his back was to me. "Be about your duties, slave." His voice wobbled. "Why're you standing there? I said go."

He's afraid, too.

He stabbed a shaking finger toward the entrance. "I. Said. Go."

Stumbling, I obeyed, fleeing to my empty chamber.

Sunlight grayed the black tent, but cool wind pushed against the cloth walls. I shivered. Without rugs in my room, without a cloak, the coming winter would find me cold.

Hooves thudded past. Was Balaam leaving? Why?

"Girl." Arseen's quiet voice reached me. "The others have gone for pack animals. We need to break camp before they return." When I didn't join him, his voice sharpened. "Sanipu's room. Now."

Arseen stood rigid just inside Sanipu's room. In my rush to join him I rammed into his back. The sweet rosemary scent of his robes cloyed in my nostrils. Before I could dodge away, he spun and caught my wrist. "You said you cleaned."

"I did."

"You. Did. Not."

My chin drew in. "I smoothed the rug and heaped the cushions together—" *And folded Sanipu's disgusting robes.*

"That's tidying." Arseen's nostrils pinched. "You didn't clean."

My hands and arms felt numb. "What—" Words clogged in my throat. "What do you mean?"

He sniffed, brown eyes studying me from hairline to bare feet. "Didn't you shake the sand out of the rug?"

No. I longed to scream it at him.

"We'll have to clean before we can pack up." Arseen stooped to grasp one short edge of the rug. "Take the other end, you slow thing. Help me."

Heat rose to my hairline. He knew my name, and he called me

"thing" instead?

Arseen raised his arms and flicked them upward. The rug rose toward the ceiling and jerked out of my hands. He groaned. "No, you fool. Raise your end when I'm lowering mine."

I tried to do as he said. My arms and shoulders ached long before he seemed satisfied.

"Now we roll it for packing on the camel." Arseen squatted, sent me a chill look. "Help me, slave."

My palms dampened. That tone—as dismissive as Balaam's, as derisive as Sanipu's. As contemptuous as my father's.

"Today, girl." Arseen dropped the rug and glowered.

How I longed to draw back one foot and kick him. Instead I knelt and folded the unwieldy rug.

Arseen rocked onto his heels. "It's crooked, you stupid girl."

Fumbling, I tried to fold it evenly. *Why is he—*

"Bael's name, you're slow." He struck at my face, but his hand wobbled at the last moment to slide along my shoulder. "Move, I'll do it. We can't pack a sloppily rolled rug, it'll come undone."

He'd hit me. Just a glancing blow, but— When I stood away from him, he tossed a sack at me. "Stuff the cushions in here."

While I packed the cushions he folded the rug, then flung the spare robes at me. His nose wrinkled. "Wash these while you still have a convenient source of water—no. They'd still be wet when we leave and rot the storage chest." He shrugged. "You'll have to wash them at our new camp, and hope the water source isn't too far away."

But he'd been so glad this camp had a spring. What happened? Then I understood. *I happened.* It no longer mattered to him because he no longer had to lug the water. Alone of all the men, he knew my name. And he chose to think of me as a slave. As—nothing.

We packed Balaam's room next. The moment we entered, Arseen jabbed a finger at the sand trails on the red and black rug. I took my place at the far end and took hold of the rough edge, ready to shake it clean. We finished packing Balaam's things faster than Sanipu's. At the entrance to his own room, Arseen swung to face me. He spoke over the top of my head. "I prefer sorting my own things, girl—slave. Leave me."

Gladly. I retreated to the scant shade of the brush that grew by the spring. Leaf shadows flickered around and over me. I could almost imagine Aunt Kupo's calloused palm gentle on my head. What would she say? My name, for sure. The leaf shadows filtered over me.

All of a sudden, I stared up into the tree. There. And there. Oh, there. Heavy, red globes. Fruit. Spit pooled in my mouth. *Food.* Food within my reach. I pulled and twisted three of them from the branches. It took all my self-restraint not to gobble them at once, but I secreted them inside my robe. Bound my rope belt tight to keep them against my torso.

Once, long ago, I'd drifted out to the garden, found my aunt seated on the fountain coping. "I'm bored."

She'd nodded. "Shut your eyes." I heard the sound of wood snapping, and then Aunt Kupo pressed three twigs into my hands.

"Find the trees these came from."

I stared around the garden at all the trees and decorative shrubs in the garden.

Aunt Kupo chuckled. "Take your time."

I selected one stick.

"Don't you want to take them all?"

I shook my head. One at a time would be easier. The twig exuded a thread of scent. Somewhere close by, I smelled the same odor. Turning in a circle, I found a tree with bark like my stick. I stepped closer to crush one of the leaves. Racing to Aunt Kupo, I rested the twig on her knee.

She snorted, eyes flying open. "Wha—"

"It's from that tree." I pointed.

"The cinnamon tree. Let's see how you do with the next one."

This time I crossed and re-crossed the garden until my robes were sticky with sweat. At last, I found a tree with bark that appeared the same, and returned to Aunt Kupo.

"Well?"

"A pomegranate?"

She dipped her head. "Yes. But the pomegranate isn't like the cinnamon tree. The cinnamon gives us its bark to flavor our food, and for medicine. The pomegranate only offers us its fruit. The bark and wood, its roots, are poisonous."

Now my hands fisted in the sand as I stared up into the slender tree. The tree with poison wood. Poison roots.

A pomegranate.

CHAPTER TEN

COULD I BREAK OFF THE SKINNIER ROOTS? I knelt to scrabble with both hands, tearing my finger nails, a cloud of dust and sand choking me.

I'd just bared the top of one root when Arseen called. "We need to empty the tent, collapse and fold it."

I touched the bulge of the exposed root, too sturdy to tear off. *Curse it. Curse everything.*

"Slave? Did you hear me? You come when I call. At once!"

In a moment he would search for me, punish me. I heard it in his voice. I touched the pomegranate on either side of its trunk. *It's a common tree. One will grow close to the next camp.*

Maybe.

"Slave? Slave." Arseen sounded louder. Closer.

"Coming. Master." Good thing he couldn't see my face.

JUST AS ARSEEN AND I collapsed the tent, hoof beats approached.

Balaam and Sanipu rode into camp, Balaam on his black stallion, Sanipu on a dark brown horse I'd never seen before. They each led another horse and two camels apiece. Jogging along at a loose-limbed pace, the camels wrinkled their muzzles at each other, at the horses, at the world in general. The horses, one a delicate gray and the other squat and dust-colored, pinned their ears at the camels. The chunky horse trailed even the camels. When they came to a halt, he rested a hind leg at once and switched his tail.

Balaam swung off his black stallion and snapped his fingers. "Girl." He strode toward the heaped household goods. "Pack the camels."

How? I scurried toward the nearest one.

Sanipu bellowed. "Hurry, load them." He pushed me.

I fell. Hot sand scoured my palms. Fabric whispered to the ground.

"Stop," Balaam ordered. "We don't have time."

Time for what? Next instant, Sanipu stood before me, naked. *Now? Here, in front of the others?*

I cowered in the sand. Arseen stared with parted lips at Sanipu's naked hindquarters, caught me looking at him and swiveled away, blushing.

"Don't waste time." Arseen spoke in a tight voice.

Sanipu flexed his hands. "But she's already on the ground." He sounded as surly as my cousin Tamar when she couldn't have a sweet.

Balaam chopped one hand in the air. "Time enough at the new camp. The owners of the beasts may already hunt for us."

Sanipu scowled, snatched up his robes, skinned into them.

Tears burned my lids. *Thank you, thank you, thank you.* Not Sanipu, or Balaam. Thank whatever power had protected me.

My fingers clawed in the sand. Power? Nothing had protected me when most I needed it. Nothing protected me now. Just circumstance.

One of the rolled rugs rested on the sand nearby. I squatted, tried to lift it. It wouldn't budge. Something lighter, then. Shaking,

I picked up the sack of cushions and crossed to the nearest camel. The beast turned its head to give me a disdainful look, flapping its lips and bobbing its head.

"Girl—" Balaam broke off with a grin. He caught Sanipu's shoulder as the thick man passed, and jerked his chin at me.

The camel seemed to laugh along with the men. The sack of cushions sagged to the ground while I watched the creature's lips flutter, now with flecks of green gathered around the edges. It really did look most peculiar—

The beast spat a gooey green mess right in the middle of my chest. Warm wetness seeped down my front.

All the men laughed. Even Arseen.

A blush spread from my throat to my scalp.

Balaam bent nearly double. "Go on—girl—load the—cushions." His words rose and fell against the other men's merriment.

"You heard him." Arseen wiped his eyes.

How could I have known what the stupid creature meant to do? Its vile-smelling slobber soaked me. Retching, I scrubbed my hands over the stain, gagged, then tried to dry my hands on the seat of my robes.

Balaam stopped chortling and cleared his throat. "Get to work, girl."

I fumbled with the ropes slung over the camel to find a loose end to bind around the sack. The camel grunted and shifted its weight. I jumped—was it about to spit at me again? But the creature turned away as if I no longer interested it.

Arseen chuckled as he brushed past to tie one of the chests onto the camel that had spat at me. It ignored him.

"Watch us load the beasts. You'll do it next time." When Arseen muttered it to me, Balaam whipped round, scowled. After a long moment while he considered me, he jerked a nod.

I stared hungrily at the pomegranate tree while they worked. If only I had a knife and some privacy to dig.

Balaam bound the rolled-up tent atop another camel, and Arseen loaded the rugs on the other two beasts. Sanipu, I noticed, wandered back and forth with single items in his hands, but didn't load a single thing.

At last they remounted the horses. Balaam snapped his fingers at me. "Mount up, slave." The smallest, chunky horse, thick-legged with a coarse mane and tail, stood with drooping head.

Sanipu glowered. "You heard him, girl." He leaned toward me to murmur, "Or I will see to it you don't waste our time ever again."

"I—I don't know how to get on a horse."

Arseen flung himself off his mount, marched toward me and caught the shoulder and seat of my robe. He heaved. Nothing happened.

"Out of my way, weakling." Balaam shouldered Arseen aside. His hard hands gripped my robes and swung me through the air, the scent of horse heavy in my nostrils. Balaam held me close to the saddle and shook me. "Don't be a dolt, girl. Swing your right leg over the saddle."

With the neck of my robes cutting into my throat, I fumbled to obey. The horse's ears flickered. My heart thudded as I struggled to get my leg over the spine. Would the men give me a chance to ride? To escape?

My mount swung its haunches while I gathered the reins. I tried to remember everything Singer had taught me. To move quietly, to breathe slowly. To speak calmly. "Easy, boy—"

Balaam snatched the reins from me. "She's a mare. Don't you know anything?" He remounted, still holding my reins, and clamped his legs against his mount, who sprang into a gallop.

So they wouldn't let me ride on my own.

My mare jolted after him. Her rough mane abraded my fingers, her sides rubbed the inside of my legs. Soon it felt like all the skin on my thighs had worn off. My behind ached from the mare's jolting strides. My backbone threatened to pop through the top of my head.

This—*this* was what I'd longed to do most of my life? "Please—we—must—stop—"

None of my captors seemed to hear me.

"Stop. I—must. Stop."

Arseen tossed me a look, then glanced away as if he'd heard nothing. Sanipu laughed, a sound as harsh as the hooves in the sand.

Balaam jerked his black stallion to a halt and tossed the reins back over my mount's head. "You hold me back anyway."

Fortunate that I'd spent much of my childhood watching Uncle Achior ride. I had some idea how to hold the reins. Before I managed to thread the straps around my fingers, the men booted their horses forward, Arseen and Sanipu towing the camels. My mare set off after them, each choppy stride clacking my teeth together.

Even so, a thrill vibrated through me. I was riding. And for the first time in days I was on my own. I tugged one rein toward the open desert. The mare's head still aimed at the other horses. When I tugged again, the mare leaned harder against my hold.

Balaam had loosed me because he knew my horse would stay with theirs. I was as much their captive as ever.

THE HORSES CANTERED steadily through featureless wasteland, scrubby growth patched here and there. My captors' belongings jingled and thumped against the camels, who grunted in protest.

I might as well have been a folded tent or other bundle from all the notice the mare gave of me. She thudded along, ears flopping in time with her stride. Every once in a while I lost my balance and jolted forward. When she raised her neck, ears flattened, I rasped my chin on her mane and nearly fell off. I squirmed back into place.

In the distance to one side of us rode a stream of men. In the heat of the day? Their robes whipped in the wind of their progress.

People. How many chances like this would I get? Could I shout for help? Canter to join them? The mare might leave this group of horses for another.

I focused wind-scoured eyes on the strangers, and my heart splashed into my stomach. I recognized a horse here, a robe there. *Father's men.* I nearly dropped the reins, crouched lower into the mare's neck.

When only the dust of my father's men lingered in the air, I glanced after them. Why hadn't they come closer to investigate? Oh, right. They hunted a lone girl. With a group of men, I remained invisible. I scowled at Balaam's back, teeth gritted. Because of my captors, I'd escaped Father's grasp. This time.

Arseen swerved closer to me. "Stop lagging behind or one of us will have to lead you again." He booted his mount faster.

The mare had slowed while my attention drifted. Wobbling, I flapped my legs against her sides and she forged after the others.

When the sun stood straight overhead a cluster of trees appeared on the horizon. The men veered toward the oasis. Fresh sweat seeped into my robe. Would it include a pomegranate? As we jogged into the oasis, I leaned forward to dismount like I'd seen Father do.

Balaam glared. "We're just letting the horses drink." He permitted his stallion a long suck at the spring in the middle of the trees, then yanked the reins. "Enough. We must be on our way."

There. Right opposite me. A pomegranate tree. "It—it might make a good campsite." My voice sounded thin. I fought not to look at the pomegranate.

"Too close to our last one." Balaam reined toward the desert, and the other horses followed him.

My whole body tightened, and the mare slowed, flicking an ear. Was she responding to me? I willed my muscles to soften. The mare bobbed her head, and galloped faster after the others.

"Good, good girl." Why not use this time in the saddle to practice riding? Someday maybe I'd use those skills to escape—

As we cantered through the heat and glare, I experimented. Trotting jolted every sinew, but when we cantered, now I could relax enough to let my body sway in time with the mare's stride. If I tightened my grip on one rein and looked in the same direction, the mare shifted that way. I sat still and stiff, the mare slowed, ears pinned.

Balaam glowered over one shoulder. "Keep up, girl, or we'll leave you to die of thirst."

Arseen urged his mount closer, and one camel he led wove its head through the air. Was it about to spit at me?

"Keep up or Balaam will lead your horse again. Fast. Fast enough for you to fall off and break your bones. Fast enough that when you fall, the sand will tear off your flesh." Arseen aimed a chill look at me to make sure I understood, then moved away at once.

I closed my legs against my mare's sides. She sped up. In spite of the men's nearness, I could hardly keep from singing. The reins chafed my hands. The mare's bristly sides scored my legs. Who cared? *I'm riding.*

Balaam slowed his stallion until he leveled with me. Had he noticed my experimentation? The black stallion's muzzle rose in the air, mouth agape from Balaam's cruel hands on the reins.

So much for my dream of galloping away.

"Give me your reins, girl."

"Why?" The word burst from me.

Balaam's eyebrows arrowed toward his nose.

I flipped my reins toward him.

He plucked them up, yanked his horse into a slow trot.

"Wh-where are we going?"

His eyes blazed at me. "I told you. Our new camp."

"I don't see a good camp?" Thank goodness Arseen asked.

"Follow me."

"Follow you where?" Sanipu hauled at his horse's mouth. "I see nothing."

Balaam didn't even glance at the other man, just trotted off to the left. My teeth jolted together. The mare's choppy strides seemed even rougher when I didn't hold my own reins. *Gods, I hate trotting.*

I tried to ignore my sore behind, jarred spine, and focus on where Balaam led me. Any pomegranate trees? No trees at all. We jogged into a shallow dip sheltered by three low rises covered with scrub.

"We'll camp here." He swung off his horse.

CHAPTER ELEVEN

"WHY?" SANIPU STAYED on his horse.

Arseen glanced around. "There's no water."

Long nostrils pinched, Balaam gestured toward the horizon. "A spring lies a quarter league that way. These slopes hide the camp. Now, dismount."

"They'll provide shelter from the wind as well." Arseen hopped to the ground.

Sanipu remained in the saddle for a long moment, then slid off.

Balaam looked at me. His mouth hardened. "Slave, I told you to dismount."

My knees gave way the instant my soles touched the ground. Balaam stamped across to me, snagged the back of my robes in one sinewy hand, and shook me upright. "Don't just stand there, unload the camels."

Sanipu passed me, weighed down with his treasure chest. "Move, girl."

So you can ravish me again? I stood as if my soles had taken root. Only my empty belly kept me from vomiting. He half-raised one meaty fist, and I hastened to obey before he could push me down again and—

"Offload the camels, then set up camp while I leave the beasts in the nearest village." Arseen muttered it to me as he passed, staggering under a folded rug.

Balaam smacked the back of Arseen's shoulder. "Don't explain to her."

"Don't give the lazy thing an excuse to stay idle." Now Sanipu did shove me. I staggered.

Balaam strode past. "Get to work, girl."

Lazy thing. Get to work. They sounded like I did nothing but loll around all day. I trudged toward the nearest camel, paused. Was this the one that spat on me? Warily I fumbled with its load, eyes on the beast's motionless head. Not until I stepped away from the camel did I notice what I held. The sack of Sanipu's filthy clothing.

He grinned, gestured at the heap of his belongings. "Good, you can carry them inside once the tent's ready. And wait for me there."

When I stumbled and nearly dropped the sack, he swatted my behind. "Put it with the rug from my room." He leered. "You'll recognize it, you've had your nose in it often enough."

I scurried to drop the sack where he said. Anything to get out of his reach.

As soon as the camels were unloaded, Balaam clicked his fingers at Arseen and Sanipu. "If you want to keep the saddles, take them off the horses now. Arseen, lead the beasts into the wilderness as usual."

Arseen scuffed one foot in the sand. "Can't it wait 'til the cool of evening? If I go far enough for them not to follow me back, I—"

Balaam pivoted on one foot. "Do it now."

Shoulder hunched, Sanipu stepped forward. "You're not keeping your stallion again."

"Of course I am." Balaam fastened hobbles around the stallion's hind legs.

"If you keep your mount, Arseen and I should, too."

"How many times have I told you? This beast is valuable. Set it loose, and someone finds it. Word gets back to the owner, who realizes at once that we're in the area and hunts us down." He glared at Arseen. "Be gone."

Arseen stood his ground, if scuffing one foot and staring at his toes could be said to stand. "You stole it moons ago now, I doubt the owner still hunts for the creature."

He dares defy Balaam?

"I'd hunt this stallion until I died. And if I would, so must its rightful owner." Balaam waved toward the wastes. "I said be gone."

Head drooping, Arseen tied all the other beasts to a long rope, swung onto the horse at the front of the line, and jogged away. They shambled past the low hills and were soon out of sight.

"Move, girl. Get to work." Balaam cuffed the side of my head as he crossed to the pile of his belongings.

Clutching my aching skull, I scrambled to obey. As I passed Sanipu, he slapped my head as well. "Hurry up, you creature."

"I told you to bring the tent."

Open mouthed, I gaped at Balaam. *No, you didn't.*

But Sanipu sputtered. "Why should you always get to decide where to set it up?"

"Because I know this site, I know the best way to situate the dwelling." Balaam didn't even glance up.

"Why do you always get to decide?" Sanipu's stance widened.

Balaam's nostrils flared. Now he lifted his head one slow breath at a time. "Do not speak to me that way."

"I'm not your slave." One of Sanipu's hands twitched nearer the handle of his dagger. "Don't order me about."

Balaam straightened to his full height and went still. The two men stared each other down for one eternal moment. Then Balaam loosed a hard shout of laughter. "You stand up for yourself like a man. Now." He snapped his fingers. "Don't stand about with your mouth open for the flies, girl. Get busy."

I tugged the unwieldy hump of goat's hair fabric where he directed me. Already, my muscles trembled. How would I, how could I, ever set up the unwieldy structure, even if I knew how?

"PULL THE OTHER ROPE." Sanipu paused no more than two breaths. "The other rope, slave, look what you're doing. You'll have the tent collapsed on our heads." Before he could shove me, I dodged out of his way. He smirked as if well pleased.

I searched the horizon. Arseen had ridden off with the beasts late in the morning. Now it felt like dinner time. I studied the long line of Balaam's bent back. Would Arseen return at all? Maybe he'd sold the horses and camels to the first purchaser he came across. *That's what I'd do*—Then I sagged. I was a slave. Arseen was not.

"Stop idling before I beat you, girl. Get over here and help." Balaam's voice seemed to fill the sky from edge to edge.

Yes, Master. I scampered to obey. Sanipu sneered, and Balaam tilted his head as if satisfied by my unspoken words.

By the time we raised the tent my body ached, my hands raw from the ropes and scratchy goat hair. I collapsed in the shade of the structure, legs shaking.

Balaam lifted one brow. "What're you doing? Put away our belongings."

"In the right place, mind. I don't want my things mixed up with Arseen's." Sanipu made it sound as if I'd made that mistake countless times.

"Or mine with yours." Balaam nodded.

"Get moving, girl. Or perhaps you'd prefer—" Sanipu loosened the rope belt about his waist.

No. I lunged for the nearest folded rug. As I lugged it into the tent both men laughed.

AT LAST I had the rugs unbound, spread flat and brushed free of sand. Pillows scattered on rugs. Inside the tent, everything looked as if we'd never moved from the first camp.

I rubbed one shoulder. How had I ever thought the men didn't own much? Rugs, clothing, chests, the bulky tent. I shifted to wipe the sweat from my hairline as I recalled my father's house. How had our slaves coped with all the things inside? Of course, we didn't move every couple of days—

Slaves. Now I hated the word. Had the people who'd cooked my food, who cleaned up after me, hated me as I hated my captors? Had my casual acceptance of them and their role in my life curdled inside them? Would they ever dare turn on my family? I thought of Nahash, and his pride in the stable and horses, remembered how even my mother trembled before my father, and doubted it.

"There you are."

I startled to my feet at Sanipu's voice close behind me. He studied me from hairline to dirty toes.

No—Oh, no—

He closed one fist in my hair to drag me after him. "I told you what I wanted before we left the other camp." In his portion of the tent, he hurled me to the floor.

When I tried to push up onto my hands and knees, he planted one foot in the middle of my back, hitched up his robes, and hiked mine out of the way. "Stop squirming. Keep still like a woman should."

SANIPU ROLLED off me to sprawl across the rug and pillows scattered by his earlier movements. In moments he began to snore.

It hurt to move my arms where he had pinched me. But I squirmed out of his reach, pushed under the bottom of the tent wall. As I rolled into the comparatively fresh air, Balaam's horse snorted and plunged away from my sudden appearance at his feet. He'd chosen this shady spot—the only shade for leagues—to doze.

"It's all right, boy." *It's far from all right.* I longed for that velvety, whiskered muzzle to rub across my palm, for another creature to touch me in kindness. Careful not to startle him again, I curled up on the ground. Blood seeped down my thighs, my robe clammy with Sanipu's sweat.

The stallion wrinkled his upper lip, disturbed by the scent of blood. Stepping delicately, he eased back into the shade, but kept his distance from me, one ear cocked as if keeping watch.

Hands shaking, I retrieved a pomegranate from inside my robes. Now peeling the fruit from the seeds frustrated me for a different reason. It took ever bit if control I had not to gulp it down, seeds and all.

Then the stallion swung his tapered head toward the horizon. I peered at the movement that had attracted his attention. Arseen trudging into sight. Arseen, returned.

From inside the tent, Balaam shouted. "Girl. Here. At once." The black horse swung his head toward the sound, tucked in his chin and backed up a pace with flickering ears.

The snap of fingers. "Slave, I want you. Now."

The stallion's head jerked at the sound, but I knew Balaam was talking to me.

"Girl." Balaam's shout scoured the air like a sandstorm.

Not again. Not again. The words pounded along with the rhythm of my feet as I trudged to the tent entrance.

BALAAM RESTED on his back, arms folded under his head, ankles crossed. I nerved myself to edge away. Not by a flicker of his eyelids did he indicate he knew I was still there. He spoke to the tent roof. "We need water, girl. Fetch it."

Water? "I don't know—" I swallowed against the dryness in my throat. "Where?"

With a dramatic sigh, he rolled away from me and raised his voice. "Arseen." A louder yell. "Take the girl to the well." Then Balaam snapped his fingers at me. "You heard me, girl. Get moving."

CHAPTER TWELVE

A RSEEN'S SLIM BACK DREW FARTHER and farther away as we trod across the desert. "How—much—farther—to the—well?" Even empty, the rope bucket handles rasped my palms.

Arseen didn't look back at me. "Balaam said a quarter league this way."

I felt like a seed left to dry on the stone surround of the fountain at my father's house. Left to dry and die there. Except such a seed would at least have the sound of water to sing it to its death. I had nothing. Only the flies that lit on my face, hovered around my crotch as if attracted by the dry blood. I shook my head. The flies still clung, and buzzed around my groin. I paused to drop the buckets and brush the insects away.

At the clonk of buckets, Arseen whipped around. "Quit lagging, girl. I've spent enough time in the sun for one day."

Girl. Neither of the other men could hear him. He knew my name—

"You heard me, slave."

My heart bled as surely as the wound between my legs.

AT LAST THE WELL appeared on the horizon, a low round of stone below a tree. I sped up, eyes on the distant branches. Did I recognize the shape of those leaves? The buckets clattered hollowly at my sides.

Still Arseen didn't face me. "So you can move when it suits you."

You cruel—you evil— I couldn't think of a name vicious enough. I hitched the handles up to my elbows and pressed past him, eyes on the tree. By the time I reached the well, I no longer cared about the water. Every fiber in me focused on the trunk beyond it. A pomegranate.

"What do you stare at so? Is someone there?" Arseen half-crouched, one hand on the knife in his rope girdle. "Who's there?" His voice wobbled high. "Show yourself."

"There's—there's no one." *But there is, there is. My friend, the pomegranate.*

"Oh." He blushed, then pushed me toward the well. "Fill the buckets."

The pomegranate's scent filled the air. Against the slanting light of late afternoon, the leaves shone. The fruits hung heavy and red. Shining. A reminder of the last one I'd picked at the previous campsite, and eaten before the men woke this morning.

"Hurry up, girl."

Teeth set, I filled the buckets. If only Arseen wasn't with me, I could—

"What. Are. You. Staring at?" He sounded like Sanipu.

"Nothing." I grimaced at my empty hands. Even if Arseen had stayed in camp, I couldn't take what I needed from the tree without a knife. If only I could wrest his knife away. At the thought of knocking him over the head with one of the buckets, a giggle spurted out of me to fade away across the sands.

"Why do you laugh?" Arseen lowered his voice, as if the others might hear him a quarter league away.

"No—no reason, master." I stooped to fill the buckets.

His fist bounced off my shoulder. "Hurry up."

After I filled the buckets, we set off across the featureless desert, the shallow hills on the horizon blending with the bleached sky. While I trudged through the sand dragging at my feet, I glanced back at the pomegranate tree. It lost color—became a silhouette—disappeared. Somehow, I promised myself, I'd return armed with a chopping tool.

WITH EVERY STEP back to camp, the rope handles bit into my palms. The buckets dragged until my arms felt twice as long as usual. Water slopped onto my robe until the fabric clung to my legs. Sobbing, I moved slower at every step. When I managed to jerk a look after Arseen, he was a tiny figure far ahead of me.

"Wait—" I only had breath to gasp. "Wait—for—me." I couldn't take another step. Couldn't drag my feet through the sand one more time. I squatted and released the buckets as gently as possible. They thumped to the ground with a splash that made my throat close, but they stayed upright. I dropped to the sand between them, sore hands cradled between my thighs.

"What're you doing?" Arseen shrilled at me from an arm span away.

My head jerked upright. "R-resting."

Arseen's lips thinned. "Pick up the buckets at once." He didn't say *slave*. He didn't have to. Hem whipping around his ankles, he whirled toward camp.

Unsteadily, I crawled to my feet. Stood a moment, eyes squeezed shut, body trembling.

"I said hurry up."

Sand hissed as he strode back to me. He towered over me, a slim figure limned by the sun. He raised one hand—in threat, or hesitation about what he was about to do? Then his lips flattened, and he struck me across the face with the back of his hand. His knuckles caught my cheekbone, his rings split the skin. Blood poured down my cheek.

He stood over me, feet spread wide. His face shivered like wind-blown sand. "Fetch—" His voice snagged, then hardened. "Fetch those buckets. Now." He whirled and stalked away.

With aching shoulders and palms already raw, I stooped to obey. Trudge. Trudge. Trudge. Only when he halted did I recognize the low hills that masked camp. "Hurry up, slave." He spoke with his back to me, voice raised. So it could reach the others in the tent?

Breath slicing my lungs, I plodded between the dunes.

"Girl." Arseen rushed ahead. "How dare you pass me." He raised his voice even louder. "We're the masters. Your place is at our heels." He swept into the tent.

Balaam's horse hopped around one corner. In spite of the hobbles around his hind legs, the stallion's tail plumed over his haunches. As soon as I set down the buckets, he dunked his muzzle in the water so deeply it rippled around the edge of his nostrils.

As he sucked down the water I nearly cried out. The water I'd fought to carry—would he drink it all?

"Sorry, boy." With difficulty, I worked my body between him and the buckets, lifted the cursed things once more and lugged them into the tent. Then I dodged outside to sag into the late evening shadow of the structure, eyes closed. Soon the cool of night would send me shivering into my barren little room, but for now—

"How dare you loll about here." Balaam stood less than a footstep away. His lips twisted into a smile when I winced. "Fetch wood and get on with preparing our dinner. I'm hungry."

Sanipu paced out of the tent. "Move, girl. You've kept us waiting for our meal long enough."

While I fetched water you sent me for. What could I cook, and how? And how many slaves had they starved to death? Or did they intend to feed me after they'd thoroughly dominated me?

I glanced at the billowing walls of the tent, black against the last lingering rays of the sun. I couldn't expect Arseen to help me anymore. I'd be cursed by all the gods before I'd ever ask him to do so again.

"Hurry up, lazy thing. Fetch wood for the fire." Sanipu gestured at the open space behind the tent.

"B-build a fire?"

Balaam vented a long breath. "Make a ring of stones. Gather wood. I'll strike sparks. Then you cook our food."

Sanipu chucked me under the chin with one meaty finger. "Do not dawdle. I worked up quite a hunger today." He smoothed a palm over a bulge growing at his groin.

I scurried away. Stones. Stones. How did the men expect me to find rocks in the dark? First I'd gather wood—I jerked to a halt. There were no trees. I thought of the pomegranate a quarter league away. The next time they sent me to the well, I'd gather wood for poison, and for the fire. And fruit for myself. But in the meanwhile—I'd gather scrub.

Gasping, I floundered up the slope behind the tent to the spreading patch of brush. One step in, the spiny growth snagged my legs. I choked down a howl of pain as my ankle caught on a stout plant and I nearly fell. The base of the scrubby plants grew knotted and thick. Surely that would burn like firewood? How to cut it with no blade? In the end I broke it as best I could. The twisted plants abraded my torn palms.

I worked my way downhill toward camp, robe catching on plants in the darkness. Finally I paused to study my gleanings, found a bare patch of ground and dropped the twisted branches. Recalling the blaze in Aunt Kupo's room, I feared that these would burn to ash before they heated anything. I slogged back to the scrub. When another stout stalk tripped me, I knelt and tore at it until it broke off, stomped forward only to stumble on something hard and knobby. *Gods curse it. Gods curse everything.* Then, with difficulty, I held down a shout of joy. *A rock.* Even as I hopped on one foot, hands clasped around my newest bruise, I searched the ground. Where there was one rock, others might lurk—

"Girl, what's taking so long?" Balaam's voice cut through the cooling air like the curved blade he wore at one hip.

"G-gathering wood." Stomach queasy. I plucked up the rock and left it with the bundle of sticks. Could I find more rocks in the dark?

My neck prickled with sun from my trek to the well. My back felt permanently bent. I fumbled my way back and forth across the shallow hillside, searching. Searching. The scrub snagged my robes and flesh alike. My breath sobbed in and out of my dry mouth. My throat.

What if I'd found the only stone on the hillside? Then I felt a hard bulge underfoot. *Yes.* I snatched the rock in my mangled hands.

"Answer me, slave." Balaam's voice could have carved holes in the stone I held.

"In a moment, m-master."

"Girl." How could Balaam make the word sound shorter than it was?

Maybe if I searched the hill from top to bottom instead of side to side—

"Slave. Come here. Now."

"Yes, master." At the last moment I remembered the twigs, dodged back for them. With the pathetic bundle clutched to my chest, I slogged toward the sound of Balaam's angry breath.

He stood at the base of the slope, arms folded, jaw clamped. "I've shouted for you more times than I can count."

Because you can't count very high. "Yes, master. I—I was gathering wood, stones—"

"Why would you gather stones for a fire?"

"F-for the fire circle—"

"We have stones for the fire pit with the kitchen things. Fool."

He smacked the side of my head a ringing blow and swung back toward the tent.

His horse snorted. For a moment, I comforted myself with the illusion that the horse was shocked by his master's cruelty.

"Fetch the rocks. Let me know when the wood's ready to set alight."

Fetch the rocks from where? In the tent? I shuffled into the big room just inside the entrance, where the pots and containers of food stuffs were heaped by the door. Holding my breath so I couldn't smell the food *so close, so close to me, so close,* I tried to sort through the things without clattering pots together. A bumpy-looking sack held a dozen rocks.

Sack over one shoulder, a pot clutched to my chest, I wobbled behind the tent.

"Slave. What's taking so long, I'm hungry." A wall to one side of the tent—the wall of Sanipu's room—rippled as if he'd struck it with one fist.

You're hungry? I've only eaten stolen fruit and your tiny leavings for days. Filthy swine.

I dumped the rocks on the ground and set them in an uneven circle with shaking hands.

Arseen's voice sounded light in comparison with Sanipu's. "Yes, hurry up. Slave."

The sticks looked so few when I dropped them into the stone circle. "B-balaam." Wrong. "M-master. I mean, my Lord."

He appeared at once to swat the side of my head again. My hearing clanged. Scowling, he stooped over the twigs. "Never yell for me again. You'll reveal our hiding place." Then he raised his own voice. "Arseen, more wood."

A pause before Arseen strolled out. "She's the slave."

"Do you want to eat before morning?"

"Of course."

Balaam jabbed one finger at the fire circle. "Look at this."

Another jabbing movement, this time up the hill. "Fetch more wood."

Arseen muttered all the way up the hill.

Balaam's mouth quirked. When Arseen reappeared at last, arms full of scrub, Balaam knelt by my pitiful bundle of twigs, a flint in one long hand. He struck his flint with a stone from the fire ring. Aunt Kupo usually had to strike her flint several times to create a spark, but he managed on the first try.

Balaam knelt, fed the flame his breath. Ribbons of fire spread to the other sticks. Good thing Arseen brought more wood, else the fire would've died before the men returned to the tent. I side-stepped as Arseen dropped his bristly armful beside me.

He sniffed. "Use them wisely, girl. I'm not fetching wood for you again." He stalked away.

It's not for me, you half-wit.

My stomach rumbled loudly enough for Balaam to curl his lip. "Must you?"

It took all my will to remain upright. *I'm so hungry—*

"Call us as soon as the meal is ready." Balaam followed Arseen inside.

Chapter Thirteen

FLATBREAD. THE ONLY THING I COULD COOK. Maybe. I hoped. Flour into a bowl, water from the buckets. No, I couldn't bear to carry them another step. Instead I carried the bowl to the bucket, scooped out what I needed. Back at the fire I stared down at the flour floating atop the water like pale scum. It'd work out, I'd just stir the dough longer—

"Slave." The men must've practiced shouting together.

I squished the dough on the outside of a bowl and stuck it on the fire. The lower edge darkened in moments. The part in the upper reaches of the bowl stayed pale. Raw. Then it started to darken too, and I sagged. *Thank goodness, thank goodness, it's cooking.* No, smoke curled up from the burnt bits lower down to spread a dark stain in wavery fingers up the uncooked dough. Stiff as old leather, the burnt section curled away from the pot.

"Girl."

I flinched toward their yell, then back to the fire. *Quick, quick. How to rescue the bread?* What would they do to me for not coming when called? For ruining their meal?

My back and ribs ached, my woman parts felt raw.

"Girl." Balaam's voice made me retch.

"Y-yes, master. M-my Lord." Perhaps if I turned the dough so the uncooked section came nearer the fire—

I picked up the pot by its upper rim, burning my fingertips. With a scream, I dropped it. The scorched part of the flatbread broke off into the flames, echoed by a clink as the bowl cracked. A chill raced from my bowels to my heart. What remained of the flatbread rested directly on the fire.

"Come here. Now." Balaam's voice alone. Not yelling. Close behind me in the dark. So quiet. My very bones chilled.

The stone nearest my toes was long and thin. I poked it into the bowl and dragged the broken pieces of burnt bread off the flames. With a crunch of pottery, the broken vessel fell out of the fire.

Curse it.

"If I come all the way out there, you'll be sorry." Balaam clipped every word.

With the skirt of my robe bunched around my hands, I peeled what remained of the bread off the pot. Black-streaked dough flecked with ash. The bread tattered off the shards of clay, left a sticky residue. With one toe I nudged the remains of the pot nearer the heart of the fire. Could I discard it in the scrub later, before the men discovered it?

I plopped the bread onto a platter and raced to the tent entrance. Arms folded, Balaam stood just inside. The other two sat on the rug behind him, glaring at me. I rushed to them and knelt, as our house slaves had always done. Head ducked low, I proffered the platter on uplifted hands.

Balaam delivered another ringing blow over my ear. "What. Is. This?"

Both hands pressed to my ear, my chin dug into my breast bone. "B-bread, master."

He struck the platter out of my hands. "You expect us to eat this mess?"

"Prepare more right away." Sanipu folded his arms.

Balaam sank to the tent floor. "Arseen, show her what to do. Again."

"Me? I—" Arseen choked off when Balaam scowled. "Come with me. Slave."

"Stay a moment." Sanipu's lips curled. "Before she leaves, she needs to understand how worthless she is."

Cold as deep as winter stone filled my belly. Would they beat me again? Would I survive if they did?

Sanipu lounged into a more relaxed pose. "Eat." When I didn't move, he reached out with one foot and overbalanced me. "I said, eat this slop. Now."

I crept back into a kneeling position, gaped at the ash-flecked dough. "What?"

Balaam's smile revealed his teeth. "You expected us to eat it."

Would one bite be enough? My shrunken stomach ached with hunger, only to seal closed when the soft goop clung to my fingers. I forced some of the burnt and raw dough into my mouth. Gritty with ash, it tasted of the flames and felt wet. I retched.

Arseen's bare foot caught me in the stomach. "Vomit and you'll clean it up. Come with me." He stomped to the tent entrance.

Before I could move, Balaam shouted an additional order. "While you're out there, see to my horse."

See to his horse? Not more of the precious water. Then I collided with Arseen, rigid just outside the tent. After a sizzling silence, he moved ahead again. "Certainly, Balaam." Outside, Arseen jutted his chin. "Fire's out."

The shallow layer of ash gave off no heat. As I bent over the firepit, Arseen shoved the middle of my bruised back to send me sprawling. Ash fountained up into my mouth.

With a sound like a sob, Arseen hauled me off the fire pit to hike my robes higher. *Wha—oh, gods, no. Not now. Not him.* He hitched my robes to my knees, paused, then rolled away. "Don't just lie there, collect more wood."

"H-how?" Where?

Arseen righted his robes. "The scrub, you ninny. The thicker the branch the longer it burns."

The ash in my nose brought to mind the fires in my father's house, smoke perfuming the rooms as the piled logs burned.

Arseen jerked his head at the slope. "Get moving." His lips pinched as he stooped for one of the buckets. "Waste of water, this horse." He trudged toward Balaam's stallion, dozing in the shadow cast by the tent.

At the edge of the patch of scrub, I stared about me. In the faded dusk I couldn't see individual plants any more.

"You have to go into the patch, find a plant that's grown many seasons." At the sound of Arseen's voice right behind me, I yelped. He spoke as if he hadn't just tried to attack me and failed. "Such a plant burns longer. Gather enough to dry some for the next fire."

"How do I gather thick wood with my bare hands?" *In the dark, no less.* "I have no blade." *Solve that problem, son of a dog.*

"Oh." His hand hovered by the knife thrust in his belt. "For now. For now I'll cut it for you." He sighed, as if the task were almost too much for him. "Let's get on with it."

Arms folded, he waited at the edge of the slope while I waded into the scrub to search. Almost at once I tripped over a stout plant. Clutching my wet—bleeding?—ankle, I flapped a hand in the air. "There's a thick one here—somewhere."

"Good." Arseen crossed to me, and knelt to fumble around for the plant. "Couldn't you mark where the cursed thing was?"

No, it tripped me.

"Ahh, here it is." He stooped to chop the plant just above the sinewy roots. Then he jerked his chin. "Find another one."

This time I bumped into a sturdy plant and managed to keep on my feet. My ankles felt like they were on fire. Too bad I couldn't cook with my bones. "Here."

We repeated the ritual twenty or more times. Sweat stung my eyes. When Arseen headed down the slope to camp, he left me to carry the rough wood. The jumble of it pinched my arms at every step.

By the time I struggled up to the fire circle, Arseen stood there. I could tell that his lips pinched from the tight sound of his voice. "Hurry, girl, I haven't got forever."

You have somewhere you need to go?

"Get the fire going."

"H-how?" I could barely hear my own voice.

Arseen huffed out a breath. "What?"

"I never started a fire before."

"Idiot. Go back for some thin twigs. Dry."

Idiot yourself. Why didn't you tell me sooner? The wood clattered to the ground. Arseen skipped out of the way.

"How dare you—"

Shoulders hunched, I scuttled out of his reach to the patch of scrub, felt around until I found a plant with some dead twigs. I gathered a handful, rejoined Arseen, tossing the sticks on the tent-shape he'd built of thicker bits of wood.

"Don't just fling them on, you fool." He plucked up the twigs, then peeled curls in the bark with his knife. He replaced the curl-covered sticks and struck a flint.

Faster even than Balaam's fire, the flames leapt along the partly peeled twigs and started to eat into the logs. I frowned at the angled heap he'd constructed, peeked at his face. He looked younger. Softer.

He's forgotten me. If only I could slip off to the tent without him noticing, creep into a forgotten corner, flip my robe over my face and sleep undisturbed. For a while. If only I still had a pomegranate, even one slick and reeking from a day spent hidden in my robe.

But if I sneaked away, I wouldn't learn how to build a fire and keep it burning. Hunkered on the ground, I set myself to observe.

Thanks to my lessons with Aunt Kupo, I was good at that.

Arseen let the fire burn down until the flames turned into coals, then stepped back. "Make dough."

When I poured the flour into a bowl, he gaped. "Is that all that's left?"

"Y-yes." *I must grind more in the morning—*

"That's not enough for one person, let alone three."

Four.

Arseen strode toward the tent. "There's not enough flour. She must grind more before we eat."

From inside, Balaam groaned. "Let her cook something else."

"Let." As if caring for them is a treat. Then my stomach dropped. What else could I cook?

"I'm tired of waiting." Sanipu sounded sulky. Next moment he stormed out of the tent. Light from the fire slicked along the blade of his knife. "Worthless girl—"

"Stop." Balaam lunged and caught Sanipu's arm, jerked it.

His knife clinked on the stones at the edge of the fire circle. "Or you'll do what." Sanipu's words came out in a predator's growl.

Balaam's knife was in his hand. "Give you something to remember me by for the rest of your life."

Sanipu laughed. "So I'd still be alive, would I?"

"Minus a hand."

Oooohhhhh. The imagined crunch of blade on bone sent me easing out of the firelight, belly heaving.

Sanipu's jaw jutted. "Why you—"

"Yes, brother?"

Sanipu shrugged his heavy shoulders. "Let us not come to blows over a silly chit of a girl. I grow weary of her clumsiness." He stooped for his knife, head up to keep watch on Balaam.

"To be sure." Balaam kept his knife in hand, but the point drooped. "She'll learn. No one can learn if they're dead. I want to keep you from the mistake you made with our last slave."

A chill raced down my arms, and I crouched flat to the ground. *They had a slave before me—and Sanipu killed her.*

Now I wished the two men had fought each other, wished Balaam had hacked off both Sanipu's hands. Wished they'd killed each other.

Chapter Fourteen

Arseen gripped the back of my neck. His scrawny fingers shook against my skin. Then he shook me, and I yelped. "What're you doing? Back to work, girl."

"I'm—I'm—trying to—"

"Oh, for the gods' sake." He shifted in front of me, eyes dilated, and thrust me toward the containers of food. "Prepare rice while I slice eggplant for roasting."

How much rice? Did I dump it into the frying pan, or—

"Gods. Help. Me." Arseen stomped over to me. "Use half as much rice as water, put the rice in the pot after the water boils. Cover the rice and wait until I tell you." He yanked out a small pot with a lid, scooped water into it, set it on the glowing coals, then tipped rice into a bowl.

"W-which bowl do I use to cook the rice?"

"You're not cooking it yet, you're getting rid of the dust and chaff stuck to the grain."

When my mouth parted to ask another question, he huffed out a breath. "Rinse the rice in the smaller bowl, then cook it in the pot on the fire, you fool." Back to me, he sliced eggplant on a flat stone pulled from the fire circle, his knife grating.

I had to rinse the rice, waste more precious water? We'd need more tomorrow. Tomorrow, when I might be able to get the poisonous wood I needed. The men used water like air. I tipped a grudging handful of fluid into the rice and swirled it around. A cloud of dust swam across the surface.

"Pot's boiling. Tip in the rice." Arseen speckled the eggplant with olive oil and spices, then set the slices in a covered pan to roast over the coals. "Food ready soon," he shouted.

From within the tent Balaam grunted. "About time."

"Before we starve down to our bones," Sanipu said.

You? How long since I'd eaten more than their leavings as I scrubbed the plates with sand? Or the occasional slips of pomegranate, torn from its seeds with my teeth?

Arseen flipped the eggplant with one smooth movement. Lips pinched, he returned the pan to the fire. "You'll do that, when you've had as much practice cooking as I've had."

After Sanipu killed the earlier slaves, you mean?

Arseen stood taller, or tried. "Check the rice, slave. Give it a stir."

The rice looked fluffy, and the water had disappeared. "It's— done." Wasn't it?

"Wash up so we can eat."

What? Was Arseen talking to me? I straightened just as Balaam stomped up to the fire circle. He reached the buckets, bent to dunk his hands in, and his head jerked up. "I sent you for water. Where is it?"

My mouth opened, but no sound came out. Inside I shouted, *Your horse drank it.*

"We used it in cooking. And the horse drank nearly a bucketful."

Balaam pivoted toward Arseen. "What did you say?"

In silence, Arseen slid the eggplant from pan to platter.

"What. Did. You. Say. To. Me."

"Nothing."

Sanipu strolled out of the tent, clapped Arseen on the shoulder. "Brothers. Why argue?" He sniffed. "Let's eat."

While they focused on their food and each other, I eased out of sight. Only after they finished did I creep out to clear the sturdy clay dishes back to the fire circle. I'd wash up later, but first I'd—the men had only left two pieces of eggplant. *Pigs*. Even cold, it tasted delicious, accented by the turmeric Arseen had used. I plunged my fingers into the rice bowl. Cold—gummy—clotted. I plucked a spoon, gobbled down the clammy rice before the men caught me, then went to fetch the last, scant bucket of water.

Oh, no. Balaam's stallion stood there, muzzle deep in the bucket. He gulped the last of the water so deeply his whole body rocked back and forth. The horse lifted his slender nostrils high at my approach. Precious water dripped from his chin. Only fear that Balaam would beat me if I yelled at his horse kept me silent.

The stallion lowered his head, blew sadly around the bottom of the empty bucket, then pawed it. It fell over with a hollow thud.

I remembered how Arseen and I had drunk when we reached the well. "You poor, thirsty creature."

The horse's ears flicked at my murmur. Slowly I stroked his shoulder. His warm hide quivered, as if he mistook my fingers for an errant fly. Then he leaned into my touch.

My eyes turned hot and wet. "You're lonely, too." His black coat felt silken. "I'll bring you more water in the morning."

The stallion's head lowered until his nostrils brushed the ground.

"Has no one ever touched you with kindness before?" Foolish question. When did my captors touch anyone with mercy? "Good boy." I smoothed his tangled mane with my fingers. "Maybe tomorrow I'll comb out these knots." If I could find a comb. If Balaam even owned the tools to care for the beautiful horse he'd enslaved.

The stallion breathed into the palm of my hand. Maybe tomorrow I'd ask Balaam for grooming things. Meanwhile, what to do with the dishes?

"What're you doing, mooning about my horse?" Balaam shouted.

As I whirled the stallion hopped away as fast as his hobbles allowed. Fists on hips, Balaam stood at the edge of the moon-shadow cast by the tent. "Clean the dishes, you lazy thing."

With no water? How? Thank the gods, Balaam didn't stay to watch me. As soon as I jumped to obey him, he snorted and returned inside. Then the key word he'd barked at me echoed in my mind. *Clean.* Not wash. With fistfuls of sand I scoured each pot, rubbed my fingers over it to feel for stickiness, scrubbed with more sand, then wiped it off.

The night breeze sifted over me with the chill breath of the changing season. I curled up in the shadows behind the tent and flipped the edge of my robe over my face to make myself less visible. Tonight, I'd sleep uninterrupted if I could.

Curse it. The next moment, sand grated. Perhaps if I didn't move, they wouldn't notice me? Warmth puffed my face through the robe. When I squeaked and flailed upright, Balaam's horse skittered away, nostrils flared. Moonlight shone in his eyes.

Did his heart pound like mine? Hands clutched at my breast, I climbed to my feet. "Easy, boy, you just startled me." I chuckled. "We startled each other."

He hopped closer, brushed my palm with his velvety lips. I touched his cheek. Unlike Singer, this horse didn't pin his ears or bare his teeth. He moved closer as fast as the hobbles allowed. Our faces pushed against each other as he curled his neck around me.

We're both captives. I'm as hobbled as he is.

Balaam's curses woke me at dawn. "What in Moloch's name—where's our water?"

My mouth dried to leather as Balaam advanced on me, an empty bucket in either hand. "Where's our water, girl?" He flung the buckets at me. With a clatter, they rolled against my side. The horse hopped to the edge of the scrub, hobbles clashing. One of the buckets teetered and rolled along one leg all the way to my toes. "Fill those at once." Balaam stormed into the tent.

"Curse it." The hairy rope handles rasped my palms. Only then did I realize Balaam wanted me to go back to the well. By myself.

He shouted from inside the tent. "Move, slave."

How does he know I haven't gone yet?

"You heard him." Arseen rounded the edge of the tent. "Go."

"B-but where—"

Arseen huffed out a breath that could've started a sandstorm. He jutted his chin. "That way. Keep going straight ahead."

Disguise it though he might, he was still helping me.

"Half-wit." Arseen stomped out of my sight.

Half-wit?

"Girl."

I doubted Sanipu wanted to hurry me on my way. Buckets hitched over my elbows, I fled around the small hills that hid camp.

His shout followed me. "Girl. You come when I call."

Hot air scorched my lungs. Behind me, Sanipu's roar sounded fainter with distance. "Come here at once."

I skidded down the far side of a faint slope out in the open desert, its upper edge crested with the same kind of scrub that crawled up the shallow hills behind the camp. Would this hill hide me from Sanipu's view if he looked for me? Thank the gods Balaam had sent me to fetch more water.

"Silence. You announce our presence." Balaam's voice barely reached me.

By the time I felt far enough from the camp not to worry about Sanipu following me, the buckets dragged at my arms. Would I ever find the well? Or would I wander the desert until thirst claimed me? Until Father's men found my bones?

Wait. On the horizon. A speck of green.

CHAPTER FIFTEEN

I **FOUND IT. *I* FOUND IT. A RAGGED CHEER** tore my dry throat. Next moment I could've burrowed into the sand. What if someone heard me?

Then I straightened. What if that someone was a rescuer?

Hands clenched around the scratchy ropes, I trudged toward the well. As I drew nearer, two figures in long robes turned to face me. I broke into a run. *Other people.* Someone to help me escape, sneak up on my captors, imprison them, punish them—

But when I panted up, the figures were only two women, mouths agape. I shuddered to a stop. No decent woman would run where others might see her. My cousin Tamar had told me so often enough. Feet dragging, I reached the well. Women couldn't hide me, couldn't attack my captors. I was helpless as ever.

They studied me, one tall and young, the other gray-haired and veiled. Against the backdrop of the pomegranate's green leaves and scarlet fruit, their black robes looked dusty and dim.

I forced a smile. "Good day to you."

The younger woman set down her full bucket and perched one hip on the well's stone surround. "Where'd you come from?"

The older woman frowned. "Don't be forward." But she leaned toward me as if awaiting an answer to the younger woman's—her daughter's?—question.

Oh, gods. What to say? "W-where do you live?"

The older woman stepped nearer and waved one hand the opposite direction from my captor's camp. "Our village is that way."

A village. People. *Somewhere to hide—*

"Four households." The young woman straightened with pride, as if they came from the cultural center of Ammon.

Four households. My captors would find me at once, and I knew all too well what revenge they'd take on the villagers. Did the young woman have to crowd so close to me? I craned my neck to see her face. Why must everyone be taller than me?

She smiled. "Where do you come from?" The older woman nodded eagerly, and set her bucket on the ground as if readying herself for a long talk.

What could I safely say? I blurted the name of my father's town.

The girl's brow wrinkled. "Where?"

"Daughter." The mother gave her a friendly nudge. "That's her hometown. She obviously lives someplace else now." She turned to me. "Where do you and your husband live?"

"I'm—I—" I almost said that I belonged to a group of outlaws, but caught myself in time. "I'm part of a nomadic tribe now." True, in a way.

The mother's chin fell almost to her chest. "You're from a town, and you married a nomad?"

"Y-yes. I'd best get back now. Pleasant to meet you." I lifted my buckets, ready to start on my way and realized I'd yet to fill them.

"Wait." The daughter hopped off the well. "We meet strangers so rarely. Please stay. Chat."

"What's your name, child?" The mother scanned my filthy robes.

"S-Sarah." I shut my mouth on my family name. If I told it

to them, they might talk and word spread to my father. Make it simple for him to find me and drag me back into a different kind of servitude.

I dunked my buckets so water sloshed in. "I need to get back. We're out of water." I scuttled away as fast as the weight of the buckets allowed.

"How rude, she didn't even ask our names." The daughter's voice floated after me.

My shoulders tightened. I longed to drop my buckets, speed back to her, cast myself on her bosom, and sob out my explanation—but my captors would punish me if I didn't return, and soon. With a dry sob, I followed my windblown footprints back the way I'd come.

The dry sands, marked only by subtle slopes and rare streaks of drier scrub here and there, stretched into forever before me, and to either side. I didn't dare glance back at the well, lest I drop the buckets and flee back to the women, begging them to help me. Help they were helpless to give.

My arms felt ready to pop out of my shoulders from the drag of the buckets. Surely I must be nearly back to the camp by now? But a glance over one shoulder, peek and done, revealed the low gray smear of the well on the horizon, with a hint of green above and behind it.

The pomegranate.

I almost dropped the buckets. Why hadn't I asked the women for a knife? I could've collected what I needed, instead of allowing the women to distract me.

My captors were right. I was a half-wit.

Could I leave the water here and go back? Wind blew a stinging spray of sand around my ankles. It'd blow in the buckets and spoil the water. Not to mention what Balaam and Sanipu would do if I took any longer to return.

I stared at the smear of green on the horizon. *Next time. Next time, I swear it.* Then I turned away, and quickened my steps to the camp.

I STAGGERED between the low hills that hid the encampment and veered for the fire circle.

Arseen knelt by the fire, his back to me, scrubbing plates with a sandy rag. His head shot up. "About time. I had to cook, then scour the plates. Like a damn woman."

I peered at the clean plates. Was any food left?

He bounded to his feet and hurled the gritty rag at me. "Not much left to do, but you can do it." And he stalked away.

He's worse than Balaam. Worse than Sanipu. At least they didn't pretend to befriend me one moment, then turn on me the next. I glowered after him. A snort at my shoulder made me jump. Balaam's horse stood, ears pricked, focused on the full buckets.

"Thirsty, boy?" I tipped water into a big bowl, offered him what remained in the bucket.

The stallion drank so deeply his ears shifted in time with his deep swallows. At last he raised his lovely head, water dripping, and shoved my chest with his muzzle. I shifted the bucket to catch the precious drops and stroked the horse's neck. *So warm and smooth.* I rubbed harder, and the horse danced his haunches in a semi-circle, his upper lip stretched out in pleasure, eyes half-shut.

"Like that, do you, boy?" I laughed. *Boy.* Too much like *girl.* A slave name. "What's your real name?" No. I didn't want to call him what Balaam did, if Balaam had even given the stallion a proper name. "You're black as night. I'll call you Midnight."

His ears flicked again, as if answering me.

"Glad you approve, Midnight."

With water from the bowl, I washed the last dishes. Under the guise of putting them away, I searched for something to eat and found the remains of some flatbread. I couldn't tear off shreds fast enough. With my makeshift meal stuffed up one sleeve, I retreated to the shady side of the tent. *If Midnight drinks more water, I'll have to go back to the well. I'll have to go back—and get the poison.*

I returned to the buckets, moved one closer to the stallion. "Here, Midnight." Voice low, so the men wouldn't hear me.

But he just retreated to the scrubby hillside to lip the thorny plants. "Midnight." He swished his tail, head down in the brush. "Don't you want more water?"

The horse hopped away from me, hobbles clattering. Away from the bucket I wanted him to empty.

I angled toward him, stroked his neck, before I closed one fist around the thick hair between his ears. When I tried to tug him back to camp, Midnight scrubbed his head against my body.

"Curse it—stop that." Maybe if I pulled harder?

Midnight's hooves seemed to grow roots into the ground, his forelock rasping my torn palms. *My only friend, and he's hurting me.*

"Fine, stay here." I stalked away, only to hear the brush swish as he followed.

"Good Midnight." I still didn't dare look at him, didn't raise a hand to pat him in case he dodged my touch. With the stallion at my shoulder, I ploughed downhill through the scrub. Would the men be looking for me? What if they saw me with the horse? "Here, handsome. Want some water?" With any luck the full bucket would be empty soon.

He splashed the water with his muzzle, head-butted me again, sighed, then turned away.

"Midnight, come back." He hopped away as fast as his hobbled hind legs allowed. Could I remove the hobbles? What would Balaam do if his horse galloped away?

I wanted to fling myself on the ground, pummel the sand until my knuckles bled. What was one more injury on a body already aching? Water slopped over the lip of the bucket to stain the sand dark—and then drain away and disappear. My mouth opened.

With one foot, I shoved the bucket over. Before the last of the water cascaded out, I jumped to my feet and yelled, "I'm going for more water."

Balaam swooped out of the tent. "Why do we need more?"

"Y-your horse knocked over the bucket."

Sanipu stomped out to join us. "That cursed horse. He's more trouble than he's worth." One hand hovered over his knife.

Would he butcher the innocent horse? "H-he didn't do it on purpose. He bumped it with one hoof."

Balaam blazed at me a long moment, then lifted one shoulder. "Very well. Go for more water."

Yes. Though I could've skipped, I forced myself to trudge out of their sight. How I longed to sing and dance, but the men would hear. But I couldn't help capering now and then. The clatter of the buckets sounded like music. Unlike my previous trip, it seemed only moments before I glimpsed the green smudge of the pomegranate at the well.

CHAPTER SIXTEEN

*T*HIS TIME I'LL BORROW A KNIFE *from the mother and daughter at the well.* But the mother and daughter were long gone. My buckets clonked to the ground. "Oh, no. No. No—" I rushed to the pomegranate, scrabbled in the dirt until one root lay exposed. Too stout to break off with my fingers.

Perhaps the skin of several fruits would work? But first I sat on the well coping and ate my fill of pomegranate, barely tasting the sourness. Only then did I gather the scattered pieces of skin and bundle them in a knotted section of my robe. With more of the heavy rounds tucked beside my breasts, I filled the buckets. A deep breath. I started my fourth trek across the wasteland.

This time the walk back to the outlaw camp didn't seem to take as long. Even the sting of the drying abrasions between my thighs spurred me on. After the men were dead, I'd find some aloe. Growing wild, or for sale at a market. I'd help myself heal. Now, with every step, I pictured it as my last such walk. Ever. Even the sand felt soft under my feet. Cushiony.

Back in camp, Balaam prowled by the fire circle. "What took you so long?" He jabbed a finger at the bulge in my robe. "What's that?"

"Pom-pomegranates. I saw—saw them by the well."

"For yourself?"

I couldn't look away. Couldn't lie. "Some of them."

"I suspected as much. You've pomegranate juice smeared all over your chin."

My hand flew to my face, touched the tell-tale stickiness there. "I c-c-couldn't stop m-m-myself." *I'm so hungry.* "B-but it's not just for me, m-master. I thought you might enjoy them. All of you." Had I brought enough for them all? I swallowed. "D-did I do wrong? Master." The last word choked me.

For the first time, his brows arched upward. "Not at all." He strode toward the tent. "So much for your impatience, Sanipu. I knew she'd become a good slave with the proper training." His voice retreated. "Listen how she gives thought to our comfort—"

Training? Their comfort? My fingers tightened on the makeshift pouch in my robe with the hidden pomegranate skins. Oh, the meal I'd prepare for them that night.

AS I GROUND FLOUR, I imagined each of my torturers between the stones. Balaam, chiseled mouth contorted in pleasure as he ravished me. Sanipu's gleeful face as he pinched my tenderest parts. Arseen calling me "slave" when he knew my name. The sun sank in the sky and the grinding stone nearly splintered as I smashed it into their imagined faces.

Sanipu shouted. "Girl? Where's our meal?"

The pomegranate seeds, each with its shining layer of fruit, waited in a bowl. Hands unsteady, I hurried to kneel before Sanipu. This way, I could offer them two of the fruits, and keep the others for myself.

"Why bring the food here? We usually eat outside."

They had to stay inside while I prepared the bread. "You'll be more comfortable in the cool shade of the tent."

Sanipu's mouth slackened. Then he roared, "Balaam."

I winced back a step.

"You're right, she's becoming more attentive to our needs." Sanipu sent me a glittering look. "At least at meal time."

Ugh. Back to mix the flatbread and add the skins I'd prepared. Pat the dough on a pot, set it on the fire to bake. Would the men notice my addition of shredded pomegranate skin to the bread? Should I add a reddish spice—

"Girl. Dinner."

"Coming, master." *Die, Balaam. Soon you'll die.* The bread curled away from the pot at the edges. I removed it from the flames and carried it in.

CHAPTER SEVENTEEN

SANIPU DREW IN HIS CHIN. "Only bread? Again? Where's our dinner?"

"Why didn't you bring jelly?" Arseen scowled.

I fetched the pots of assorted jellies from the kitchen area. One was pomegranate. Perhaps it'd keep the men from noticing the flavor in the flatbread? None of them even looked at me while I delivered the jelly. I slunk back to the fire, all my attention on my captors behind me. When would the pomegranate take effect? I could barely swallow the plain flatbread I'd prepared for myself. Though I listened with my whole body, no groans came. Were they dying in silence? Would they vomit, have diarrhea?

What if my captors suspected my part in their torment? My eyes darted around the barren encampment. Could I run far enough for them not to find me? Would they stay strong enough to hunt me, catch me? I shuddered. Strong enough to peel the flesh from my bones with their knives—force their stinking bodies on mine one last time.

Stop this. Stop it. Too late to question what I'd done. Maybe they'd keeled over where they sat. May each one suffer for the torture he inflicted on me, the torture done to all the women before me.

If only Aunt Kupo had told me more about the effects of pomegranate poisoning—

"Girl."

I bounded to my feet. Balaam still lived?

"You heard him, girl. Bring us food. Now."

Sanipu was also alive, and wanted more bread? More?

"Slave, do not make me come after you," Arseen blustered.

"If I come out there, you'll regret it." Balaam's voice gritted with threat.

Sweat sprang over my entire body. Balaam could still threaten me, hurt me. They all could.

"Y-yes, master." The ground seemed wobbly underfoot as I rushed into the tent. None of my captors even looked sick.

Sanipu angled his head. "I see no food." As I stumbled to a halt beside him, he slapped the back of my head.

Skull ringing, I fled back to the fire circle. Back at the kitchen area, I looked at my options, then laughed as if shards of broken pottery crowded my throat. For immediate food, I only had the two pomegranates left from my failed attempt on their lives. The two I had kept for myself. Now I scurried into the tent with them, unpeeled.

Sanipu scowled at the fruit, at me. "This is what you bring us?" He swung at me again, though this time I stood far enough away for him to miss. Scowling, he threw himself back on his elbows. "I hate pomegranate. It's a bother peeling the fruit from the seeds." He belched. "Besides, I have wind."

All my trouble getting the pomegranate, mincing it, had only gained me Sanipu's flatulence? "I'm making more bread. For you to eat with the jelly."

"Well, where is it?" Voice low, Balaam sounded at his most dangerous. Like Sanipu, he leaned on one elbow on the carpet. But he could leap to his feet in an instant.

"Y-yes, master." I raced back to the kitchen area, snatched the plain bread I'd made for myself, plunked it on a plate, and hurried inside. For once, the sight and scent of bread didn't drive me wild. I might never eat again. Why hadn't my plan worked?

Sanipu grunted. "Plain bread this time? I liked the flavored bread you brought us earlier."

He'd liked the poisoned bread? Liked it? But then, I hadn't managed to poison it, had I?

Arseen leaned forward to tear off a piece. He chewed, then waved the torn piece without looking at me. "At least she bakes better. Faster."

I'd cooked a poisonous meal for him, for them all—and they liked it. I crept out to stare into the night. What had gone wrong? Why hadn't my plan worked? The skins of the fruit must not carry enough—or any—poisons.

My shoulders squared. Next time I'd go to the well better prepared. Ready to chop roots from the tree. *But how? How?* When the thought occurred to me, I almost tipped onto my own seat. I was out here with the kitchen things alone, wasn't I? Now I scrabbled through the kitchen things for a strong knife, but even as I did, Balaam stalked out of the darkness.

"What're you doing?" He halted so close to me I felt the heat pouring off his body. "Slave. I asked. What. You. Are. Doing."

His deliberation meant trouble. My heart pounded in my fingertips. "I'm—I'm—" *What?*

"Yes?" He drew out the word with a hiss. "You're rattling about. I came to investigate."

I gagged on my tongue. "The k-kitchen things are a mess. I'm putting them in order."

He studied me. "I see." The dying firelight played over the faint smile on his lips. Back into the tent he strode. "You see, Sanipu? She grows better at her work."

Sanipu's reply made all the men laugh.

The wooden handle of the knife in my fist grew slippery with sweat. How I longed to drive that blade into Balaam's eyes, the eyes that had narrowed in pleasure as he soiled me. Into Sanipu's bulging belly, the sweaty belly that had squashed me.

No, I wanted to chop off Sanipu's male parts while he watched, then mince them to bits while he bled to death. If I could manage to find a place to set the blade on its tiny length.

And Arseen? I'd stab him deep in the heart, the way he'd hurt me. Moonlight shimmered along the blade when I tilted it. I sagged. Never could I stab the men. They'd defend themselves as if from a child's wooden toy, then take slow revenge on me.

I straightened. But the knife would help me silence and stop them all the same.

CHAPTER EIGHTEEN

THE NEXT MORNING SOMETHING HEAVY plopped on my stomach. I jolted awake and onto my feet to find Arseen smirking at me.

"Don't stand there gaping, put those away."

"W-what?" I blinked down at the laden sack humped over my body. "Wh-where?"

He gestured at the sack. "With the kitchen things, you dull creature. Where else would you store chickpeas?"

He'd started for the tent, but doubled back to kick me in the behind. "Don't lag like that, stir yourself."

"W-where did you g-get chickpeas?"

He sighed. "From a market, of course. I replenished our chickpeas. Now put them away."

He'd gone to a market without me? So much for buying aloe, or other herbs to help me heal—wait. A village large enough to have a market was within range of our camp?

Arseen clapped his hands once. "When I tell you to do something, do it."

THAT AFTERNOON Balaam poured the remaining water into bowls, jerked his chin at me. "Carry these into the shade of the tent, then fetch more water."

I launched to my feet, and his eyebrows swooped into his hair. "You seem excited. Why?"

Curse it, I appeared too eager. "Water, again?"

"Again." He glowered at me. "With an extra person in camp, we use more water."

He blamed me? Me? They hadn't once fed me, much less offered me water!

Head tucked down, I gripped the rope handles. "As you say."

When I reached the well, I dropped the buckets to jig in place, then froze and looked about. Had anyone seen me? No—no one in sight. First, as always when I visited the well, I drank my fill. Then I filled the buckets, and wiggled the knife from its hiding place in the hem of my robe. Threads dangled from the frayed slit.

The whole garment stank of my sweat, of Sanipu, of misery. As soon as possible, I'd get another robe and burn this one.

Under the pomegranate tree I dug with cupped palms to expose the roots. "Old friend, I'm sorry for what I must do." Would the tree die because of my efforts to kill the outlaws? I paused, one palm pressed to the trunk. I hoped not, but that couldn't stop me. Wouldn't. I wiggled the blade into a root and sawed away.

The knife stuck.

Was it too dull for the job? *No. No. I will do this. I will.*

Damp hair clung to my neck and temples as I chopped. My shoulders and arms ached when the root finally broke free into the dirt. "Yes!" With raw hands, I pried it loose.

Did I dare risk chopping another? I couldn't bear another meal while I waited for the men to die, only for them not to oblige. This time I chose a skinnier root and hacked at it. My palms left smears of blood on the knife handle.

How to carry the water and my two chunks of root? I gazed

toward the campsite, as if I could see Balaam and Sanipu striding toward me. Or had I stayed away so long they assumed I was dead of thirst and sun?

Could I chop the wood fine and bundle it into a makeshift pouch in my robe? No, I couldn't take the time. Balaam and Arseen would beat me bloody, then let Sanipu take his pleasure on my limp body.

At last I bundled the roots into a fold of my robe, filthy hem gripped in one hand, then fumbled for the buckets. At least the cloth cushioned the rope handle.

With the coming of winter the sun stood low in the sky, but I sweated as I staggered into camp. Balaam and Sanipu waited for me, just as I'd imagined, with Arseen just visible inside the tent entrance. Balaam stormed up, robes whirling around his lean legs, and slapped me across the face.

Only fear of an immediate return across the desert kept my hands fixed around the handles. "W-why—" *Don't question him. Don't.*

"What took you so long?" Sanipu fisted his hips.

Balaam's mouth pinched. "Indeed."

"And what's that concealed in your robe?" Arseen stamped out of the tent to grab my makeshift pouch and feel the lumps of pomegranate root. "Wood. She fetched wood as well as water."

Balaam let his hand fall to his side. "Did you plan to burn it?"

What could I say? "Y-yes, master."

"You see?" Balaam made a satisfied sound. "She's learned to plan."

True.

Sanipu sniffed. "We'll see."

Yes, you will.

Only Arseen remained while I let the wood fall from my robes. He prodded the roots. "Why did you fetch such damp wood?"

Would he figure out why I wanted it? Notice the sawed ends

of the roots and wonder? "It's thicker than the scrub wood." The knife in my hem seemed to glow like the moon.

"This will take forever to burn, even if you feather the edge with a knife." Arseen shrugged his narrow shoulders. "Not my problem." He strolled away.

I studied the chunks of pomegranate root. After they made such a fuss over burning the wood, I'd have to burn the skinnier piece. But what if, as Arseen predicted, it wouldn't burn? Perhaps—I placed the root close to the fire circle to dry out.

Now to prepare the other, thicker chunk. I kept checking over one shoulder to make sure none of my captors could see as I propped the pomegranate wood on the flattish rock I'd used to mince the pomegranate skin, then pried the knife out of my hem.

My efforts at the well had dulled the blade so it wouldn't cut. Curse it. I imagined gnawing the root into fragments. *Then I might die, too.* I looked around me.

With one of the fire circle stones I bashed the root over and over again. At first I heard only the juicy sound of rock striking damp wood. Nothing happened to the root. Sweat ran down my neck to soak my robe. Would the men hear? Investigate? I smashed the stone one more time with my trembling arms. The root fragmented. For an instant I stared, unable to believe it. Then I chopped the pieces as fine as I could with the dull blade and searched the dishes for a jar with a lid.

It held a little sumac—I knew from the faintly sour odor—but I tipped that out, then carefully brushed every last fragment of pomegranate into the jar.

ON THE THIRD NIGHT after I fetched the roots, I snatched up the jar. Welts from Sanipu's pinching fingers ridged my breasts and belly, my cheek felt splintered from Balaam's fist, my woman parts burned.

With a flat stone, I reduced the chopped root to powder.

NEXT DAY, BALAAM disappeared around dusk. After full dark, he returned leading a thin ewe.

"Where'd you get that stringy old thing?" Sanipu made a dismissive gesture at the creature.

Balaam sniffed. "Sheep wander away from villages all the time. The shepherds won't miss it."

If he expected applause for his valor in capturing the old sheep, he didn't get it. "Butcher it, Arseen."

Arseen's mouth fell open. "Why me?"

"Why not you?" Balaam's lips twisted. "You're too fussy of your pretty, pretty robes."

With drooping shoulders Arseen muttered something, and went into the tent. Sanipu fingered the ewe's matted wool. "You might've stolen a sheep that wouldn't break our teeth while we chew."

Balaam's eyes narrowed. "Do it next time, see how you fare."

Arseen returned, a pole with a narrow cross bar at one end. As Balaam passed him on the way inside, the leader said, "Show the girl how to kill the ewe and butcher it. She'll kill the next one."

"Yes, get on with it." Sanipu sniggered as he followed Balaam to the tent.

Arseen scowled at me. "What're you staring at, slave?"

"T-that." I pointed to the pole.

"Watch and learn." He approached the ewe, who hadn't stirred since Balaam dropped her rope. He hoisted her up the pole, tail up. Her hind legs kicked feebly as he stretched tall to thread her back hooves through loops of rope on the pole's cross section.

She flailed a moment or two, then grew still as if exhausted, her fleshless head lolling. Arseen left her there a long time. At first, her forefeet occasionally tapped the post, her matted wool shivering. Gods, but she was scrawny. Her bleats stabbed me like needles.

These outlaws think me as helpless as this ewe.

At last Arseen walked back to the hanging creature. As casually as he'd dip a mouthful of hummus from a bowl, he drew his knife across the animal's throat. Blood gushed. A few hot drops fell on my feet and I gagged at the coppery scent. In childhood, I'd witnessed countless animal sacrifices in the temple. But Arseen hadn't used any incense, prayed, or invoked the gods in any way.

Now he glanced at me. "Step closer. I'm not showing you how to gut a beast ever again." While the dying beast gave her last few twitches, he slit the belly and tugged out her red and blue entrails. Tossed them on the ground to ooze. My own guts roiled.

"Take the offal and bury it before it draws scavengers." Arseen stooped and plucked up the heart and liver, dropped those prized organs into a bowl. "We'll eat these." When I didn't move—too sickened to do so—Arseen jerked the bloody blade at me. "I told you, remove the mess."

My hands rose to clamp over my trembling mouth. *Move that disgusting mess? How?* How to do it without touching anything?

Arseen began to peel off the ewe's stringy flesh, only to straighten and snap his fingers. "Get on with it." A pause. "Slave."

Dog. My belly tightened. My captors killed the ewe with the same nonchalance with which they raped me.

I planned to poison them. *But I take no pleasure in it, I only want to free myself.*

Arseen's knife hand stilled. "I told you to bury that offal." His mouth turned down. "Or shall I call for Balaam to motivate you?"

Hug the guts to myself, or get beaten. Which? I raced to the kitchen area.

"What're you doing?"

He broke off as I hurried back, a large platter in my arms. I set it on the ground, shoved the entrails onto it with one foot. They felt warm and slimy. Breath held, I carted my filthy load at least a hundred paces from camp. There I lowered my burden to the ground, scraped a hole, and tipped it in.

Did Arseen call Balaam even now? I rushed back and placed the gory platter by the fire pit on my way to Arseen.

He flicked a glance at me. "You dirtied the platter." He sliced the last bit of meat off the ewe's bloody bones. "Hope you paid attention. You'll butcher the next animal we eat."

But I don't know how. I kept my eyes lowered so he couldn't see the hate in them.

"Stringy meat is best stewed."

"Yes. *Master.*" Did he hear my contempt?

CHAPTER NINETEEN

NEXT EVENING I CARRIED THE STEWED MUTTON into the main room of the tent. Arseen scowled at the platter. "Isn't that the dish you used to—"

Curse it, he knew I used it to cart away the ewe's guts. "I washed it twice, dried it in the sun."

"Very well." Arseen's lips squeezed tight.

Balaam'd already served himself. "The slave used it for what?"

Bent over the platter, Arseen twitched one shoulder. "Doesn't matter. She cleaned it." He stuffed mutton in his mouth.

Yes. Eat it all. I hid my fists in the skirt of my robe.

"Good to eat meat again." Sanipu's cheeks bulged.

"I'm glad you appreciate the meal I've made for you. Master." I kept my head down, so they couldn't see the hate in my eyes.

Balaam straightened. "How dare you take credit for the meal? I brought the meat."

My heart pounded. *Please, let the pomegranate take effect before he beats me.*

I cringed. Nodding, Balaam lounged against the carpet. "Be gone."

"Yes, master." Wait—he preferred "My Lord." Didn't he? *Soon it won't matter. Soon.*

Arseen's voice rose above the soft rattle of dishes on the carpet. "You stole it, but I butchered it."

And I cooked it. I cooked it, and more. I bowed the way slaves used to do when my father stalked past. Had they hated him as much as I hated my captors? I doubted it.

Beside the fire circle, I paced for what felt like half the night, though the clink of plates still sounded inside the tent. Would I hear the first groan soon? Were their faces flushed, as Aunt Kupo had told me happened to pomegranate poisoning victims? I fingered a twist of dried pomegranate skin fallen by the fire circle.

"Girl." Balaam's shout sounded less vigorous than usual. "Get in. Here."

Each word sounded thick. Blurred. When I shuffled into the tent, Balaam curled on one side, a hand pressed to his flat stomach.

Every moment I'd chopped pomegranate root, every moment I'd ground it to powder, had led to this moment. Now I remembered his fist pounding my flesh. *Do you ache, master? Do you hurt as much as you hurt me?*

Sanipu coiled on the opposite side of the rug, whimpering. Again, I recalled his reddened face above mine, his sweat spattering me as he tore in and out of my woman parts. The rug burning my back and legs.

At first I didn't see Arseen in the shadows. Was he already dead?

Balaam lifted his head. "What—was in—that stew?"

Did he suspect? "The mutton, master."

"Then why. Why. Does. My belly. Ache?" Balaam tried to rub his stomach.

In the shadows, Arseen groaned. "And mine." His words disintegrated into the sound of vomiting.

"And mine." Sanipu rolled so a slant of moonlight from the door fell across his greasy face. "It must be. The mutton."

He sounded steadier than the others. I sidled toward the tent flap.

Balaam moaned. "I need—I need—" There was a loud squirting noise, and his face twisted. "Gods, I've shat myself."

"My head. Pounds. Like a drum." Sanipu flattened both hands to his temples. "Fit to burst."

"I've—fouled myself." Balaam hitched onto one side. "Fetch—clean—robes." He panted a moment. "Slave."

You're dying because of me, not the mutton. Then Sanipu whimpered, and I closed my mouth.

"Girl." Balaam flicked one hand toward his chamber, as if he hadn't the strength to flourish as usual. "Fetch—clean. Robes. Help. Me. Change."

I didn't move. Sanipu twisted on the rug. "Obey. Him. Girl."

"Now." Balaam's peremptory tone faded.

"Yes, master." My lips tingled as if I'd eaten pomegranate root, too. In Balaam's room, I paused a moment, heard Arseen cry out.

"So you've. Beshat yourself. I've vomited. Down. My best. Robe."

"This. Poi-son. F-food." Sanipu's voice shook.

Gods. I rolled under the goat hair wall into the open air. The night breeze brushed over my fear-bumped skin. Moonlight gleamed on the sands, the subtle curves, of the landscape all around me. Where? Where? Where to run, where to hide?

"Girl." Balaam croaked as I fled up the hill to the patch of scrub.

CHAPTER TWENTY

I WADED TO THE FARTHEST EDGE OF THE SCRUB, flattened myself into the scratchy brush. This time I didn't heed the way it snagged my clothes and flesh. I covered my ears with both hands. Even so, Sanipu's gurgling shrieks pierced the night, mingled with Arseen's high wails. I couldn't hear Balaam. Had he already died?

Footsteps rustled the scrub, and chilled even my bones. Had Balaam managed to follow me? Find me? Would his final act be to drive his sword into my heart? I huddled lower. Maybe he couldn't see me in the dark.

Then warm, horsey breath swished over me. I wobbled to my feet. "You."

Midnight hopped a step closer, as near as his hobbles allowed. *What're you doing?* His alert stance asked the question as if the stallion had spoken.

"Oh, good boy. Good boy." I pressed my cheek to his, and my tears streaked his coat. "Oh, Midnight, it's so awful. I d-didn't know it would be so awful." The last word stretched into a howl, quickly bitten off. Could the men still hear me?

Then I realized I could no longer hear them. Well, hear Sanipu and Arseen. Had they all died at last? Haltingly, I straightened to peer down at the tent. It took a long time for me to force my wobbly legs to carry me to the fire circle. Longer still for me to fumble the sack I'd left hidden and ready over one shoulder. To creep into the long goat hair structure, a low, dark shape against the moonlit sky. Would my captors lie twisted in the final agony that killed them? Part of me longed to stand over them, to glare down at their dead bodies. To know I was safe at last.

But not yet. I couldn't bring myself to approach them yet. I poked a rag-wrapped stick deep in the embers. When it lit at last, I shuffled to the back of the tent. Stood a long time, body vibrating to my heartbeats. At last, I made myself bend. Crawled under the wall into Sanipu's room. It took three attempts before my wobbly fingers managed to heft the lid of his treasure chest.

Even in the dimness, jewels glinted. When I thrust my hands into the chest, I felt a golden cup, coins. I half-expected Sanipu to march in, box my ears. 'Just what do you think you're doing? How dare you, slave. Girl."

It took all I had not to cower. Not to peer over one shoulder. *Take the cup.* Fistfuls of coins and jewels slid out of my sweat-slickened hands into my sack. It grew heavy.

In my memory, I heard the men screaming.

I tiptoed into Balaam's room, paused, trembling. On a deep breath, I made myself stomp across the carpet where he'd torn away my worth as a woman. Gold, silver, jewels crowded to the top of his treasure chest. Sanipu's treasure had only reached halfway.

This time I forced myself to be deliberate. That rope of azure gems. More coins, this time only those of greatest value. A few bracelets and armbands studded with jewels, a ring with a translucent green stone. Last I took Midnight's bridle, coiled against the front of the trunk. More jewels glinted on the brow band and the bit shanks. Small wonder Balaam kept it with his prized possessions.

Stolen goods. Stolen by the men. Earned by me with every in-stant they kept me enslaved, earned by my cleverness in setting myself free. *Earned a thousand times over,* I told myself.

As I slung the jeweled bridle over one shoulder, I remembered Balaam kept the saddle near the entrance of the front room. Where the men had died.

Get it. Get the saddle. Go. The men could do nothing to stop me anymore. Go. Go now. But my feet refused to move. Much as I savored the knowledge the men would never harm me again, what if one still lived? Managed to wreak revenge on me?

But—not fetching the saddle meant I must ride Midnight bare-back.

Don't be a simpleton. Get the saddle. Then I'd examine each man in turn, imagine how agony had gripped him.

Next time they'll know female doesn't equal helpless. I paused. Frowned. Wait. There'd be no next time.

"What're you doing, girl?" I whipped toward the entrance to the room, braced to see Balaam looming. He wasn't there.

He wasn't there because I'd killed him. Killed them all. Now I was stealing. Stealing.

My chin lifted. I was only stealing from them. My defilers. My torturers.

In any case, the dead couldn't own things. Just as they no longer owned me.

For the first time in my life, no man could order me about. Not Balaam, not Sanipu, not Arseen. Not my father. I felt as tall, and as strong, as Uncle Achior.

The treasure no longer reached the upper edge of Balaam's trunk. I stepped back, shut the lid. I eased it down, still half-afraid my captors would hear me. With a shake of my head, I decided that I would sell the jewels, and keep the coins to start my new life.

I'm a thief like them. No, the men had stolen my innocence. They'd taken the coins Aunt Kupo had given me. Left me with no other way to care for myself. I stalked away from Balaam's treasure chest, torch held before me. Maybe others would find this encampment, pick it clean. People who came to investigate the odor of death, then stayed once they discovered the treasure farther inside. I'd never know.

After a pause for thought, I returned to Sanipu's room. Circling the space, bent double, I poked among the clothes and debris on the carpet, then straightened. Nothing of value here. Only his stink. The stink of the agony he caused. I headed for Arseen's room, only to slow my steps and listen. Aunt Kupo had once mentioned that pomegranate poisoning sometimes caused paralysis. Maybe all the men were sprawled across the tent's front room in contorted poses, still alive but unable to move while the poison worked in them—

No. No. I wouldn't, couldn't think of that right now. I dodged into Arseen's room, flung back the lid of his trunk, stiffened. He had as much treasure as Balaam. I'd imagined Arseen's chest as the least full of the three. Then I focused, and realized the trunk held fewer coins. Fewer jewels. Only thin copper or brass bracelets, most without even semi-precious stones. Some wooden carvings of animals, some small rounded jars.

When I picked up one of them, the odor of cinnamon tickled my nose. I spun in a wild circle, certain Arseen stood just behind me. Almost I flung the jar back in the trunk, but what if the thing shattered? Filled the room with his fragrance? I tucked the pot in the trunk so gently it almost made me scream. Without willing it, I took up another pot and the scent of jasmine drifted around me. Flooded the cloth chamber. When I set it down, the pot jostled another that exuded the strong odor of frankincense. Choking, I slammed the lid. I didn't want anything Arseen had owned.

Did I have enough goods to secure my future? The bag weighed so much I could barely hold it. Wait—a noise drifted to me. A soft clatter. Did one of my captors still live? Would he stagger in? Slash my throat?

Sack heaved over one shoulder, I ducked under the back wall to flee into the night.

The instant I stood up into the open air, a movement jerked at the edge of my vision. Something, someone, approached around the far end of the tent. I whirled to face it with a gasp, the make-shift torch tumbling out of my shaky grip. "No, m-master, don't—"

The stallion's hobbles rattled when he hopped closer. Tears gushed down my cheeks. "Midnight, it's you. Only you—" I dropped the sack to fling my arms around the stallion's neck.

I'm a poisoner.

He breathed warmth along my cheek. Only my hold on his long mane kept me upright. "Good horse, oh. Good, good horse." I kissed his muzzle. "Come on." I burrowed in the sack for his bridle.

As Nahash'd done with my father's horses, I held the bridle at the top so it hung down, weighed by the bit. I slid it over the front of the stallion's face until the bit bumped his lips. He clamped them, head high. My feet dangled as he craned upward with my hands clamped just behind his ears, lifting me off the ground.

The stallion sidestepped and brushed my fallen sack. It jangled, and he snorted, bounding away from the unaccustomed noise. My hands slipped down his face. In a moment, I'd fall on my behind and he'd dodge away. I worked a finger in the corner of his mouth and jabbed his gum. He resisted a moment, then lowered his head with a sigh and opened his mouth. Feet back on the ground, I slid the bridle into place. Reins still in my hand, I moved to his hind-quarters to unfasten the hobbles.

Now to mount.

Midnight's withers, the bony bump at the base of his neck, were too high for me, even if I hadn't had the sack weighing me down. What to do? Lead the stallion to the base of the hill and try to hop on from there, or—the buckets. They could do me a favor for a change.

I led the stallion to them, turned one upside down, and perched atop it. With one leg over his back, a clink from the bag made Midnight swing sideways. I teetered off my perch.

A few coins had spilled out. As I bent to poke them back inside, my stomach gurgled. Gods, I was hungry. "Curse it."

Sack left by the bucket, I led Midnight to the fire circle. There I wrapped the last of the flatbread in a scrap of cloth, returned to the bucket. With the sack snug against my side to muffle it, I climbed onto the upturned bucket again. Pushed off with all the strength in my legs, gripped his withers with the crook of my elbow and his mane with that hand. Dragged myself on just before Midnight tossed his head and sidestepped again, quicker this time.

The treasure sack rattled. His head and neck stiffened. Tension rippled down his spine against my seat and legs.

"It's me, Sarah. You know me. You like me. Now—" I sucked in a deep breath. "Walk."

His muscles shivered, but he didn't move.

"Walk." I raised my voice a little.

Still Midnight didn't stir.

"Come on, Midnight." I recalled Uncle Achior on his gray stallion, Desert. He spoke to his horse, but did more as well. I squeezed my legs.

He bounded forward. The bucket clonked over. My sack clanged, and the stallion spurted ahead even faster. My fingers knotted in his mane. "Whoa, Midnight. Whoa, boy."

My voice fluted up. I took a breath, fighting not to slide over the smooth black shoulder. "Whoa. Please whoa—" The stallion bounced along for a few strides, then broke into a trot. I shot onto his neck. His mane scraped my chin.

"*Idiot. Don't you know anything?*" I heard Arseen so clearly I ducked one shoulder, and squinted back at the camp.

Hidden by its low hills, I could no longer see it. The tent where I'd suffered the loss of my innocence, not just of my body but of my spirit, might as well have not existed. I turned my back on it. Forever.

"Good boy." Midnight's slender neck stretched before me, only open desert visible between his pricked ears. This time I squeezed my legs gently and spoke to him at the same time. "Walk, Midnight."

He set off at a walk. My body tightened automatically, and he jerked to a stop that slid me toward his shoulder, but I caught myself. For a little while, I just sat there until Midnight and I breathed in rhythm. Then I nudged his sides with my calves. He took a delicate step, another, so different from the plodder I'd ridden when the men moved camp.

Midnight's ear swung back as if to watch me while he stepped along in a wavering circle. I only needed to tense for him to halt. When I remembered how Balaam had so often jerked the bit to stop the stallion, I nearly wailed. *Ignorant swine.*

Eventually, I learned that if I looked where I wanted to go, Midnight walked in that direction. After a while, when the stars began to fade, I made a little chirrup, and Midnight broke into a jog so smooth my treasure sack didn't even rattle. I still half-expected Balaam to shout after me. *"What're you doing, girl? Get off my horse."*

"Let's go, boy." Another cluck, a soft squeeze of my legs. My horse bobbed his head and trotted faster, his strides nothing like the harsh trot of the mare when the outlaws kidnapped me. In spite of my bruises, in spite of the dragging knowledge that I'd committed murder, only the uncertainty of who might hear kept me from singing.

CHAPTER TWENTY-ONE

HOW MANY TIMES HAD I FALLEN ASLEEP aching from my captors' brutality, and pictured galloping away from the camp forever?

Now I found the reality quite different. While dawn lightened the sky, I twisted one hand in Midnight's heavy mane. The desert stretched all around me, from horizon to horizon. Strange how different it looked from this higher perspective. Except for the hiss of sand under the stallion's hooves, silence hung around us like a heavy cloak.

The silence of death.

Stop. Don't think about it.

Where could I go? The women from the well lived in a village, but according to them it contained only a handful of houses and nothing else.

"Idiot girl." Arseen's voice scolded inside my head. I sat a little taller on Midnight's swaying spine. The village near the well might be tiny, but surely someone there must know of a market in the area.

Earlier in the season, the sun would've burned from high in the sky until my hair melted off my head and down my back. But now the sun barely warmed me. Even so, my sweat mingled with Midnight's to dampen the skirts of my robe. A green smear appeared between his ears. The pomegranate tree. The well.

It seemed days before we jogged up to it. I needed to reach it, needed to ask for directions to the closest market town. At the same time, I shrank from speaking to strangers. Exposing my filthy robes, my filthy self to anyone—Midnight slowed and halted, ears pricked, as if he knew we'd reached our destination. From his back, I saw a huddle of roofs beyond the pomegranate.

"This way." I looked and leaned a little toward the houses, but Midnight's hooves seemed rooted to the ground. He craned toward the well and huffed.

"Come on. This way, Midnight." Did I dare kick him forward?

He took one springing step toward the well and nickered outright.

Oh. "You're thirsty." In spite of the cool breeze, my ears turned hot. How quickly I'd thought to kick my only friend, force him to my will. Just like Balaam. Another glance around assured me no one could see. I rode Midnight to the well and slackened the reins while he lowered his gorgeous, tapered head and drank his fill.

When he raised his head again at last with a deep sigh, a little steady jogging brought us to the cluster of hovels beyond the pomegranate tree. What should I do? Yell for help? Dismount and knock on a door?

From behind the nearest hut, a child appeared only to jerk to a stop, eyes rounding. Boy or girl? The dusty robe and bare feet gave no clue. "Mother! A horse. Someone on a horse. Here. In our village!" The child stumbled closer, one trembling hand extended toward Midnight.

A girl, from the piping voice. I remembered that same impossible longing at sight of Singer or Desert. The desire for a strength and speed beyond anything offered by her feeble, female body. Of course she would gawk at a horse, any horse, in her isolated huddle of poor hovels, especially a stallion as fine as Midnight. *Curse it.* I'd made myself memorable before I'd even spoken.

Chin on my breast bone, I tried to make myself invisible. "Can you direct me to—"

A woman rushed out of the hut. "How many times have I told you not to yell for me? How many times do I have to tell you not to yell for me? Wait until we're face to face like a civil person—oh." She peered up at me through wisps of dark hair going gray. "May I help you?"

How long since someone spoke to me in respectful tones? The woman didn't seem to see my soiled robe and knotted hair. Or did she speak to someone mounted on a horse, and therefore worthy of deference?

Before I could answer, an old man limped out of a hut on my other side. "What're you jabbering about, I'm trying to sleep." Then he saw Midnight and stiffened. "A horse. What's a horse doing here?" He didn't say it, but the words hung in the still air. *And such a fine one.*

"Please." I stared at Midnight's mane. "Where's the nearest market?"

"What're you doing on a horse?"

I turned toward a new voice, light, female. Familiar. The young woman I'd met at the well stood behind Midnight, a bowl in her hands.

Before I could draw breath, the little girl stepped nearer Midnight, and raised that trembling hand to his muzzle. Trembling, not with fear, but excitement. I could see it in her parted lips and glowing eyes.

"I like your horse," she said, voice so soft Midnight didn't so much as twitch his ears.

"Get away." Her mother marched over, yanked the back of her robe. "He could bite you. Horses are dangerous." Her eyes glinted at me through tangles of graying hair.

The old man's head bobbed. "Or it could kick you all the way to the well."

It. I'd best stay mounted, ask directions, and ride away.

"Why're you gawking?" The older woman—the mother—I'd met at the well crossed from a hovel off to one side, a bunch of basil held loosely. "You've seen a horse before."

"Not so close." While I was distracted, the little girl had crept even closer to Midnight. Now she teetered onto her toes to straighten his forelock. "His long hair feels so different."

It's his mane. I longed to tell the girl, but the less said, the sooner they'd forget me.

"I've chores in plenty before nightfall. Don't the rest of you?" The child's mother turned away, paused. Clapped her hands so sharply Midnight flinched. "Come along, I've tasks for you, as well."

"But Mama—the horse—" The girl stroked his neck, and her mother doubled back to jerk her away.

"I said come along." They returned to their hut, the girl staring back at Midnight, steps lagging, until they disappeared inside.

The older woman from the well eyed the man. "I heard you fussing about your daily sleep. Why don't you go do it?"

"Just leaving." The man limped back into his hut, reminding me of Aunt Kupo. Why didn't he have a stick? Maybe he couldn't afford a fine polished one like hers, but—

Soon only the mother and daughter from the well remained with me on the dusty strip between the few houses. "Now." The mother smiled. "It's just us." She set down her basil. "My name's Dadu, what's yours?"

My hands tensed on the reins. Midnight jerked his head. For an instant, I pictured galloping away without another word, but if I did, the villagers would never finish talking about it. If my father's men ever came here, the villagers would recognize my description, tell all they knew of me—

Dadu stepped closer, tugged the hem of my filthy robe. "Slide off that horse so we can talk at our ease."

Her daughter nodded. "Where did you come by such a fine horse? That must be a good tale."

Dadu scowled at her daughter. "For shame, daughter, introduce yourself before you ask questions of our guest." She shifted her frown to me. "Why do you keep mounted? Join us, we'll make you comfortable in our home."

Her daughter took a cautious step toward me. "I'm Meesha."

She'd given me her name. Now what? If I told them my real name, and Father's men came looking for me—*Give a name not my own.* "T-tamar." Curse it, why had I used my pretty cousin's name?

"Greetings, Tamar. Now come inside for some tea." Dadu grinned. "Then you can tell us your adventures."

What would she say if I told her the truth? I hesitated, and Meesha tugged my hem. "Please, get off your horse, rest awhile."

Dadu saved me. "Daughter, I think she needs to get to the market to supply her family."

"Oh." Meesha's face crumpled much like the little girl's had. Why? My whole body tightened, and Midnight side-stepped. Dadu hurried out of his way.

Just standing here, I put them in danger of trampling. And more, I put myself doubly at risk. I heard the echo of Balaam's voice. This stallion was stolen. Not only might the villagers pass on word about me to my father, they might let Midnight's owner know I had him.

Meesha pointed east. "That way."

"For shame, daughter. You offer help thus? I raised you better." Dadu stepped to Midnight's shoulder to peer up at me. "Ride east five leagues. Smoke from the town's cook fires will guide you."

"Thank you." The dry syllables escaped somehow.

Dadu patted my knee. "No matter, visit us next time you pass. Gods be with you."

MIDNIGHT'S STRIDE ate up the distance. A smear of smoke appeared on the horizon before midday, and his muzzle lifted to smell the air. I stroked his neck, proud to dare release my grip on his mane, even with one hand. "I'm lucky to have you."

Or was I? What about the reactions of the people back in the village? Midnight carried me faster than I could walk, but—

The stretched eyes of the little girl. The adults' remarks. Midnight made me unforgettable. In spite of my eagerness to reach the market, I eased the stallion down to a walk. A single tear disappeared into his mane.

I had to sell him.

CHAPTER TWENTY-TWO

THE SACK OF GOODS JOSTLED MY KNEE as Midnight jogged into the town. A town, not just a village. Shrinking as small as I could, as if keeping my shoulders rounded and my eyes lowered had ever kept me out of trouble, I brought my stallion down to a walk. Just ahead, the market spread before us, far larger than the one in my father's town. So many people, such a bewildering tangle of goods for sale—

But the place smelled familiar. Spicy. Smoky. As if Aunt Kupo might march into sight, her stick thumping the ground while she peered at the goods in every booth, judging which wares looked best and buying according to her wisdom.

Tears smeared my vision. I halted, slid from my horse's back, and led him forward. Aunt Kupo was far away. I'd never see her again. Never hear her voice or the thwack of her stick on stone. Never hug her. The stallion crowded close, and I stumbled away from him. My hip jolted a booth, and the metal wares on display jangled. I darted an apologetic glance at the vendor. "S-sorry."

He shrugged. "No harm done." He indicated the bracelets of beaten metal before him. "Perhaps you'd like something pretty? My prices are the best in the market."

My hands tightened around the top of my sack, which clinked. "I'm here to sell, not buy."

His thin brows arched. "So? How much do you want?"

"You've not seen what I have yet."

The vendor's rotten teeth showed in a wide grin. "I like surprises."

Do you? I upended the sack on the wooden lip of his booth. The golden cup spun across the rough boards, sending his wares skidding. Coins from my sack bounced, jewels glittered in the sunlight. Behind me, Midnight skittered backward with a snort.

The vendor's jaw dropped. "Where did you get a treasure like this? How?"

"I—I—" What could I say? "I inherited it." True, in a way.

He studied me from dusty toes to tangled hair. "Inherited?"

"Yes." Midnight bumped me with his muzzle. His touch gave me courage. "Five thousand for the jewels and such. I keep the coins."

"Five thousand?" The vendor stepped back a pace. "There's not so much money in all the market. Five hundred." He reached grubby fingers for the cup.

I recalled Aunt Kupo bargaining in the marketplace. "For that much you can have the cup." The jewels would bring more from a jewel cutter, anyway. If the town had a jewel cutter.

He drew back as if the cup had burned him. "Five hundred for the cup. And all the rest."

"No deal." Scooping my goods back in the sack, I turned as if to walk away. Took a step. Two. So much for my bargaining skills.

"Wait. How much for just the cup?"

I turned back slowly, as if reluctant. "Six hundred."

"A moment ago I offered five." His lips drew in to hide his teeth.

The spirit of Aunt Kupo seemed to stand at my shoulder. "That was a moment ago."

A short man with robes redolent of horses stepped in front of me. "Is your horse for sale?"

"Hey." The vendor in the booth moved to join us. "Wait your turn. I'm bargaining with this girl, not you."

The short man stepped closer. "Is your horse for sale?"

"Y-yes." Though I'd hoped to say goodbye to Midnight before I sold him.

"Speak up." The horse dealer's mouth twisted. "Why am I bargaining with a girl?" He peered around me. "Where's your husband?"

My breath sounded like cloth tearing. "I'm not married." At my elbow, I glimpsed the gleam of Midnight's eyes. My only friend's eyes. "But my horse is for sale."

The man touched Midnight's shoulder with a reverence I'd rarely seen outside a temple. "Come with me."

"But I want that cup." The stall vendor's outraged shouts faded behind us.

We followed the horse dealer through the market, out the other side. I stopped, Midnight at my shoulder. "Do you not have a booth?"

The dealer doubled back to me. "No use to have a booth. My place lies just outside town." He kept one hand on Midnight's neck while we passed houses, none as big as Father's, but larger than the hovels in the village near the well.

Midnight nudged me, as if asking why I walked beside him instead of riding. My fingers knotted in his mane. *Goodbye, my friend. Goodbye.*

As we reached the edge of town the stallion tensed, ears pricked, to give a ringing neigh. A dozen different horses answered, and Midnight burst into a jog, shouldering past me. He jerked me a number of stumbling steps forward until I managed to untangle my fingers from his mane. Why—

Then I saw the dealer's pens. Large ones full of mares with foals, a few smaller pens with solitary horses, probably stallions. Every horse shone with health and good feeding.

The scent of horses flooded the air. Their skin, their coats, their dung. The warm sweetness of their breath. Every inhalation reminded me of the stable at my father's house. Of Desert. Uncle Achior. Of Nahash giving me the horse hair, and of my eager desire for freedom—

The horse trader stopped, leaned against the nearest pen. "I can offer you a thousand."

A thousand? I shook my head. "Such a fine stallion should fetch more." Shouldn't he?

His lips pushed out. "A horse's owner could recite its bloodlines ten generations back. Can you do that?"

While I struggled for an answer, Midnight gave another neigh, then pawed with a mighty arc of one foreleg. "Easy. Easy, boy." I led him in a tight circle. By the time we faced the dealer again, I hoped my breathlessness excused me from answering his question.

Even surrounded by all these horses, I could smell the dealer's robes, permeated with the strong odor of horse sweat. He scooted onto the nearest fence and let his feet dangle. "I'm the only trader for a hundred leagues in any direction." He gripped the rail so he could lean back a bit. "You're the first woman to try to sell me a horse, and I've bought and sold horses since my voice deepened."

"You asked me if Midnight was for sale—"

"I expected a male relative to negotiate with me."

Silence hung between us. "My father d-died." Pause. "The horse belonged to him."

The dealer studied me down the length of his nose. "And you have no male relatives. Well, I've made an offer. A thousand."

With difficulty, I kept my eyes level with his. "Five."

"Why do you counter for a smaller amou—" He wobbled, nearly fell, and gripped the fence. "Five thousand?" His voice shook with outrage. "I don't have so much coin on the place. Most of my worth is in the horses themselves."

He clamped his lips. "Twelve hundred."

"Three thousand." Once again, Aunt Kupo seemed to guide me. *Herbs or horses, it's all the same.*

"Did I not just tell you I've no such sum?" He managed a shrug, but the corners of his mouth quirked. "Your horse would be worth more with a saddle."

He's enjoying this. He thinks I know nothing of bargaining. "Midnight's worth at least three thousand on his own."

The dealer sputtered.

I held up one palm. "Very well. Fifteen hundred, and my pick of your horses."

He erupted into such noisy laughter Midnight stepped back a pace. "I knew you'd prove entertaining."

Entertaining. My body thumped with dread. Could I scramble onto Midnight's back and escape before he—"W-what do you mean?"

"You've ridden that wonderful creature, and you expect me to believe you want one of my animals?"

This very visible creature. I laced the stallion's reins around the fence the dealer sat on. "Yes." Fighting not to wail, I walked away. Midnight tried to follow. I heard sand scrunch, the fence creak when he reached the end of his tether. He nickered.

Midnight. Oh, Midnight. I tried to focus on the penned horses before me, but they smeared into a blur of shifting colors. Chestnut. Brown. Dun.

As I left my beloved stallion behind, I thought about the kind of horse I needed.

While I hesitated, the dealer hopped down to nudge me toward a pen. "Try one of these."

The enclosure held a dozen or so animals, smooth-coated and blooming with health. From neighboring pens the stallions all watched me with pricked ears and heads held high. Just beyond this corral the mares nursed their young. But the horses just the other side of the fence from me barely raised their heads.

"They're geldings, quiet and easy to handle. Soldiers sometimes choose them for that reason to ride into battle. A gelding doesn't get—" He glanced back at Midnight, who craned now toward the mares. "Distracted like a stallion."

"Why?"

The dealer looked away, a blush rising up his throat "Never mind." He sounded strangled. "The thing you need to know? A gelding's quiet, easy to handle."

Just what I wanted. "How much would my horse—" I needed to stop thinking of Midnight like that. "How much would the stallion bring with a saddle?" Can I go back there, face the dead bodies of the men I killed? My stomach clenched.

The dealer's mouth twisted. "You won't catch me out that way. What if I name a price and you bring me a worthless lump?"

Balaam's saddle. Embroidered with scarlet and gold thread. The saddle my tormentor sat in. Touched. To bring it here, I'd have to touch it, too. Sit in it. "It's not a worthless lump."

"I won't pay for a saddle I've never seen."

Better earn more while I could. "Very well. Eighteen hundred for Midnight—the stallion. Plus the most reliable of your geldings. Plus when I bring you the saddle, you pay me what it's worth.

"Reliable?" His gaze flicked to a stone-colored horse, round-bodied and short. Like me. The opposite of Midnight in every way. "You want a horse for yourself?"

"With no father to protect me, what choice do I have? On horseback I can escape danger quickly."

"True enough." He jerked his chin at the little gelding. "Do you want to try him?"

Try him? What if my father's men came asking after me? I'd made myself memorable enough already. "I'm sure he's fine."

"Oh. Well." The dealer ducked into the enclosure and

approached the gelding with one cupped hand held out. The gelding strode over to him, ears tipped forward, and nosed into the man's outstretched palm. I half-expected the horse to turn away when he found no grain. Instead he mouthed the dealer's sleeve in a friendly fashion, and allowed himself to be led to the fence by his forelock.

"He's friendly, you see." Once out of the pen, the dealer fetched a bridle. The gelding opened his mouth for the bit, even lowered his head for the crown piece to slide over each ear. "Want a saddle?"

I thought again of Aunt Kupo's dealings in the marketplace. How much would a saddle cost? "I'll make do without."

"Very well. Wait here while I fetch your money."

He retreated across the compound to a small mud brick dwelling, and returned with the amount I'd asked for. As he handed it to me, he winced. "Many deals like this and I'll be out of business."

The coins clinked into my sack. How would I mount? No respectable woman allowed a man not of her family to touch her. I'd used buckets to climb aboard Mid—the stallion. I saw no buckets lying around, but there was the fence.

To my surprise, the gelding seemed to know what I wanted when I led him alongside it and climbed up the rough wood. He positioned himself beside the barrier and waited for me to slide onto his back. But my robe tangled around my legs, and my sack swung awkwardly.

"Let me help you—"

"Thank you, I'll manage." Again, the gelding seemed to know what I wanted. He sidled even closer to the fence, and I managed to clamber on, face hot, smoothing my robe down my legs as best I could. "You've trained him well."

"I train all horses to stand while mounted." The dealer stroked the horse's shoulder. "Few took to the lessons as well as this one."

The warmth of my new horse seemed to spread in a radiance throughout me, from my legs on his sides all the way through my heart. "Does he have a name?"

"I gave up naming horses long ago. That's for you to do." He ran a hand under the gelding's mane with a final pat.

How the gelding behaved would reveal an apt name for him. "I'll bring you the saddle by nightfall."

As we walked away from the dealer's place, a horse whinnied loud and long. I thought I recognized Midnight's voice. *Where are you going? Come back. Don't leave me.*

"Oh, Midnight. Midnight." My hands tightened on the reins, and my new horse halted. After a pause to study his ears, I eased the reins. The gelding bobbed his head, then set off again at a steady walk.

We crossed the desert back toward my captor's camp. Though the sun stood overhead, the air stirred in a soft breeze. Neither my new mount nor I sweated, as we would have earlier in the season. For a half dozen leagues—I hoped—we negotiated the slithery dunes, occasional streaks of scrub. As we drew nearer the site, my thighs tightened with anxiety. The gelding took longer strides, one ear turned to face me. *You want this? To go faster?*

Yes. I tightened my legs again.

Midnight would have burst into a gallop that unseated me. The gelding shifted into a steady trot. When I grabbed his mane, that ear turned back to me again. *Did I do wrong?*

With a deep breath, I settled onto his back. My new horse's strides seemed less springy than the stallion's, far flatter than the mare's jolting ones. Looking forward between the sand-colored ears, I aimed the gelding toward my captor's camp. Who would've thought I'd return less than a day after leaving forever? My hands clenched on the reins and the gelding dropped into a walk.

As we rode closer to the hidden encampment, he took shorter and shorter steps. Could he sense the evil that clung to the place? By the time we crept between the dunes that hid the tent, I could've walked faster than he did.

The camp seemed so quiet without Balaam's gritted orders, without Sanipu's shouts. I halted by the entrance. It took all my will to slide off the gelding's back, so solid and warm. He nudged my shoulder. *What's wrong?* He might as well have spoken.

"You deserve a name." The gelding had none of Midnight's glamour. The color of sand or stone—"That's it. Rock. I'll call you Rock."

Well, I could delay entering the tent no longer. Rock tried to follow. "Wait, Rock. Wait here." If he trailed me into the tent, the stench of death might panic him. Would the men already stink?

I tugged my robes over my nose and mouth, forced my feet to carry me inside. Rock took a step or two after me, then halted when I held him still.

Shaking all over, I forced myself forward. Through the tent entrance. Did I only imagine it, or did the structure already sag, loose on its moorings?

The saddles waited near the doorway. As I hefted the embroidered saddle onto one hip, I saw a humped shape near the entrance to Balaam's quarters. Without meaning to, I focused it. Was it—no. Only Balaam's torn robe, stained with vomit. As if he'd ripped it from himself while he crawled into his room to die. I tried not to imagine him, not to picture each of them, succumbing to the poison I'd fed them.

Would Balaam have managed to drag on clean robes, only to soil them as well? My stomach churned. Had any of them suspected? Had they known they died because they'd thought a girl an easy prey?

Now I straightened. "No." They'd brought death to themselves.

I broke away from the limp robe and rushed back to the saddle. Should I try to take all three? Perhaps I could take an extra one for Rock—

Sit where Sanipu had sat, or Arseen? I'd rather deal with Rock's knobby spine every day for the rest of my life. *Just take the one worth money and get out of here.*

But I turned again to that limp, stained robe. My own belly rose to my throat, but I clamped my teeth and crept into Balaam's room. I had to see him. Had to see all that cruelty brought to death. To nothing.

CHAPTER TWENTY-THREE

HE WASN'T THERE.

I felt cold to the tips of my hair. *Somewhere else. His dead body must be somewhere else.*

From Balaam's room I forced myself into Sanipu's. His lifeless body sprawled in a contorted position on the rug where I had so often twisted beneath him. He would never rape another woman.

I pivoted away and stumbled for Arseen's room. The stench of diarrhea wafted out to me before I reached the doorway. Pausing, I ducked away. No need to look. He'd never yell at another slave.

But Balaam was nowhere in the tent. And—I forced myself back to his room. His treasure chest stood, open and empty.

"Rock. Here, Rock. Here." Lips numb, I called my horse, and fumbled my way to the tent entrance. Did Balaam wait just outside for me, ready to spring? Unable to feel my feet on the muffling rugs, I lurched past his saddle unseeing, every breath like shards of broken pottery in my throat.

Even if Balaam had left the camp, I knew he hunted for me. I could have no doubt what would happen when he did. What he'd do to me. Rape—torture. His fists. His knife. And finally, his sword. Would he pierce my belly and leave me to bleed to death?

Or would he strike my head from my shoulders? With one swipe of his blade, or in cruel, tiny blows?

I dithered in the doorway, terrified to step into the open.

My gelding still waited for me, one hind hoof resting toe down. That hip sagged. Rock stood shorter than Midnight. On a ragged sob, I tottered into the moonlight and lunged for his back, legs flailing in a way that would've sent Midnight veering off at a gallop. As we trotted out of the camp, I scanned for Balaam's footprints. The hidden entrance into the encampment was the most logical way in, but on foot Balaam might've gone anywhere—

Rock halted so suddenly I almost fell. Did he fear Balaam too?

He doesn't know the man exists. No, Rock had only halted because my body tightened.

Now I unlocked my muscles one by one, and lightened my grip on the reins. Rock turned one ear toward me, questioning. I closed my legs against his ribs. *Go.* At once, my horse broke into his loose-limbed trot.

We crossed the desert back to the market town. Only as we rode into it did I remember Balaam's saddle. I'd forgotten and left it in the outlaw encampment. So much for getting more money from the horse dealer. I'd never return there. Not for anything. Not even if the horse dealer offered me double Midnight's price.

People crowded the market. Women in plain robes, women in fine embroidered robes and thin veils, men both old and young, the occasional giggling child. I waited until Rock reached a gap in the masses and dismounted. He might tread on someone, or bump into a vendor's stall. Where could I leave him?

Not at the horse dealer's, where I'd have to explain why I hadn't brought the saddle. Plus I'd see Midnight again.

Just then a man pushed past me. In the jostling mob that was nothing new. But he led a bay gelding with knobbly joints. They threaded through the crowd to a gap between buildings.

I followed the other horse. The opening between the houses

was dark and narrow. Like the alley where the outlaws first seized me. Teeth gritted, I entered the skinny space, one hand gripped in Rock's mane, focused on the sunlight at the far end.

At last I reached a small stable yard. The man had already unsaddled his mount in a lean-to shelter on the far side. While I watched, he slid the bridle over the horse's black-edged ears, shut the door. When he turned, he went rigid. "Who're you?"

"I need a place to leave my horse while I'm in the market." I stuck my hand in the bag at my hip and groped for a coin. "Would this repay you for sheltering him while I shop?"

His left eyebrow arched high, but he shook his head. "My stable's only big enough for one horse." Then he darted another look at the coin. "But perhaps—" With some scrap wood, he barricaded his horse in the back half of the little building. "Bring your horse in. Leave your bridle on the peg with mine."

"Thank you." Rock shouldered past me to breathe into the bay's flared nostrils. Both horses squealed and half-reared, the saggy ceiling so low neither could rise high. Maybe this wasn't such a good idea. If the horses took a dislike to each other, they'd kick the makeshift partition to splinters, and then the entire structure would collapse on top of them.

After a few more squeals, though, Rock and the bay nuzzled each other, then settled side by side with a sigh. I swung away to search for a place to hang up my bridle. "Back soon."

My coin closed in his fist, the man was already walking into his house. "Take as long as you need."

I STUDIED THE MARKET from the mouth of the alley, and felt chilled in spite of the sun. So many people. If Balaam were here, how would I know? He could slip up behind me, unseen, and slide his knife between my ribs, then stride away as I fell, limp and dead. Or he might grasp my wrist and drag me away with him. Enslaved again. At his mercy for as long as he chose to keep me alive. I gagged. *I'd rather he killed me at once.*

The vendor in the nearest booth glanced my way. "Want something new and pretty to wear? Come closer. See my beautiful embroidered robes! They've got matching veils, too. See?" The woman lifted the edge of the multi-colored stack of cloth before her, and held up one thin veil. She wore a pink robe, garishly embroidered at neck and wrists, with a gaudy yellow veil over her face.

Fresh clothes. "Y-yes." I stepped closer to examine her wares.

Snarled threads in the embroidery, uneven weaving in the cloth. My cousin Tamar would've wrinkled her nose and stalked away in insulted silence. I couldn't afford to be picky.

I hesitated over a deep blue robe with paler blue trim, then glimpsed a dove-colored one at the bottom of the pile. Gray, with slightly darker embroidery. Dull. Unmemorable. Perfect.

"Lovely." In spite of her trilling voice, the vendor's eyes remained flat. "That's my favorite."

Then why hide it at the bottom of a stack?

"You'd like a veil to match." The vendor rooted through veils, edges frayed from rough handling—or poorly stitched to begin.

"Don't trouble yourself. I want a cloak, not a veil." A dingy brown or gray cloak, with a hood to hide my face.

She stiffened. "I don't sell cloaks."

Good. "How much for the robe?"

The vendor studied my ragged appearance, and put out a hand to the gray robe to draw it away from me. "Twenty and five."

Clearly, she didn't expect me to be able to pay for it. "Ten."

Her hand slid off the gray robe. "Don't insult me. Forty."

My back itched as if Balaam stood close behind me. Not bartering would make me more memorable, but—I thrust one hand into my sack, and counted out twenty-five coins. "You won't get more than this from me."

While she scrambled for my coins, muddy eyes alight, I tucked my new robes under one arm and marched away to change before

Balaam found me.

I hustled through the crowds as best I could, paused when people jammed up to watch a street performer. I didn't even glance aside. What did I care about a sword eater? Another few steps, and the woman in front of me snatched a small boy by the shoulder of his ragged robes.

"Give back my coins, thief." She shook him so his bare feet almost left the ground.

"I don't know what you mean—"

She twisted his ear. "Liar. Give back my money."

My fingers pulsed as if under a hammer. It took all I had not to push past and dash away. And then I saw them, hung from the frame of the stall just ahead of me.

Cloaks. Hooded cloaks.

The rest of the market melted away. The people who sweated, swore, and shoved seemed to vanish. The woman's curses at the pickpocket existed as a vague noise, nothing more. Drifting like fog, I moved closer to examine the cloaks.

Gray. I fingered the nearest one, edges of the thick fabric doubled over on itself and hemmed with sturdy stitches. The vendor, a thin man, glanced at me and away.

"Excuse me." It took all my breath to speak above the rumble of the crowd swirling past. "How much?"

The vendor didn't glance my way. "That's a man's cloak, not for a little girl like you."

Little girl? The ache between my legs from my captor's last assault throbbed. I hadn't felt like a little girl in lifetimes.

"It's for my— " I choked on the word. "Father. His birthday. How much?"

One bony shoulder twitched. "They're all twenty."

"Very well." Dropping the correct number of coins in his outstretched palm, I tugged the cloak into my arms. Where could I change? Perhaps in an alley—no, I'd never make that mistake again.

In the end I changed in Rock's temporary stable. New robes brushing my dusty skin, weight of the cloak muffled about me, I barely noticed the floor beneath my feet. After I patted my horse's neck, I stepped through the door and tripped on the hem of the cloak. It dragged on the ground. Who cared? I felt invisible. Invincible.

Until I returned to the market, and first one person, then another, trod on the excess fabric. When I stumbled and almost fell for the third time in a half dozen steps. I stopped. What to do? To take off the cloak meant exposing myself to Balaam's searching gaze, maybe to Father's men, if their hunt for me had brought them so far. My shoulders rippled. What choice did I have? I bunched the excess fabric in my raised hands, and set off to buy what I needed.

Pots. Cookware. Bowls. Food. I tripped on the tent-like edge of the robe. *Curse it.* Oh—a goat-hair tent. Like in my captors' camp, but not black. Dun-colored. One that would blend with the desert sands. I looked over my shoulder, as I had looked over my shoulder countless times already today. In this disguise, Balaam wouldn't recognize me. Would he? Perhaps he stood right behind me—

Cringing, I stole a peek over my shoulder again. And there— a booth of pottery. Platters. Stacks of bowls in a variety of colors, even some cochlear, the mouth-sized scoops protruding from straight handles. One or two looked big enough to stir stew.

"Buy some nice pottery for your dowry?" The stringy vendor shifted a pot closer to me with a skinny finger.

Dowry. How had he recognized me as a woman? "Something like that." Shoulder half-raised, I examined his wares. As I bent nearer, someone jolted into me. Balaam? I spun to face a sturdy woman. She muttered an apology and hustled away.

I snatched the closest bowl, then selected the rest of my cooking things. My fingers throbbed with cold so I couldn't feel the glaze on the pots, certain I'd smell Balaam any moment, feel his hand grip the back of my neck. "These. How much?"

The vendor asked a price.

Shaking my head hard enough to see to either side of me, I offered five coins less.

He pushed out his lips. "Well—"

I stepped away. "I'm sure there are other pottery sellers in the market."

"Phaugh. Oh, very well." He waved a hand at the pots I'd chosen.

No reason to lug them along with me. "I'll fetch them after I finish my other purchases."

His lips curved. "Certainly. For five more coins."

One hand fisted on my sack, as if the vendor might snatch it from me. "You'd charge me for keeping them here?" I waved a hand at them. "But they're already here."

"And now they belong to you, not me." He shrugged. "Take them with you."

"Never mind, I'll—"

"Very well, you can leave them here for three more coins." His eyes crinkled with enjoyment.

My shoulders hunched. "One."

"You drive a hard bargain. One it is."

"What?"

He blinked. "One coin. You get your way."

I get my way. I started laughing and couldn't stop. *Now I live in a world where I can say what I want.*

The vendor stared at me as if my hair had caught fire. I snorted into silence and tried to prim my mouth into sober lines. "Fine." I dropped the coin in his hand and turned away, then back again. "Which vendor sells the best foodstuff in the market?"

He plucked his lower lip. "Booth at the end of this row for fruit. For the best sheep, go to—"

"Sheep?"

"Mutton, after your menfolk butcher it."

Mutton. Meat. Knives. Blood. An image of Arseen butchering the old ewe flared in my mind, and I fought not to retch. "Just vegetables. Rice. Fruit. Jam."

His head tilted. "Most womenfolk make their own jam."

Of course. With a nod, I headed for the end of the row, wove through the crowd until I reached a booth of fruit and vegetables. No vendor sat inside.

Maybe they'd come back at sight of a customer. A heap of pomegranates aglow in the sun made me shudder. Would I ever eat one again without remembering? Beside them, artichokes, Aunt Kupo's favorite. I selected the ripest one, then a few less ripe. Who knew when I'd find my way back to a market? Better buy enough to last a week. A bin of chickpeas stood in front of the booth. I bent to pick the best. After cooking for my captors, making food for myself would be easy.

"How may I help you?" A man little taller than I was slid into the booth.

"These, please." Choices heaped between us, we haggled.

After we agreed on a price, the vendor scooped my purchases into a cheap basket and handed them over. With the hood of my cloak tugged over my face, I pushed back into the crowd.

How to carry the pots back to my horse without dropping them? My feet slowed. How could I transport everything on horseback if I couldn't hold Rock's reins? Someone bumped into me and I flinched.

In my mind's eye, I pictured a secure campsite. My pots neatly stacked by a fire circle, my foodstuffs safely stored inside my tent—wait, where did people buy tents?

Lips numb, I crossed to the vendor who'd sold me the new robes. She swiveled toward me at once. "Don't you want a pretty robe to—oh." She glowered. "No refunds."

No refunds? "I just want—"

"Move along, little girl." She gave me her back.

Girl. I stomped to the other side of the booth. "Where can I buy a tent?" Someone who sold cloth goods must know.

Her brows raced up her low forehead. "People do not make tents to sell, they make them for themselves." The vendor turned her back once more, to lean toward a young woman in robes dyed a soft green, probably with crushed leaves and stems.

"A lovely young woman like you must want lots of—" The vendor's potential customer kept walking without even a sideways glance. The vendor glared at me over one shoulder. "Stop scaring off my potential customers. Move along."

My feet scuffed the ground as I trudged back to Rock. How did one make a tent? When I tried to picture the walls of my captor's dwelling, I couldn't bring them to mind. Instead of the goat-hair walls, I recalled Sanipu's weight crushing me, the rough fibers of the rug scraping my back and hips. I felt again Balaam's hot breath on my throat, saw Arseen's disgusted face.

I fled down the alley to Rock. If only I could flee from my memories so easily.

CHAPTER TWENTY-FOUR

NO MATTER HOW HARD I RAN, I couldn't escape the words pounding inside me. *I killed them.* Aunt Kupo had raised me to heal, not kill. What would she say if she learned what I'd done with the skills she taught me?

Now I froze at the edge of the stable yard. "Curse it." *My pottery.* I trudged back for it, every inch of my skin tingling. Would I come face to face with Balaam? With my father?

Back in the market, the crowds had thinned. At the potter's booth, I didn't see my purchases. "Where are my things?"

"Right here." He stooped to heave a skinny sack into sight. "Packed them up for you. Easier to carry this way."

How? If the bowls and spoons and so on were just stuck in a sack, they'd break—might even be broken now.

"Tore some old sacking into pieces, put a layer of that between each pot, then put your goods into one of the narrow sacks my wife stitches up for me. That'll keep them upright until you reach your destination." His smile filled his thin face.

Oh. "Thank you." So much for him trying to cheat me. "Here." I dug out another coin. "For your trouble."

"Thank you, Miss." He turned to a woman bent over his pots. "How might I help you? Best pots in the market."

Only after I returned to the stable and bridled Rock did I falter. How could I mount my horse with bags of food and pottery in my arms? I stood there, stymied, while Rock complicated things by whinnying and jostling me as he tried to rejoin his buddy in the stable.

"Rock. Stand. Still." I would've yanked the reins if I'd had a hand free.

My gelding trod on my toes with another ringing neigh.

The back door creaked open a notch. "Trouble?"

It took all my strength not to collapse on the ground, sobbing, while Rock rampaged around me. "I can't get on my horse—"

The stable owner joined me. "Not with your hands full. Fix it so your horse carries the goods for you and you can hold the reins."

When I gaped at him, he took the sacks of food and pottery—and the stolen treasure—from me, twisted the bags closed, then knotted the tops together. "You see?"

Not really, no.

He sighed. "Look." Carefully he hefted the sacks over Rock's neck, so they hung on either side of the gelding's neck and down his shoulders. When my mouth sagged, he shrugged a little. "I've loaded some goods in my time. Now bend your leg and I'll boost you up."

When I raised one knee in front of me, he stepped back. "Has no one helped you mount before? Bend your knee, lower leg sticking out behind you."

Stomach jumping, I obeyed and reached for Rock's mane. Next moment, I was on his back. "Thank you. Thank you so much."

His head dipped. "I did nothing. Good day to you."

Rock whinnied all the way down the alley, the other horse calling after him. "Quiet, Rock. Quiet, boy." I smoothed a hand along his tensed neck.

At least I had fewer people to dodge in the market now. Rock settled as we rode out of town. At the edge of the settlement I turned him in the opposite direction from my captors' camp. "Let's see what's out here, Rock."

One of his ears swiveled back toward me and he whinnied so hard I felt the flutter against my legs. He neighed again, bobbing his head.

Then I heard many other horses reply in the distance. I stroked his neck. His hide twitched under my touch, as if I were an errant horse fly. "Your friends at the horse dealer miss you too." Did Midnight scent me on the wind?

The sacks bumped Rock's shoulders and jostled my thighs as he tried to scoot sideways toward the unseen horses. I took a firmer hold on the reins. "This way."

We left the town far behind. Was I taking Rock into the desert to die?

His pricked ears gave me courage. *We'll make it,* he seemed to say.

At last I smelled growth, the mineral odor of water. Peering about me, I saw a clump of trees, dark against the darkening sky. An oasis. When we reached it, I slid to the ground, knees sagging at the impact.

What to do for shelter? I flipped back the hood of my cloak, only to draw it up again. The evening felt cool and dry, like most nights in this season. I pictured myself asleep and exposed on the ground, vulnerable to Balaam. Anyone who crept up in the night. Pictured Balaam's rising delight when he found me. Would I wake to his weight on me? Would he stab me to death in my sleep, or after I awoke to find him on top of me? Inside me?

I gagged. *Think about something, anything, else.* I forced myself to puzzle out the problem of my campsite. While I did, I tugged off my cloak. It swirled out in a circle.

I stared down as it dangled from my fist. For an instant the cloak had looked like a tent. Tomorrow, in the daylight, I'd prop it up like one. For now I curled under its shelter and eventually fell asleep.

Soon after I drifted off, the quiet sound of shifting sand jerked me awake. *Who's there? Balaam. He's come for me.* I forced my eyes open. Could I roll aside, dodge the blade poised to dive into my breast?

"Oh. It's you. It's only you—" The last word rolled out on a sob. Rock stood over me, ears tipped forward, his soft eyes focused on my face. It never occurred to me to worry that he might tread on me. His warm bulk stood between me and danger.

I rolled over, and slept.

I was married. A husband of my own choosing, not the old man selected by my father for the benefit of his business. No, this handsome, young man honored my knowledge of herbs and plants. He honored everything about me, including my body. He lay on me in the dark, his back muscles rippling against my embracing arms and legs, his belly hot and damp against mine, his chest warm on my breasts. We moved together in unison, he moved against me, inside me, and I moaned in pleasure—

Then his muscles, his bones, the very shape of his whole body, even that linking us so intimately, changed shape. I felt it, could somehow see it happen from above us where we entwined on the bed. Even that changed, became the filthy layer of rugs, discarded clothing, old food matted with tangled jewelry. The warm tongue deep in my mouth went rigid and unforgiving. Stopped sliding with mine and jabbed against my throat, while the stubby man-root raked my most vulnerable softness. My lover's warm maleness shifted into rankness, into Sanipu's reek. Sanipu savaged me, and horror of horrors, I embraced him—or the beloved now lost to me.

My own screams woke me. I tore upright, arms and legs flailing as I hadn't been allowed in the outlaw camp. *Nothing. No one. I'm alone. Safe. Safe?*

"R-rock?" Frightened by my thrashing and shrieks, my gelding must have galloped away, perhaps all the way back to the horse dealer's. Then his hooves shuffled near, his warm breath puffed over me. *"Don't worry, I'm here."*

"Oh, Rock. Oh, Rock." I wobbled to my feet, hugged his sturdy neck. Wept into his rough mane, and let his solid warmth seep through me while I wept.

I **WOKE** in wan light. At once I drew in my arms and legs. *Where am I? Will my tormentors attack me as I lie here—*

Then I remembered. *Free. I'm free.* For the first time in what felt like years, I didn't have to jump up, prepare breakfast for my captors. For anyone but myself. No sweating, grunting, hairy man would fall on me, dig pain into my core.

Free. Free. Free. Giggles boiled out of me as I rolled to sit and stretch. Pale pink tinted the eastern horizon. Rock dozed just the other side of the gleaming spring. This oasis seemed smaller than the first chosen by my captors, and not as well hidden as their second. Did Balaam know of this one? Would he find me here?

I burst to my feet. "We need to move, Rock." Right away.

My fingers fumbled with the bridle. Rock stretched his head beyond my reach, ears twisted, jaw clamped. *Slow down,* his actions told me. *Take a breath. Think.*

I sank to the ground and hugged my shaky knees. Did Balaam know this place, or did I just imagine he did? Another study of the landscape. No town for leagues. And it had water. Shade from a few trees, most welcome since I had no tent. *Balaam won't find me here. I'll move before he does.*

Now to turn my cloak into a tent. But how?

Shade. Trees. Trees—fallen branches.

I foraged beneath the trees, grateful none was a pomegranate. *Will I ever eat a pomegranate again?*

With an armful of sturdy branches, I sought the best location for my makeshift tent. In the shade of a juniper, near the water for easy bucket refills. My fingers closed over my palms, still abraded from my captors' rope-handled buckets.

Perhaps the side of the tree opposite from the water would serve me best. If Balaam or my father's men found this place, they'd be less likely to see me.

What will I do if Balaam appears? He'd come at me, lips peeled in an evil grin—Vomit scorched my throat at the image. Well, if he or my father's men found me, I'd run to Rock. I was no longer helpless, I had a horse. I could gallop away.

And leave my pots and foodstuff? Yes.

Besides, what made me think Balaam'd choose this oasis out of the whole desert? *I'm safe. I'm safe. I can risk it.*

Rock bumped his muzzle against my shoulder, ears flopping.

"Good horse. Good Rock." I stooped to prop up my cloak with the branches.

When I finished, it looked like a cloak propped up on sticks. But mine. My home. And I'd birthed the idea and made it real by myself. I'd never had a home of my own before.

The world is mine to explore. Mine. What foods did I like best? What new ways could I prepare them? What kind of clothing did I want to wear, what colors?

The life I'd lived under Father's roof, the life Aunt Kupo lived, were both limited by his attitude that we existed, like everyone else, to please him.

Now I live to suit myself.

I made a fire circle, heaped deadwood nearby. *Much easier than my captors' campsite—* No, I'd not compare my life with what came before.

The propped-up cloak hung lifeless. It needed an entrance. I hitched the east-facing section upward. Balaam never oriented the tent the same direction twice. I would always set up my dwelling to face the sunrise, so dawn woke me. When I settled permanently,

I'd build a fenced area for Rock—

My toes curled into the sand. I'd pictured Balaam on foot, but by now he'd have stolen a horse. The nearest horse dealer had Midnight. Balaam would see his stallion, know I'd been there? Then he'd visit the market. Learn which way I'd gone. He could be right behind me, mounted on Midnight and coming fast.

The horizon blurred as I scanned it for that malignant figure galloping toward me. A warm touch on my shoulder made me shriek. I veered around, and Rock skittered away, nostrils flared.

Hands clenched, I tried to calm myself. "Sorry, Rock. Sorry."

My horse edged farther away, ears stiff. Sweat darkened his neck. I eased up to him. "You're all right, Rock. We're all right."

A glance over one shoulder showed only empty desert. *Balaam's not there.* But if he was following me, I knew Rock couldn't outrun the stallion. I might as well stay here.

CHAPTER TWENTY-FIVE

THAT NIGHT I COULDN'T BRING MYSELF to crawl under my propped-up cloak. If Balaam found me, that'd be the first place he'd look. So I plucked the cloak off its sticks and clambered up the rock outcropping just beyond the oasis. There, I hunted around until I found a niche just wide enough for me to sit on the ground, and tucked myself into it.

The stones dug into my back where I propped myself against them. Insects buzzed about my eyes, tangled themselves in my hair. "Stop it. Stop!" With their incessant buzzing, would I even hear Balaam if he came?

My elbows bumped into the cliff face as I shifted around, trying to find a comfortable position. With a strangled cry I sat up, hair a damp tangle over my face. Wait—I'd made noise. Had anyone heard? I peered over the edge of my hiding place and saw only my gelding's shadowy bulk, my household goods. Was I a fool to hunker up here, stones prodding the bruises Sanipu bequeathed me? Perhaps I should risk sleeping on flat ground, in the shelter of my cloak.

While I worked up the courage to move, I fell asleep.

I jolted awake with the moon straight overhead. Dawn felt far away, the buzzing insects were still. Only the gentle splash of the spring broke the silence. So what had woken me? When I eased up in my hidden niche to peep down at my camp, all my breath rushed out.

In the darkness, a dark figure stomped to examine my cookware. The grind of his feet in the sand, the clink of pottery, must've wakened me. Night hid his face, but I knew him from his sharp movements, his impatient search through my foodstuffs.

Balaam.

Cold pulsed through me. I pressed against the stones as if I could become part of the cliff by will alone. As if I could ever hide from him. Balaam flung down one of my new pots. It shattered as he stomped away from my makeshift kitchen. Faint reflection from the stars slicked blue along the blade in his hand. A dark shape shuffled closer to him. *Rock, don't. Don't go near him.*

Then I recognized the horse's delicate ears, the proud arch of his neck. Midnight. Balaam had got him back. Stolen from the horse dealer? Probably. I sagged on the outcropping.

As the stallion hitched closer to my tormentor, a gust of tears shook me. *Midnight, how could you do Balaam's bidding?*

Midnight squealed and struck out with one foreleg.

"Silence." Balaam cuffed the stallion, but Midnight flung his head up out of the way and called out again.

With a tentative nicker, Rock answered.

Balaam's laugh, low though it was, sounded clearly through the night. "So, you're her horse. Where is she, hmm? She can't have gone far without you, not this time of night." He raised his free hand and caught my horse by the forelock. "Since you can't tell me, you'll help me leave a message for her." He angled the sword as if to drag it across Rock's throat.

A mew escaped me. *Run away, Rock. Run away from him.*

Then the stallion shouldered Balaam aside, teeth bared. My tormentor fell to the sand, sprawled and cursing. Before he hit the ground, Midnight tore a strip of hide off Rock's neck. My gelding grunted, half-reared, and scuttled away.

Still swearing, Balaam scrambled up to hurl his sword after my gelding's haunches. The weapon clattered on the stones of my fire circle. "Not worth it anyway." He retrieved the fallen blade. In the dark, his teeth gleamed. "I've better things to do."

What if he looks up, sees my head projecting from my hiding place? I flattened against the stones, for all the good it'd do. When the sun rose, Balaam would discover me.

My stomach threatened to spew up the simple meal I'd eaten before bed. My hands clamped at my sides. If only I could find a loose rock, big enough, heavy enough, to drop in silence. Crush Balaam's skull.

After all my plans, my dreams of freedom. Tears striped my cheeks to pool under my chin. I couldn't bear it, that Balaam had reappeared to snatch my life from me. Again. If I'd had a knife with me, I'd slash it across my own throat. Why hadn't I brought a knife up here with me for protection?

Instead my only sharp knife rested with the other kitchen things at Balaam's feet. Though even if I held it, what good would it do? Unskilled with weapons, soft-bodied, I didn't reach Balaam's shoulder. *No wonder he thinks me no challenge.*

Then I straightened a little. I wasn't helpless, I'd killed two men. What could I do to save myself now?

The shadowy figure below me thrust the sword through his rope belt so it swung ready at his hip. He hovered on the balls of his feet a moment, then marched straight for the rock face.

He's seen me. I pressed my forehead against my arms. How long before his hand closed on my shoulder? Would he run me through with the sword? Force himself on me one last time? Hurl me off the rocks and stalk past my broken body to his horse?

Nothing happened. I peeked up, couldn't see him anywhere—

oh. He stood right below me at the base of the formation.

If I breathed hard, he'd hear me. If I moved, he'd come for me at once. By the time the horizon pinkened with dawn, my body ached from keeping still. Light spilled into the oasis.

Balaam gave a half shout of frustration and flung out of hiding. I nearly peed myself. "It's no use." He strode up to Midnight. The stallion jerked away to the end of his reins. Balaam wrested the stallion's head down with one fist, hurled himself onto the horse's back. Swore. Bounded down, cursing, and stooped to unfasten the hobbles.

At once, Midnight flicked his heels into the air a breath from Balaam's nose.

"Damn your worthless hide—" Balaam yanked the reins.

Midnight reared. His tormentor fell again, and the stallion galloped out of the oasis, dragging Balaam, who still clutched the reins. Sand spurted into Balaam's face as the stallion fled into the open desert.

It took everything I had not to whoop with joy. *Go, Midnight.* I hoped Balaam choked to death on sand, that his arms pulled out of their sockets, that his elbows blew apart in a spray of blood.

I jigged in place at the image, only to gasp and go still again at the aches wakened throughout my body by a sleepless night spent cramped and on my feet. With frequent pauses, I worked my way down from my hiding place.

So much for my first home. Hood shading my face, fingers fumbling, I tried to stack my breakable goods. On the bottom, one vessel shattered. The handle snapped off the large spoon. On the other side of the spring, Rock's head shot up when I swore. My usually mellow gelding snorted and jumped backward.

Curse it. I couldn't return to the market; Balaam might lie in wait for me there. Who knew when I'd find another market to replace these things?

I took a sticky breath, another, until I grew steady enough to load the kitchen things without mishap. To pack away my food. Tie both sacks over Rock's neck, like the stable owner in town showed me.

A final scan of the oasis, and I focused on the sticks that'd propped up my cloak. If my time in captivity taught me anything, it was that few trees grew in these wastelands. So I plucked the sticks from the ground to tuck them in my treasure sack. They were treasure, as much as any gold coin.

Then I mounted Rock and rode away from the oasis for good.

CHAPTER TWENTY-SIX

A SOFT BREEZE STIRRED THE SANDS as the day wore away. Rock trod along under the low autumn sun. Though only three days had passed, it seemed a lifetime since I fled the oasis—several lifetimes since I'd escaped my captors—but only the week before, I had been their helpless slave.

Now I reined in Rock. Should I go back to the outlaw encampment, hide there? It was the last place Balaam would think to search for me, and at least I'd have a roof over my head. I hesitated, while Rock stood patiently waiting my next signal. Once in the camp, what would I do with the stinking bodies of Sanipu and Arseen? Bury them in the sand? My empty belly clenched, and I let Rock keep going straight ahead.

As evening darkened the sky, I thought of my father's favorite god, Moloch. Should I thank the god that the sun wasn't as high or hot due to the change of seasons? Make a sacrifice of some of my precious grain, since I had no animal to kill?

No. Had Moloch stretched out a powerful hand to me when my captors raped me? Beat me? But what could I expect of a god who demanded the sacrifice of children? Probably Moloch had looked on with enjoyment while the outlaws tortured me—

I straightened so abruptly Rock halted again. *That's the god of my father. I can worship any god I like.*

Rock swiveled an ear back at me. After a pause, I released my breath in one long sigh, then nudged my horse with my legs.

Which god? Which god do I choose for myself? Frowning, I reviewed all the gods I knew. They were all harsh. Why? Because people like my father worshiped them? Or because such people imagined gods like themselves?

And my captors? Remembering the casual way they'd butchered the old ewe, I doubted they'd worshiped any deity at all.

Now I halted Rock at a slight dip in the landscape. No one would seek me out here. No need to unpack my household goods; I'd move on as soon as I woke.

I settled on the ground, cloak already pulled over my head, and chewed a stiff piece of elderly flatbread, left over from a previous meal. When I finished and curled flat on the sand, I fought to ignore the grinding in my stomach. *Go to sleep. It's not the first time you've suffered hunger.*

Curse it, would I never cease to remember my time as a captive?

It took most of the night for me to fall asleep. Eventually I flipped the hood off my face to stare up at the stars. Fresh air flowed over me, and I sat up. This felt wonderful. Why did anyone sleep sealed up inside?

Then I thought of the treasure chests full of my captors' thievings, of my father's heavy furniture and countless goods. *Greedy people need someplace to hide their treasure.* To hide what they did to those in their power. I sank down to sleep again, this time with the hood off my face.

At last dawn woke me from a restless doze. A desert lark's piercing sweet song cut off when Rock yawned and his bit chingled.

"Oh, Rock, I never unbridled you." How could I treat him with such carelessness? "I'm sorry." I lunged to my feet to stroke his drooping head, and his lax ears fluttered. The day stretched ahead of us, waiting. I swung onto my gelding's back and his head rose, his ears perked. "Walk on." I nudged him forward.

If men like my father, my captors, chose to live inside, why did good people like Aunt Kupo do so? *Because they live in the world ruled by those other people. By men.*

At that instant, I decided not to seek out a tent, not to deny myself the pleasure of open air and space. I would decide how to keep myself warm from the winter winds when the time came.

For days I rode from sunrise to full dark. Balaam might expect me to flee in a straight line, so I traveled in different directions each day. In the shelter of darkness I visited village wells, filled a jug stoppered with a plug of cloth so I could drink by day. To stop where people could see me in daylight might leave a trail for Balaam to follow. I whispered to Rock, lest my voice carry over the wasteland and lead my father's men to me.

Then one day a smudge of green appeared on the horizon, with no smoke from fires hovering above. I aimed Rock for it. The sun burned low in this season, but the trees offered a break from the chill breeze. As we drew nearer I saw the oasis offered water and— my heart clutched—a couple of pomegranate trees.

Every fiber in my body tightened. Rock stumbled. Eyes shut, I made myself loosen my muscles. Someday I'd grow used to the sight of that tree and its fruit. Maybe someday.

I dismounted, pulled the laden sacks to the ground, and removed Rock's bridle. He shook himself until dust flew out of his coat. He'd never proven hard to catch, but could I catch him quickly if I saw Balaam on the horizon? I half started after Rock to tie him to a branch, stopped. Took a sticky breath. If I limited Rock's need to wander, to browse, that made me no different from Balaam's cruelty to Midnight. The way he left the stallion constantly hobbled.

I left my household goods in the bags. Ready for me to sling over Rock's neck and escape if necessary. It made the oasis a temporary refuge, not a home.

That night, stretched out under the stars, images of my captors' camp as it must be now crept through my mind. Sand sifting over their belongings. The tent flabby and sagging. Had wild animals torn the bodies apart, scattered the bones?

Stop thinking about it. Stop.

I heaved onto my other side, but couldn't find a comfortable position. *They're dead. Well, two of them are dead. Sanipu'll never pinch my nipples, pinch any woman's nipples.*

That night, I dreamed again of a lover. Though I couldn't clearly see his face, his mouth met mine, warm and gentle. His body, firm and lithe, pressed into mine, and I cried out with longing as he slid into me. *More, oh more. Harder. Faster. Deeper.* My hips rose to meet him, thrust for thrust, and rotated—but then. Oh then. His living voice broke into an evil chortle. The palms spread warm over my breasts twisted and began to pinch. The glide of his maleness shrank but didn't shrivel. His body grew heavy.

Sanipu jabbed himself into my woman parts with rough stabs. "I knew you were a slut all along. Cry out for me now. Scream." He laughed, and twisted my nipples until I thought they'd tear off. "I like it when you scream."

I froze in place. *Wake up. Wake up!* Sanipu tried to dig deeper into my body, but his inadequate part prevented him. "Come on, slave. You want me. Say it." He cuffed my head. "Say it!"

I woke. I couldn't move, then felt the weight of my cloak tangled around my legs and body, pinning my arms to my sides. I bolted upright, clawing the fabric off me. I couldn't bear even that reminder of Sanipu's body on mine.

Rock crept closer in the darkness, whiffling through his nostrils. *You all right?*

"No, Rock, I'm not." Why? Why did I dream of wanting a man, wanting to lie with a man? Willing. More than willing, I recalled with a shudder. Eager. Joyous. Acid burned in my throat. Never. I'd never touch another man again. Never allow one to touch me. Never. *While I'm awake, anyway.*

Dawn found me still awake. Still tired. I squeezed my gritty eyelids closed, but the sunlight glowed pink through them. Then I stiffened. A scuffling sound came from my sacks. Cautiously, I peeked under one lid. Balaam? No, a scrawny dog with matted fur, scrabbling at my things.

"Stop that." Stumbling over my tangled cloak, I lurched toward him. The dog aimed one desperate look at me, then scampered away with his tail clamped between his scrawny haunches.

I staggered to my bags. "If you've stolen my food—" The top of the sack with my dwindling supplies remained tied shut, though loosened threads fluttered where the dog's claws had torn.

When I turned toward him, the dog cringed back. "You get out of here." Then the dog peered at me, belly flat to the ground, and I understood. "You poor thing. You're just hungry." I knew how that felt.

At first the dog stayed rigid, well beyond my reach. Lips peeled away from the teeth. Bunched shoulders. The deceptive wavering of the tail, friendly-seeming. Until the dog sprang for the nearest ankle. I knew the signs too well from memories of my father's dogs. Maybe this dog would run away. Or he'd attack me.

"It's all right, boy. I promise not to hurt you. Sorry I yelled at you before."

The dog quivered, head low to the ground. Beneath his ragged coat his hips jutted, with sores visible through his patchy fur. Someone had beaten him.

Beaten. Starved. Bile scalded my throat. I stepped closer. The dog tensed, but didn't move. I crouched, slowly, and kept my voice soft. "I won't hurt you."

One tattered ear twitched at my low voice. He whined.

I reached for a piece of the leathery, tattered remains of my flatbread, and offered it to the dog.

Drool edged over his black lip, but he didn't creep near enough to take the bread.

"All right, then." I flipped the morsel toward him.

The dog yelped and dodged as if I'd thrown a stone.

"Poor creature."

One eye on me, he crept to the bread and snapped it up, already withdrawing. He licked his jaws, tongue startling pink against the faded fur.

I took out more bread, frowned. Even a canine would have difficulty biting this. In the end, I hacked it to pieces with a knife and threw him the bits. My first half-dozen tosses had him ducking behind trees, but then he crawled closer to catch each tossed mouthful out of the air. His slender whip of a tail twitched, then wagged.

When I hesitated over the last piece, he yapped. *Hurry up.*

I laughed and flung him the bread. "Soon you'll grow fat again." I held out one hand. The dog took a tentative step closer.

I kept that hand extended as the dog belly-wiggled forward, one painful body-length at a time. Sweating from the effort of remaining motionless, I at last felt his whiskers brush my palm, the coldness of his nose.

"Good boy—"

He cowered. Rolled belly upward, lips crinkled.

"It's all right, boy, I won't hurt you." *I'll never hurt you. I only ever hurt anybody else to save myself.* In memory, I felt the wooden spoon handle dig into my palm while I stirred the ground pomegranate root into the mutton stew.

I wiggled my fingers to free them from the memory. Right now I needed to focus on what to call the dog. "Boy" reminded me of Balaam's roar of "Girl." I sank to the ground. "I won't hurt you, I won't—"

The tip of his tail flickered.

My arm ached from holding it out so long. Just before I let it sag into my lap, the dog wiggled close enough to lick my fingertips, then shrank back. *He hopes I have more food—*

He squirmed a little nearer and licked my hand again, whining. His tail wagged harder.

Could I pat him?

The instant I reached out to him, he yelped like I'd kicked him and tore away, vanished like a thief.

Thief.

Should I name him something I didn't want him to be? I stood to shake dust from my robe. "I'll risk it." If he responded. If he came back. "Here, Thief."

He peeped at me from beyond the trees. His tail lashed hard enough to smack his haunches. Wonderful—I'd found his name.

"Here, Thief, here." I smacked my thigh.

Thief took a small step toward me, only to drop flat to the ground and whine. *How do I know I can trust you?*

I had flour for flatbread. I poured some into a bowl, added water, stirred. At first Thief cringed away from my rapid movements, then crept closer.

"Good dog. Good Thief." He'd learn his name if I used it.

By the time I patted the dough on a vessel ready to bake on the fire, he'd wriggled closer to watch. Drooled when the scent of bread filled the air.

By the time I eased the bowl off the fire, Thief rested his head by my foot.

CHAPTER TWENTY-SEVEN

THIEF SNAPPED UP THE FLATBREAD I tore off for him and bounced around me in a circle. Tail wagging, mouth parted in a doggy grin.

"Sorry, Thief, the rest is mine."

He jumped up on me for an instant, ears perked.

"Well—" I knew the aching grind in the belly. I tore another wedge for him. "Here."

Thief barked, tail wagging until it blurred. When I hesitated, he frolicked around my legs, barked louder, demanding me to stop teasing him. Begging for something more substantial than flatbread.

"Rock." I called my gelding. *"Rock."* Oh no—had my gelding wandered away into the desert? Would I never see him again? When Rock strolled into sight over a slight slope, I nearly cried with relief.

Thief stopped gamboling about me to press every bit of himself flat to the ground, staring up at the approaching horse. He whined. Scooted backward away from my gelding.

"It's all right, Thief. He's our friend. Friend." I patted Rock's neck, tried to do the same to Thief. The dog only squirmed away from me even faster.

Thief yipped every time I touched Rock as I readied him for the errand. *Are you crazy? Keep away from that thing.* When I clambered up on Rock's back, Thief growled.

As I started off at a walk, the dog's cries increased. *Get down, don't you know how dangerous huge dog is? Stop riding it right now!*

Midnight would've unseated me, and probably trod on Thief in the bargain. Rock just cocked an ear at Thief's ruckus and set off at a placid walk. Whining, Thief trailed after us. I jounced a little on Rock's back, and my gelding tilted back one ear at me. I had a horse and a dog. For now.

I SEARCHED the horizon for any sign of smoke. Signs of a village. Thief kept pace with Rock, grumbling low in his throat all the while. *Listen to me, get off that thing. Now!* At last I saw a spiral of smoke so frail I almost missed it. Only as we approached the huddle of houses did I halt Rock. What if Thief ran away and never came back?

The place was too small to have a market. Smaller even than the huddle of four houses I'd visited on Midnight. Two huts opposite each other, with barely a track in between. At least Thief couldn't get lost in a crowd. Halting between the houses, I wondered how to get meat for Thief. No one came out of any of the huts, no woman visited the squat well. At last I slid off Rock, chose a house, and sped toward it. Thief hunkered to the ground, ears pressed to his skull.

"I'm not mad at you." I took the last few steps and tapped on the door. It shivered in its frame like a too-firm knock would splinter it.

A little boy opened it. How strange to have someone look up at me. Usually I had to tip back my head to see another's face. After what felt like a long silence, I crouched until the boy and I were on the same level.

"May I speak to your mother?"

Finger in his mouth, he didn't answer. His hair looked shorter on one side of his head than the other.

"Is your mother—"

"Who's there, Ben?" A woman with frazzled hair came out of the shadows, a pair of brass scissors in one hand. Snippets of hair clung to her robe.

"Sorry to interrupt while you give your child a haircut."

She glanced down at her scissors, brushed her robe. "What do you want?"

"Could anyone in the village sell me meat?" No need to tell her it was for a dog.

The scissors chirped as she opened and closed them. "Don't your menfolk provide for you?"

What to say? I just shook my head.

"Well—this morning my husband butchered a rabbit for our evening meal. I've chopped the meat ready, you can have some of that."

I glanced at Thief, hovering by my heels. He might've caught and eaten a rabbit before. "Perfect."

The woman returned to the kitchen. Ben stared up at me, eyes huge in his triangular face, then ran after her. "Nama, Nama, wai' for me—"

Should I follow? Thief leaned against my knee and whined. I touched his head with chilled fingers. "Don't worry, I'm getting meat for you," I whispered.

The woman returned with a wooden box, a handspan across and about as tall.

She jerked to a stop in front of me, half-turned to snap at the boy. "Stop stepping on my heels." At that instant, a baby wailed inside the house. The mother sagged as if her bones had turned to pulp. "Gods help me." She turned to answer the cry, and her body showed the bulge at her waist.

The baby already here sounded so young. I glanced at the toddler. The mother must've been my age when she birthed him. Not unfeeling to him now—just overburdened to breaking. "Let me help." I held out a hand to Ben. "Want to play a game?"

He wound both arms around his mother's thigh.

"Tchah." She nudged him toward me. "Ask what she wants to play." The last word drifted behind her as she hurried away.

With a deep breath, I squatted down to his level on the dirt floor. "Let's play—" My cousin Tamar and I had played finger games in bed, after the maid took the lamp away. "A finger game."

Now I sank all the way to sit on the bald ground, and offered the child my open hand. "Can you touch a finger to my palm before I close my fist and catch you?" I remembered Tamar's taunting call, and made my voice friendly. "Bet you can't. Bet I catch you every time."

His chin wobbled. "Will you—will it hurt?"

"I'd never hurt you." *Hurt anyone. Ever again.* "Like this, look." I poked one finger into the opposite palm and closed my fist. "Got it."

The boy peered after his mother. "I promise to catch your finger softly." An idea. "If I can catch you at all. You look pretty quick."

Ben hopped closer, dipped a finger into my cupped palm.

I closed my hand slowly. He whipped his hand into the air so fast he almost batted my nose. "I did it, I did it, I did it!"

How long since I'd laughed like this, full and loud? My insides felt like a dry river bed flooded with sudden rain. Next time, I dared close my hand faster so I nearly caught his finger. "Almost got you that time."

"But you didn't, you didn't, you didn't," he sang.

The next time I closed my fist fast enough to grasp him for an instant. His flesh felt soft and warm as butter left in the sun.

"Again, again, ag—"

"Ben." His mother stood an arm span away.

Absorbed in my game with the child, I hadn't even noticed her return.

"Don't take advantage of her." A blush sped up "Nama's" throat to her forehead. "Sorry, I forgot to ask your name, or give you mine. I'm not used to adult company."

Neither am I. "Please, don't worry about it. I'm Sarah."

"Sarah." She dipped her head in response, and a hot shiver bolted through me. Someone said my name. Then her mouth twisted. "Days and days and days with only Ben to talk to, and the baby always crying—"

"What's your name?"

Her head tilted up slowly, she stared at me as if she'd never seen another woman before. "Do you know how long since anyone asked me that?" Then everything about her drooped. "No, how could you imagine? Ben calls me Nama—"

"Because it sounds so much like Mama."

She shook her head once. "No, Ben says it's because my husband sometimes uses the word—I mean, my son just calls me that."

Now I remembered how my father had used the word "namus" to shame my mother. Namus. The loss of a man's pride through dishonor. I held out my hand. "What's your name?"

Could she blush any harder? "Liah. Call me Liah."

"Call you Liah?"

She switched the infant to her other shoulder. "I know that's a well born woman's name, but my name is so long and complicated. In my own home—I mean, my husband's home—"

With one firm step, I closed the distance between us. "Glad to meet you, Liah."

"Oh." Her arms tightened around the baby. "I'm honored to meet you, Sarah. What must you think of me, forgetting to introduce myself or ask your name?" Her lower lip quivered, and Ben sidled around to peer at me suspiciously.

"Alone with a toddler and a baby—" *With another on the way.*

"Of course you don't know what to do with yourself."

I thought of my own mother, remembering how my cousin Tamar and I'd raced around. At least the women in my father's house had each other and slave—servants to help them. Had anyone helped Liah since the baby's birth?

"Sometimes after the children fall asleep at night, I realize I haven't brushed my hair all day." She handed me a small wooden box with a fitted lid. "Meat's already chopped."

Probably the best vessel she owned. The most useful. "I'll bring the box back to you."

Liah dipped her head, baby dozing against her shoulder. "You know where I live." She stepped forward to nudge the door open with one hip.

As I stepped out of the house, she whispered, "Thank you for your help with Ben."

CHAPTER TWENTY-EIGHT

THIEF HAD SQUEEZED HIMSELF against the base of the house, whining. When I reappeared he gave an ecstatic bark and leapt on me. "Good boy, Thief, good dog, you stayed here." But my mind lingered on the woman still inside. I pivoted, one fist raised to hammer on the door, remembered the sleeping baby, and tapped with my fingernails. Liah opened the warped panel a crack.

"I'll bring your box back, I promise."

"Yes, so you said." Liah swayed in time with the infant's soft breaths. Ben peeped at me, then ducked into the skirts of his mother's robe.

Thief clung around my ankles, as if I might disappear inside once more. "Maybe you can play with my dog next time, Ben, if you'd like?"

The boy edged nearer. "'s."

"Good." I straightened to smile into the young mother's face. "I look forward to it."

She shifted her baby a little and held one hand out to clasp mine. "Me, too."

"Come, Thief." I returned to Rock, tethered to a fig tree opposite. He stood in the sliver of shadow cast by the tree. As I swung onto his back, I promised myself I wouldn't bring only Liah's box when I returned.

As I mounted Rock, Thief bounded up to lick my ankle, tail lashing hard enough to wiggle his whole body. I nudged him down with my foot. "Off, you'll tear my robes."

Thief dropped to all fours and sat at Rock's feet.

"Good dog. Good Thief." I hugged the little wooden box. It felt polished smooth by time. No doubt inherited for generations. "This is for you."

It took all my concentration to ride with the reins in one hand and the precious box of rabbit meat in the other. Rock ambled along in a wavering line. I prodded him in the right direction with my legs, leaned the way I wanted to go. His wandering pace settled into a business-like walk. I smiled as I thought about what I would give Liah when I returned the box. When next I visited her tiny— "village" sounded too big a word. Settlement? I nodded. The settlement, too small even for a headman—I stiffened so suddenly Rock jerked to a crooked halt.

A headman. When I'd visited the well near the outlaw camp all those times, why had I never thought to ask for the village headman? Asked for help? Told the men of the danger so near them, asked them to send for every male relative they possessed, so they could seize my captors? Imprison them? *I didn't need to kill them at all.*

I sat on Rock's back, and the cooling breeze of twilight chilled my wet face. *Arseen was right. I'm a dull-witted creature.*

I grew limp with crying, and even Rock grew restive. Tail switching. Shifting to rest one hip, then the next. At last he set off for my camp on his own, at a cautious walk, one ear turned back to me. *All right?*

As we drew nearer to the trees, Thief's ruff rippled. He growled low in his chest.

"What's the matter with you?" There must be some other predator hidden among the trees—

A predator. The tiny hairs down my back quivered. I stiffened, and Rock's strides grew jerky. Thief erupted in a frenzy of barks and dashed ahead of me into the oasis.

It couldn't be. It couldn't. Balaam—

"Thief." He ignored me, hopping forward to do battle with—what? "Thief. Stop."

Ears flattened, he bellied back toward me, his whine thin. Pleading.

Then a squirrel answered Thief's challenge with an insolent chitter. My dog quit his apologetic squirmings to leap ahead into the trees. Branches rattled as the small animal plunged up a fig tree.

A squirrel. The "predator" is only a squirrel.

After I slid to the ground in the oasis and loosed Rock, I built a fire in a shallow hollow of sand. When it burned to glowing coals I seared the meat in a pan, shredded it, mixed in dried grain from my stores, and put it down for Thief.

Only then did I allow myself to examine this small oasis. Not as good a spring as many, just a thread of water bubbling from beneath a stone. And fewer trees, no doubt a reflection of the scant water supply. But its lack of appeal meant my pursuers—Balaam, or my father's men—were less likely to notice it.

I smiled, hugging myself in the dark. "I'm home." And I set about unpacking my bags.

Well after dark that night, Thief barked. Eyes gritty with sleep, I rolled over, and kicked off my cloak. Thief faced the darkness, tail stiff. My feet contracted so hard my toes pinched sand. I couldn't see or hear anything, except the echoes of Thief's hysterical yaps.

Balaam? Father's men? Both?

Then Thief plunged to the base of one of the trees, growled. Frantic scrabbling up in the tree. Leaves and bark pattered down. My dog bounced around the trunk.

Every fiber in my body went lax. "Bad dog. Bad." I fumbled under my cloak again. Thief finally stopped harassing the wild animal—the squirrel—again to curl at my feet, but dawn tinted the sky before I shut my eyes again.

Yes, this time he'd chased another small animal. But next time?

CHAPTER TWENTY-NINE

Two days later, I fed Thief the last of the rabbit. He chomped it down in about five bites and looked up at me, licking his jaw. *More?*

"Okay, boy, let's see what we can do." I mounted Rock and set off for Liah's to return the box. Thief crowded my gelding's heels until Rock lifted a hind hoof and waggled it at him. My dog took the hint, loped off to one side, and stayed there.

Only after I swung off Rock's back at Liah's doorstep did I remember the promise to myself to bring her relief from endless pregnancies. Almost, I crept back to my camp to fetch—what? None of the herbs I had in stock would help her.

Then I focused on the weeds sprouted along the base of the house. No, not weeds. Not to someone with eyes trained by Aunt Kupo. Laughing, I darted forward to tear up handfuls of wild carrot. Liah's relief grew on her own doorstep. With the ragged bouquet clutched in one fist, the young mother's precious box tucked under my elbow, I tapped on the door.

This time Liah opened it herself, neither the baby nor Ben in sight. "It's you." She focused on the wild carrot springing every which way from my fist. "You've brought me—flowers?" Her head angled toward the place they'd grown. *Not even flowers from far away, but my own scrubby weeds.* She might as well have spoken.

"These will help you with—the problem we talked about the other day." She frowned in puzzlement. "Your many pregnancies. Collect the seeds of the wild carrot, and take a small spoonful of them every night, or every time after your husband lies with you."

A blush swept up Liah's neck from her robe to her forehead. "I cannot do that. My husband would see. Would stop me."

"It's easy, I'll show you—"

"You don't understand, if my husband suspects what I'm doing, he'll beat me." Her blush burned hotter.

That stopped my burbling words in mid-flow. I knew the thud of male fists raining down on my body all too well. Almost, I let the wild carrot fall to the ground, then tightened my fist. "There's another way."

Liah stepped away from me into the house, shaking her head. "Thank you for thinking of me, but no." She lifted a hand to close the door between us.

"Wait—" I pushed inside after her.

"Hush, you'll wake the baby."

She looked so exhausted, so fearful. I wanted to hug her, to rock like she was a little girl. "You drink tea, don't you? Of course, everyone drinks tea. Dry wild carrot leaves and make tea with them every night and morning after—" *Put it tactfully.* "After you and your husband have been together as man and wife."

Liah took a half-step closer. "So simple?"

"Just that simple."

"But—how does it work? I drink tea all the time, and it doesn't—"

"Wild carrot makes your woman parts slippery inside."

She nodded. "I see. Will it work even if—no matter if—my husband wants to—every night?" The blush rose again.

"Drink the tea as often as your husband—" *Just say it.* "Couples with you."

She giggled. "Then I'll drink so much I'll burst."

A chill shot through me. I remembered how my captors forced themselves on me again and again. I could've gotten with child myself. I could be with child right now.

I thrust the box at Liah with hands that could hardly hold it. "Here. Thank you for the meat."

"You're very welcome—" She stiffened at a tearful wail behind her.

No need to remind her to take the tea. Reminders aplenty howled in her ear every day. I leaned over to kiss her cheek. "Take care, my friend."

"And you." She clasped my hands in hers a moment, then wheeled away to answer the sobs.

I fumbled my way out of the house. What would I do if I found myself with child by Sanipu? Or Balaam? Would I recognize the father of such a child in its face?

My stomach chilled and clenched tight. My whole body seized up so I couldn't mount Rock.

Bent double, I stared down at the dust at my feet. My mouth turned dusty too. *I can't, I can't, I cannot!* Not only could I not afford to take care of such an infant with my new vagabond life. I would never be able to bear the sight of a child with Sanipu's thick-lipped, leering face. A boy who would grow to have the same hectoring voice. A boy who would grow into a bully—

Well, I didn't have to, did I? I'd helped Liah, hadn't I? I'd help myself if I needed to do so.

I crossed to the hovel. Pulled more wild carrot to process the seeds, dry the leaves when I returned to my own encampment. Then I swung onto Rock, clicked my tongue. "Let's go, Rock. Thief."

WALKING BACK into my campsite, I halted Rock to eye my belongings. Maybe I should move on? Even as I considered it, Thief burst into the scant brush beyond the trickling spring, silent and eager.

"Thief, stop annoying that poor squirrel—"

At that moment, my dog trotted out of the spindly thicket, head held high, squirrel clamped in his jaws.

"Oh, no—let it go—drop it. Drop."

Tail swaying, he dropped the creature at my feet. It squeaked and paddled its forefeet. Blood oozed from tooth marks in its belly. Its tail twitched, and with a final cry, the squirrel stilled. "You've killed it. Bad dog—"

Wait. He'd provided meat for both of us. "Good dog. Good, good dog." I dismounted Rock, then retrieved my sharpest knife.

CHAPTER THIRTY

IN DREAMS THAT NIGHT, I clasped my faceless beloved close. Cried out with joy, with ecstasy, as he drove into me. I opened myself to him, body and soul, as his own moan of release filled my mouth—and his body thickened in my arms. The clean scent of his masculinity changed into the reek of Sanipu's filth. My ecstatic shrieks became the terrified screaming I'd never dared give while my captors ravaged me.

I heaved beneath him. Fought the way I hadn't, couldn't, back then. Worked my bent knees between us and sent him catapulting off me. Sanipu soared into the air—and vanished.

Wakened by my own fierce yell, I scrambled upright to peer around my peaceful encampment. "And never come back!" I shouted it into the night, and Thief rolled over to stare up at me, only to flop back down with a sigh. I hugged myself. Like me, my dog was healing. I settled back under my cloak and dropped into sleep at once, with no dreams.

At dawn, I woke with my dog's comforting weight pressed against my feet. I burrowed my toes in Thief's fur. "Good dog."

My dog wiggled up to lick my chin. When I patted him, his tail thumped the ground. I gazed into the pale blue sky above. *If only I'd thought to ask for the headman at the well village. Begged him for help escaping my captors*—I might live in that village now. Might serve as the village healer. As a healer people travelled to for help.

No. I sat up so sharply Thief scooted away from me, not in a spurt of fear, but with an irritated huff. *You're not making me very comfortable. Naughty owner.* After a pause, he gamboled off into the trees. I stood, swaying with my hands clasped between my breasts. Certainty poured through me. *No, it's too late to second guess what I did.*

As I stretched to my full height, Balaam burst from behind the fig tree, lips peeled from his teeth. His heat scorched through my robe as he hauled me against him.

He's here. He's here. Balaam is here.

His sword edge kissed the pulse leaping in my throat, his breath burned my ear. "Every day, every moment, I've hunted you. Planned what to do when I had you at my mercy. Now I've watched you sleep, planned to ravish you until you could no longer walk. No longer stand."

Where's Thief? Why had my dog not warned me?

"Planned to slice bits off you until you begged. Died. As my brothers died."

"I— I—" Curse it, I couldn't get the words out.

Balaam spun me around, hands like stone on my shoulders. "You killed them. You tried to kill me." His breath, spiced with the thyme and salt of za'atar, spurted hot over my face. His stubble rasped my cheek. "But. You. Failed." He shoved me to the ground.

This is it. My last breath.

But his sword didn't slice my throat. At last I dared twist to look up at him. He wasn't there.

Balaam had fallen to the ground two arm spans behind me, clutching one thigh. Sweat dewed his face, his chiseled lips squared in agony.

"You're—" I worked saliva into my mouth. "Hurt?"

"It's. Nothing." He struggled to rise. "Fear for. Your. Own. Life." Blood stained his robe in a wide circle around his clenched hand. "Not. Mine."

The heat I'd felt blazing from him was the heat of fever. My spine stiffened. I climbed to my feet, breathing like I'd just climbed the stairway from the courtyard of my father's stronghold to the roof top pleasure garden. "You—you cannot order me anymore. I'm not—" I swallowed. "Not your slave anymore." *I'm no one's slave.*

As I started to turn away, he fumbled at his sword handle. "Where do you. Think. You're. Going?"

"Where I will. Away from you." *Again.* "To live my life." The life Aunt Kupo had prepared me to live. Aunt Kupo—she would ask him. "How did you hurt yourself?"

Balaam twitched one shoulder. "While I took back. My horse—" *Stealing. I should've known.*

"—the horse dealer. Guards posted." His head jerked forward, brows arrowed toward his nose. "I wouldn't. Wouldn't have been. There. At all. If. You hadn't stolen. My. Horse." Balaam surged halfway to his feet, teetered, and sagged again. His chin jerked higher. "Come. Here. Girl." He stabbed one wavering finger at the ground before him.

Poisoned blood works through his body, poisons him. I'm the strong one now.

I stood still. "N-no." I forced my clenched fists to open. Forced my voice steady. "No."

"Do. As. I. Say." This time he made it to his feet, only to topple. The smell of blood strengthened. It saturated his robe.

"Your wound's infected."

His sword wavered. "Nonsense."

"I can smell it from here. You're bleeding, dizzy. Weak. The edges of the wound are hot and puffy, aren't they? If you don't get to a healer, you'll lose your leg. Or die." Aunt Kupo, her bent old fingers, gentle and firm, guided by the wisdom of years of experience. "A gifted healer would help you." *Help you live, you stubborn fool.*

He just pointed a finger. "Come. Here." The words jerked out in the rhythm of his shivering.

"I could help you." *What? What did I just say?*

Balaam gaped at me.

What had I said? "My aunt taught me all about herbs. I could—"

His chin tucked in, sharpening the beak of his nose, tightening the skin over his cheekbones. "Herbs. That's how. You killed. My brothers. Tried to. Kill me?"

My rounded shoulders answered for me.

"Why give you. Another chance?"

"You murdered my spirit." *And savaged my body, you and your "brothers."*

Balaam jerked out a laugh jagged as broken pottery. "I hear. Your hate." He coughed. "You'll never. Touch. Me."

That much was true. "I'm free now. I freed myself." I spread my feet, fists on hips. "We're even."

"My brothers. Are dead. Because of you."

"And I can never marry because of you." He didn't know I'd never wanted to marry anyway. "My aunt taught me about herbs and healing. Let me use that knowledge as she intended. Let me heal you." If he refused one more time, I'd mount Rock and ride away, I'd—

Thief gamboled up at that moment, tail lashing, mouth wide in a triumphant grin. *I had a wonderful time chasing squirrels.*

At sight of Balaam, my dog went rigid between one leap and the next, paced forward a single threatening step. *Who are you?*

"Thief, no." I caught him by the scruff as he shouldered past me. "Calm down, he's a—" I gagged on the word "friend." "Calm down, we're safe." *Safe?* My fingers trembled. Maybe I should just open them, let my dog rip this man to pieces.

Thief stilled, but growls quivered in every fiber of his body. Balaam's jaw drooped almost to his breast bone. "You. Stopped. Your dog. From. From attacking. Me."

"Of course."

Balaam kept still a long moment, then inclined his head. "Do. What. You will. To me."

How often had I heard my father give an order in that tone, as if the one serving him should feel blessed?

Thief's grumbles faded into silence. With my hand clasped on his ruff, I retrieved what I needed. When he relaxed enough for me to risk letting him go, I took out my precious bulbs of garlic. "Show me your wound."

Balaam's lips compressed. "Do not. Speak to me. Like that." He gasped for breath. "Who. Are you. To. Order me?"

I stalked toward him. "The person whose skill could save your miserable life."

Thief punctuated my statement with a rumble low in his chest.

"Thief. Down." With a creaking whine of protest, my dog dropped to his belly. "Good boy. Stay."

Balaam's mouth opened and shut.

The garlic's papery skin crinkled in my clenched fist. "I can't heal your cut without seeing your leg." *You never seemed shy before.*

While he blushed, I knelt beside him. My hand reached for his robe, hovered between us. I couldn't make myself touch him.

"Here." Every movement stiff, Balaam tugged his robe out of the way. "Get on. With. It."

Head down, I peered at the wound. Puffy edges raw as uncooked meat. Pus and blood crept down his thigh.

He started to press his hands over the cut and I gripped his wrists. "Don't touch it." *The wound needs to be clean before anything else,* Aunt Kupo's voice rang in my head.

When I stood to fetch and heat water from the spring, Balaam sneered. "You retreat from a little gore? Some healer."

I filled a pot with water, built a fire. "A hot compress first to draw out the infection." Plus if I used plain water on him to start with, he might relax.

When the water boiled, I dropped in a cloth, but when I approached him with it, Balaam winced away. "Heat on a cut?" Fear sharpened his voice.

Not so tough now, are you? I pressed the wet cloth onto the wound as he tried to twist away from me. As I'd tried to twist out from under him so many times. "Leave this on until I tell you." I turned away to mince garlic.

When the scent rose on the air, he spoke. "Garlic? You. Plan. To flavor. Me?"

Busy chopping, I didn't even look at him. "Garlic draws out infection."

"Then why." He paused for a raspy breath. "Why not use. It with. The hot. Water."

"Garlic works best raw." I made myself meet his glower, lifted my chin. "Let me do this."

His gaze fell away from me. He sagged. "Very. Well."

My touch gentled. *Under all that bluster, has he always been afraid?*

He half-turned his head and shoulder while I worked. Only when I removed the garlic and took up the cinnamon and pot of honey did he stiffen. "What's that?"

"Honey and cinnamon paste for your injury."

"Honey? Cinnamon? I'm not a sweetmeat."

You're telling me. Something cold and wet brushed my ankle. I jolted and smeared honey on Balaam's arm instead of his leg.

"Mind what you do, girl."

Thief squirmed up to flatten himself against my thigh, upper lip peeled back as he growled at Balaam. I grabbed him as he burst past me. His teeth grazed my wrist.

Balaam grizzled out a laugh. "Some protector."

"Yes." I tipped my head to study him. "Had I not stopped Thief, you'd be on the ground with your throat torn open." I applied cinnamon and honey to his cut.

"Enough. You've done nothing but make my robes sticky." Balaam twitched away from me.

I took his wrist. "I'm not done." As best I could, I wrapped a clean cloth around the cut. "That should keep your robe clean." *As clean as it ever is.* "Find a healer to look at it in a day or so."

He scrambled to his feet and gaped at me. "Another healer?"

"Yes. At the next place—" *You stop to steal something.* "Down the road."

Balaam dropped back on the ground. Thief growled but didn't move. "I will not expose myself to the eyes of a stranger. A stranger who could talk and endanger me. I go nowhere until this heals. You will see to it."

He meant to stay in my camp? Now I gaped at him.

He flourished a hand in the air. "How else am I to make sure you haven't poisoned me?"

Curse it. "You won't be comfortable here."

"At last, you're concerned for my comfort." His lips quirked.

"I—I—" *What?* "I have no shelter from the night air."

Balaam plucked at his lower lip, scanned the oasis. Then he climbed to his feet. "A healer needs to examine the wound in a day or two?"

Yes. Yes. Another healer. Far away. Go far away. Never come back.

"Very well, I return tomorrow or next day." He jerked a nod, mounted Midnight, and galloped away as I crumpled forward with a sob.

CHAPTER THIRTY-ONE

I CROUCHED, ROCKING IN PLACE. Thief whined. I hugged him tight, his fur rough and warm against my cheek. "Thief. Thief. Thief." He squirmed onto my lap. "Balaam found me. He found me."

And I lived.

NEXT MORNING I jerked awake. Scanned the graying horizon. Nothing and no one. Balaam hadn't returned. Not yet. I baked flatbread for breakfast, but when I wedged some in my mouth, I couldn't chew.

At last I stood, picked up a stick. "Here, Thief. Can you catch it? Catch, Thief." When I made as if to toss the stick my dog crouched, tail wagging, and yipped. He darted after the flung stick the moment I threw it, then circled me, head high.

Balaam forgotten, I tapped my thighs. "Here, Thief, bring it here."

He raced around me and finally dropped the stick at my feet. I hurled it for him again. Again, harder. He snatched it from the air with a triumphant bark. This time he returned it to me at once. As

I lifted it to toss again, hooves gritted behind me. I froze.

Balaam.

But when I turned, a caravan of camels and horses approached the oasis, camels laden with rolls of fabric, vast containers of food, and other goods. Toward the rear of the caravan more men in plain garb bestrode other camels, while a man in finer robes sat a fine horse at the front. And at the center, in the most protected spot, rode a slender, diminutive figure. I peered at her. Yes—a girl about my age, in robes thick with embroidery and braid. Jewels glinted around her neck, wrists and fingers.

As the first camel trudged into the oasis, Thief scuttled behind me with a whimper. He cringed against my legs, a warm, vibrating lump.

"They're just animals like you." Then I remembered camel spit sliming my face. "You're right, they're nothing like you."

The man in fancy robes, mounted on a bay stallion, must've heard me. He craned to look around the small oasis, stiffened, and jogged away from the lumbering camels to halt at my side. "You make camp here as well?" He frowned at my meager household goods and tangled cloak.

Ears pricked, Rock left off browsing to jig up to the bay, who pinned his ears and squealed a challenge. The girl's trim gray mount loosed a neigh so deep I knew she was a mare, and jogged closer, but with her head turned towards my gelding, ears pricked. A number of the pack camels twisted their faces, but the girl passed swiftly enough to avoid being spat upon.

The bay stallion squealed another challenge and struck out with a forehoof.

"Hush that noise, you split my head." But the man stroked the glossy bay shoulder before he swung to the ground. While he held the stallion a camel driver dismounted and hurried to hobble the bay in a few practiced moves, easily evading the dancing hindquarters. Another camel driver helped the girl dismount.

The mare bounced toward Rock until she hit the end of her reins. Spinning around the servant who held her, she loosed a frantic neigh. The stallion's muzzle crinkled. With glaring eyes he lunged at the mare, teeth bared. Rock skittered away as if he feared the stallion would punish him next. The stallion tore a strip from her hide before the handlers could stop him.

The merchant clapped his hands. "See to the horses, especially that bite mark." Then he peered at me and around the small oasis. "Your husband has gone off to hunt?"

So tempting just to nod. But if they lingered I couldn't sustain the lie. "I'm alone."

The girl stepped closer, eyes wide above the veil she wore in protection from the sands. "Your menfolk allow that?"

"I—my—" It felt like everyone in the caravan, even the camels, stared at me. "My husband died."

The girl clasped my hands in her soft ones. "Widowed so young."

"Yes, he was much older than—" I glanced at the merchant. "Yes. An accident."

The merchant nodded. "We're sorry for your loss. My name is Tobiath. My wife, Hycania." He gestured at the girl.

She squeezed my hands. "Your name?"

"S-sarah." All around us the camel drivers set up half a dozen tents. Why had they stopped to make camp so early in the day? Before I could ask, Tobiath glanced at my cloak on the ground.

"Where's your dwelling?"

"I don't have one." When Tobiath's brows rose and Hycania gasped, I hurried on. "We lived in a village. A rich man owned most of the houses." Could that happen? "When my husband died—"

Hycania embraced me. "You poor dear. As long as we remain, you must stay in one of our tents. Mustn't she?"

Tobiath answered her appeal with a smile. "Of course."

All around us rose goat-hair tents even larger than my captors', and again I wondered why a merchant caravan chose to halt so early in the day, and at such a tiny oasis. Even if the oasis provided the only source of water for today, it made no sense to linger.

Ears flickering, Rock edged out from behind a tree, nearer Hycania's gray. "I'd best tie him up for a bit." No sense leaving my gelding at the mercy of Tobiath's stallion.

"We have hobbles aplenty. Let one of the camel drivers see to it for you."

"Hobbles." *Balaam.* "No." I took a big step toward my horse. "Rock doesn't wander when we're alone. I'll keep him tied to a tree just until he grows used to having other horses around."

Tobiath studied me a moment, then raised his hands. "As you will it."

LATER, HYCANIA showed me into a room of the tent she and Tobiath shared, then withdrew for me to settle in. I lined my housewares along one of the inner walls, smoothed my cloak on the heaped rugs already there, and flopped on top of them. Far from reminding me of my captors' encampment, the goat hair walls seemed to shield me. Would Balaam even return once he saw the caravan?

Thief wriggled under the tent's front wall to settle beside me, his head on my stomach. "We're safe, boy. Safe."

At that moment hooves galloped close. Thief drew away from my tensed body with a whine. By the time I reached the front of the tent, Midnight surged into sight around the thickest patch of greenery. The smirk on Balaam's face stiffened at sight of the tents and men. His mouth sagged.

Thief tightened a moment, then turned aside and settled into the sand with a little grunt, as if he couldn't bother to make a fuss over one more person.

Midnight had halted at the edge of the trees, head high. Balaam sat there, his ragged beard jutted out. He raked all the activity in the oasis with hot eyes, then glowered at me. He jerked Midnight's bridle as if to ride away just as Tobiath saw him and bellowed a greeting.

"Yet another visitor to this sweet gem of an oasis?" He swiveled toward me. "Perhaps you should establish a caravanserai here." He swung back to greet Balaam. "Do not be put off by our numbers. Come, water your horse, refresh yourself."

Balaam hesitated—delicious, the sight of Balaam hesitant! Then he booted Midnight up to me, bent nearer from his stallion's back. "Who are these people?"

His voice gritted. I gripped my hands together until the knuckles ached. A scream of joy clawed in my throat. *He can't hurt me. He can't threaten me with the caravan here. And he knows it.* "A merchant caravan stopping here for—" How long could I say? "Days. Many days."

Midnight switched his tail irritably as he side stepped away from me. Why—I remembered how sensitive the black stallion was, how quickly he mirrored his rider's tension or ease. *Balaam's nervous.*

"I shall return tomorrow." Again Balaam made as if to wheel Midnight away, only to jag the stallion in the mouth and fling himself off beside me, staggering. "No, you shall heal me now." He muttered, "After all, I can mount and be off in a moment if need be."

Head angled, I studied him. "Really? I cannot help you unless you sit and hike your robe out of the way."

He goggled at me. Swayed from foot to foot before he finally plopped down at my feet. "Very well. Be quick."

Who'd have thought Balaam and I'd ever want the same thing? As I peeled away the bandage, Tobiath approached.

"What's to do?" He watched as I unwrapped the bandage from Balaam's wound, and bent to study the cut. Then Tobiath burst out laughing, whirled to face the others scattered around the oasis. "Our luck's in! She's a healer."

A great shout rose up as every man hooted with joy. Thief yapped as they all rushed to encircle Balaam and me. As more and more men gathered around us, Balaam crouched. Hand trembling, he adjusted the hood of his cloak so it shadowed his face.

Now he knew how it felt to be outnumbered and helpless. My hands stilled on Balaam's wound. Why did the caravan act so excited to meet a healer? Then one of the camel drivers strode up to me and hitched his robe to his knees. Red bumps dotted his skin, a few swollen with pus.

"My flea bites are worse than yours, let her see me first." Another driver pushed himself close to me and rolled back his sleeves to reveal ropy arms speckled with flea bites, most of them connected by ridges of reddened flesh.

Balaam cowered in his cloak and sent me a pleading look. Pleading? Balaam?

Tobiath beamed down at Balaam. "Pardon us, please. We've itched ever since our stay in a shoddy caravanserai three nights ago. Torment. But you arrived first." He shooed the others back. "She's already helping this man. We must wait our turn."

The camel drivers groaned.

Tobiath made gentling motions with his hands. "We've waited this long. Another little bit won't hurt us."

As the men drifted away from me, one muttered, "Seems like a lifetime to me."

"You? I've scratched myself until I bled."

Balaam kept silent while I examined the edges of his injury. Already, a faint line of new flesh edged the cut. "This looks good." I wiped away the remains of the old poultice.

"Will it scar?" His voice couldn't have reached even the nearest camel driver, but he glanced over one shoulder nonetheless.

I recalled the scars roped along his body. "A fresh poultice will reduce the chance of that. Then I'll bandage it and you can go."

He flicked a look at me. "Get on with it. You'll not rid yourself of me so easily." He tilted back his head with an attempt at his old arrogance, but his voice quivered.

It took all my will not to giggle. He didn't budge as I built a fire, heated water, cleansed and poulticed the wound. When I finished, I drew back. "Return tomorrow."

His cheek twitched. "I'll return in—" He checked the number of armed men in the oasis. "—a few days."

"Please yourself." I withdrew to the tent.

Tobiath coughed to announce his presence. "He doesn't seem grateful. Riding off like that without even thanking you. Or offering payment"

What to say? I turned to him. "Our history is complex."

"Oh?" His brows rose up his broad, lined forehead.

"Let me see to your flea bites." At the edge of the oasis grew a number of aloe vera plants. "Come with me."

The rest of the caravan gathered around as I broke off a leaf and squeezed the gel over the flea bumps on Tobiath's hand and arm. His face slackened with relief, and at once the camel driver who'd stood close to me earlier gasped. "So easy? We've ridden past hundreds of those plants. Thousands."

"It takes knowledge to heal. Sarah knew the plants could help us and we did not." Tobiath drew back from me with a smile.

Though I stayed outside to supervise, the men were soon treating their own flea bites. Once again I withdrew into the tent. The walls bellied in the cool wind. And once again, Tobiath cleared his throat just before he stepped into the room with me.

"I couldn't ask you about this outside." Even in the dimness of the tent, his face looked red.

Puzzling. Ask me what?".

"I need your help—" He sidled closer. "You've shown yourself so skilled. I'd—I'd—perhaps you can help me with—with—another problem."

"Of course."

Tobiath's mouth worked a moment. "No doubt you wondered why we stopped so early in the day?"

I nodded. What could that have to do with his mysterious problem?

"Hycania felt ill this morning. I hoped—well, I hoped—so I promised her a rest as soon as we reached an oasis. Then one of the of the camel drivers felt uneasy in his stomach as well."

"So—oh." If a man felt nausea too, then— "So Hycania isn't—"

Tobiath sagged in place. "She must not be. I suspect they both ate something at breakfast."

"You want me to help them?"

"No. I mean, yes, if they're still in any discomfort. Naturally. But. We've been married a whole season, and Hycania hasn't— I mean, there's no sign she's—" His whole body drooped. "This morning, I so hoped—"

How would Aunt Kupo respond to a call for help with such a problem? Not by tittering like a fool. I squeezed down my nervous giggles, tried to keep my expression suitably serious.

"My bride is so young. So beautiful." Everything about him sagged. When he spoke, his voice sounded scratchy and dry as wind through scrub. "I want her—so much. The wanting itself—" His face blazed red. "Often—well, sometimes—defeats me."

"I'll do what I can for you." Herbs that increased blood flow, perhaps? *But first of all, I'll talk with his wife.* "Send Hycania in to me."

Tobiath jerked upright. "You're not going to tell her what I said?"

I shook my head. "Of course not. Be easy." I gestured him toward their rooms.

CHAPTER THIRTY-TWO

I FETCHED MY URN OF LAVENDER BUDS from its place against the wall and waited. A little later, Hycania edged through the doorway. "Tobiath said you want to see me?"

"Please come in." At that moment, Thief wriggled past her and lolloped up to me, wagging his entire back end, to bump his head against my palm. *Pat me, pat me, pat me now.* When I didn't respond fast enough to suit him, my dog glanced at Hycania and whined.

The merchant's wife hopped into the room. "You're so lucky to have a dog." She stooped to pat Thief. "What a good boy. Good, good boy."

He cringed at her loud voice, but pressed up into her touch as she stroked him from head to tail.

"I've always wanted a dog, but Tobiath says the road is no life for one." She dropped to the rug beside me. "Why did you want to see me?"

"Your husband—" I broke off to fiddle with the lid of the lavender jar.

"My husband?" Her brow furrowed.

"Yes. He said— that is, he's worried—"

"What could worry him that he'd speak to a woman about?"

I tried to remember how Aunt Kupo spoke to embarrassed patients. *Be matter-of-fact.* Would it help me get through my own embarrassment? "He's concerned about your illness this morning. What it might mean."

Hycania blushed to her hairline. "No, it wasn't—I mean, I'm not—I just ate something that disagreed with me." She bent to rub Thief's head, eyes down. Before I could speak, she stumbled on. "I wonder. Do you have a medicine—maybe an ointment that I could use—you see, when my husband—comes to me in the night, I—he—"

"Yes?" I struggled to keep my tone practical. What was this?

"When he—approaches me—" If possible, she blushed harder. "I am not—ready—as my mother told me a wife must always be."

Oh. Both of us hid our faces by patting Thief. "I see." In spite of all my efforts, my voice wobbled. Nothing Aunt Kupo taught me as a child prepared me for this.

But my time as a captive had.

I straightened away from Thief. "His man part tears into your woman parts?"

She reared up to stare at me. "Of course not, he is kindness itself. But I experience—discomfort."

What could help? I thought again of how my captors had used my body. Olive oil, perhaps? I thought a moment longer. "Talk to him."

"Talk to him about what we are doing? Oh, I couldn't, I couldn't ever—" Hycania covered her mouth with both hands.

"Not about—that. Talk to him about his day, about yours. Get him to talk to you." If I'd tried to do that with my captors, I'd have gotten a fist to the jaw, but Tobiath wasn't an outlaw. "Show him who you are, what you think and feel. Get him to reveal the person he is, as well." *Learn to know each other. Become a person to him.*

Her full lips quivered into an almost smile. "Thank you. I'll try."

"And have a saucer of olive oil beside the bed."

Hycania frowned. "Why? We'd have eaten long before."

"In case you need—" Never had I found it so difficult to speak briskly. "To ease things along."

"To ease—oh." Her giggle burst out, high and sweet. "Yes, I see." Then she leaned toward Thief. "Now. Tell me about your dog."

THE CARAVAN FOLK set up a fire pit near the spring. That evening I carried my food stuffs and kitchen things to it. Even laden with goods, I strolled along. I hadn't moved so freely since the outlaws had dragged me from the alley with a filthy sack over my head. Not since my days in the garden with Aunt Kupo.

Would I ever see her again? *Only if Father's men find me.* Thief whined at my heels as I hunched forward to hold in a sob.

When I walked forward again, my legs moved as if I ploughed through knee-deep sand. At the fire, Tobiath lifted both hands in greeting, only for his smile to fade. "You're sweating. Are you all right?" Before I could answer, he gestured to two of the camel drivers. "Help with her things."

"Let me." The camel driver, whose flea bites I'd first treated, shouldered aside the other men. "Don't trouble yourselves, I'll do it." His lean face reminded me of someone—who? It lit with a smile as he scooped the jars and pans out of my hands. "Here you go, lady."

"Th-thank you." *Don't be an idiot. He's no danger.* I fought to unfreeze my locked joints from his nearness. Healing a man was different from having him loom toward me. Clutch my body with his arms. Breathe over me— then I realized who the camel puller reminded me of, and gasped. Uncle Achior. His leanness, the powerful scent of animals, even the unexpected sweetness of his smile.

Tobiath stared at me, his brows lowered. "What's amiss?"

I forced myself to move. "N-nothing. Not a thing. It just occurred to me I've been rude. I made myself smile at my helper. "What's your name?"

My face and neck felt hot. Why hadn't I asked the camel driver his name when I helped him earlier? Why hadn't I asked every one of them their names? Camel drivers were people, too. Not furnishings. Not stone.

He dipped his head. "Ehud."

"I thank you, Ehud."

Grinning, Ehud withdrew from the fire.

As he did, Hycania joined us from within the tent. "Oh, no need for you to cook." She turned to her husband. "Surely Sarah can join us in our meals while we stay here?"

"Of course, my dear."

She sank down beside him in a flutter of embroidered robes. "Tell me about your day, husband." She slanted an anxious glance at me when Tobiath just gaped at her. "What's the best thing that happened to you today?"

"Well—I suppose—" He glanced around the oasis. "This place. I've always liked this oasis, small as it is."

Hycania nodded.

Go on. She said nothing, just peered from her husband to me.

"Why?" I asked.

Tobiath blinked. "I suppose because it's so small. So unexpected, like a jewel discovered in a sack of grain."

I jerked my chin at Hycania. *Go on, say something.*

"That's why I like it here, too. Part of the reason." She smiled at me.

He loosed a mighty laugh. "Let me change my mind. My favorite part of the day was having my flea bites seen to."

"Yes. Yes indeed." Ehud strode out of the shadows to flop down opposite Tobiath, who leaned across to clap the camel driver on the shoulder.

Hycania glanced from Ehud to her husband, and her brows drew tight.

Maybe talk with the whole group might ease talk together when they returned to their tent? Leaning toward Ehud, I said, "So your bites are better?"

"So much better! Look." He pulled aside his sleeve to show me.

Tobiath bared his bites for his young wife's inspection. "See how they've improved?"

Hycania stroked a gentle finger beside the fading bumps. "Yes, husband. I do." She slipped a glance my way, then dimpled up at him. "I do indeed."

THE CARAVAN STAYED two more days. Two days with people and fires all around us. Thief no longer braced when someone else moved. On their last evening in the oasis Tobiath edged up to me, voice low. "It seems I—won't need that—" He peeked over his shoulder at Ehud and the other camel drivers. "That—ointment after all."

Good for you, Hycania. "That's wonderful."

In the flickering light of the fire, Tobiath's face reddened. "Thank you for all your help."

Had Hycania told him of my suggestion to her? Surely not.

He hastened to say, "With the flea bites."

I bent my head. "Of course."

THE NEXT MORNING Hycania joined me at breakfast. "Thank you for all your help. I can never repay you." She ducked her head, then met her husband's adoring gaze across the fire pit. "Before we pack up to leave, we want you to go through our goods and take all that you need. Anything you desire, it's yours."

Anything? "You're too kind—"

"Not at all." She shook her head so briskly her curly hair almost tumbled out of its confinement.

Tobiath joined us. "Please, do as my wife bids. And I swear to you, in every village and town we visit, we'll praise your knowledge and skill."

"We'll tell them where you live and send them to you." Hycania hugged me. "And I'll bless your name every night," she whispered.

"Think nothing of it," I murmured.

"Everyone in the desert should know where to find such a fine healer." Ehud crossed to us.

He assumes I'll live here always.

"Not just us, you healed that man with the cut leg."

"Please." Hycania clasped my hands in her soft ones. "You helped us. Let us help you. It is no bother for us to spread word about you. To direct people to where you are."

If I remain here, Balaam will always know just where to find me.

A healer, Tobiath and Ehud had called me. The caravan could see to it I had a steady flow of sick people, injured people, worried people, coming to me for aid. "Yes, thank you." I bowed to Hycania, and fought not to skip in place. *This is what Aunt Kupo trained me to do.*

"The first thing—" Tobiath gestured to Ehud, who bent and retrieved a roll of goat-hair fabric. Grinning, Ehud dropped it at my feet. "Your tent."

"I don't have a—" A tent. To sleep on my own, inside a shelter. Then I understood and wheeled to face Tobiath. "You can't give me a tent. It's too much."

"No." Hycania embraced me. "It's not. Every time you sleep in its shelter, know my husband and I thank you." She stepped back. "Now choose all else you need. Go on." She nudged me toward their goods.

"Don't you need the tent?"

"That tent dates back to an earlier time, when the caravan was larger. We no longer need it, but you do."

But—a caravan tent. "It'll be too big for me alone." Thief joined me, and my fingers knotted in his fur.

"Not at all." Laughter edged Hycania's voice. "A room for sleeping, a room for eating, and a room at the front of the tent where you'll heal the people we send you." She turned to the camel pullers, clapped her hands. "Set it up for her."

Ehud and the others got to work at once.

"No, please—you don't have to do that."

"Nonsense, you can't raise such a big tent by yourself." Hycania laughed at the thought.

"I still think it's far too big for me alone."

Tobiath raised his brows. "Who says you'll always be on your own?

Hycania nestled closer to him with a happy sigh.

Her husband gestured at their goods, his free arm around her. "You've work to do, too. Please, Sarah. Choose."

"It's too much." I stepped back and trod on Thief's paw. He yelped and shot off to lick it.

Ehud paused, his arms full of tent. "After those nights we spent itching? Giving you everything in the caravan wouldn't be enough."

To my surprise Tobiath nodded. "Don't think of them as gifts, think of them as payment. You're a skilled healer. Take what you've earned."

What I've earned. How would Aunt Kupo respond?

Hycania jerked her chin toward the well-built fire pit. "I saw what you used to prepare your meals." She swiveled to Ehud and the others as they finished setting up the tent. "Spread the kitchen wares out for her to make her choice."

With much jingling of pottery, the men set a dizzying number of pots, platters and eating dishes out on a blanket. I stared at the shining plates. "There's only one of me. How could I ever eat off so much?"

Tobiath and Hycania laughed. He touched her cheek. "If nothing else, we pass this way a few times each season. Take the plates and so on. We'll help you eat off them when we visit."

Aunt Kupo's voice sounded so clearly in my ear, I almost turned to embrace her. *You share with me, I share with you.*

Where to begin? Then I noticed a soup pot, glazed a rich cobalt. But—such a large pot? *I can keep it simmering for days. Add things to it so it always tastes different.*

"Your favorite color, yes?" Hycania set the cobalt pot to one side of the blanket. With care, I selected six plates, then straightened. She shook her head and nudged me toward the pottery again. "More."

Only when my selected stack stood ten plates high did she allow me to turn away. She stood close beside me, cheeks dimpled, a cobalt robe over each arm. Two plain robes of undyed cloth draped each of Tobiath's arms as well.

"So many?"

Hycania shook her head, dark curls dancing. "You need plain robes for rough work, when you don't want to stain a fine robe." She edged closer to murmur, "Just think of us, as I will of you every night when my husband and I—talk before sleep."

Clean robes. I gathered them close. "Yes, please." At the longing in my own voice, I took a half step back. "I mean, thank you for your kindness." Then I smiled at the camel pullers. "Thank all of you."

Hycania's laughter filled the oasis. "You're not done yet." With Tobiath at my other elbow, they led me to their supply of chickpeas, olive oil and so on. "Take all you need."

"Your personal store, no, I couldn't—"

Tobiath stepped behind me, preventing retreat. "We insist."

CHAPTER THIRTY-THREE

I STARED AFTER THE CARAVAN as it dwindled into the distance. At last I could no longer tell the camels from the horses. Tied once more to a tree, Rock loosed a whinny. *Come back, my friends, come back.*

I tried to hug his warm neck, but Rock jostled his quarters and sent me back a pace. *Alone. Alone. Why am I fated to remain alone?*

Rock whinnied again.

I sobbed. "Oh, Rock, I miss them, too."

Another horse answered him close behind me, and Thief barked a warning. I whirled, already certain who I'd face from the brassy note of the other horse's voice. Midnight. Balaam.

Midnight jigged into the oasis, head tossing from his rider's tight hold on the reins. Balaam's brows creased. "Why is this tent still here? I watched the caravan leave."

"They gave it to me and set it up before they left."

"Such a large tent for one girl? How stupid."

For one girl alone. Alone with—him. I stiffened taller. "No, how generous of them. Now I have a room to sleep in, a room to eat in, and a room for meeting with patients."

"Oh. Well." Balaam scanned the oasis. Shrugged. "Let's go in, then." He hopped down from Midnight, hobbled him. "You will see to my wound in there." He headed for the entrance.

Go into a tent with this man? *Never again.* I didn't move. "You haven't had treatment for several days. I need to stay out here, in case I need to heat a compress."

He swung round to face me with a scowl. "I don't need another poultice."

"That's for me to decide." Could he see my body swaying in time with the bang of my heartbeat? I sank down near the fire pit. "Come here."

He stayed in place a moment or two, then sighed, drooped, and did as I said. "Very well."

I wiped off the old layer of ointment from the pink line of new flesh and left off the bandage. "There." I stood without haste, though I longed to bolt away from him, screaming.

"That's all?"

"You're healing well. You can go." *Go now.*

"I don't need to come back?" He stayed motionless.

With difficulty, I kept my voice level. "No."

"Oh. Well. Good." He turned to leave, then paused to swivel back to face me.

Oh no, oh no. Now it's coming, his vengeance. Only now, after I helped him grow strong again.

"But—I'll tell others about you. Though, of course—" He leaned closer and almost smiled. "I don't talk to many people."

Now Arseen and Sanipu are gone. "Of course." *Not in your line of work.*

He shook his robe so it went sliding down his long legs, lean and seamed with scars. "Even so. Even so, sometimes I meet men with need of healing. I'll send them to you."

Wonderful. A stream of bandits, rapists and killers. Should I thank him? *Please go.*

Still he hesitated. "I've no way to pay you."

"You—" As if he could ever repay me for my stolen innocence.

"For healing my wound." His eyebrows angled. "If I get hurt again, I'll come back."

Oh joy, I might see him again.

When I said nothing, he jerked a nod. "You've nothing to fear from me. We're—level." Then he wheeled away at long last. Moments later Midnight galloped away.

And don't come back.

ONLY LONG AFTER Midnight had vanished over the horizon did I stop to wonder. Why did I still bear so much hostility toward him? Yes, he'd stolen my innocence. Beaten me. But because of him, I not only knew how to care for myself, I had shown myself to be a healer to the caravan, who would spread my name across Ammon. This part of it, anyway.

Like Balaam said, we were level.

No, my resentment held a deeper meaning. I prowled into my spacious tent, into the coolness of its shade. Perhaps—perhaps Balaam served as a horrible reminder. I killed Arseen. Sanipu. Meant to kill Balaam himself. *He reminds me that I'm a killer.*

I sagged to the ground, sand abrading my knees through my robe, but I couldn't bring myself to make the effort to shift onto the rug an armspan away. All the other choices I could've made surged through me. I could've asked the villagers for help. Asked them to seek out a priest and other men of power and justice.

I curled in on myself, weeping. *If only I'd never abused the power Aunt Kupo taught me, turned the power and wisdom to heal into the power to kill. To murder.*

Thief belly-crawled toward me, whining, and pressed himself onto my lap.

"Oh, Thief. Thief—" I hugged him, rocking while I wept. My tears sparkled on his fur. He dug his head into my bosom at first, then twisted to lap the tears from my chin. My sobs finally faded.

Balaam lived. He lived with a whole, sound leg because of me, because of all my beloved aunt had taught me. "That balances, not just him and me, but myself with myself." I'd believe so, anyway.

As the sun set, I heated water over the fire. In the healing room of my tent I let the warm water soothe my aching eyes and heart. I dipped the clean rag again and again, smoothed it over myself until my fingers wrinkled. First I slipped a plain robe over my head, only to peel it off again and try on one of the fancier robes.

I looked down at myself, but could get no sense of the fit. When I raised my arms, the robe didn't pinch or bind across my bosom, though the sleeves trailed a bit too long. Did I look like a fine lady? I chuckled. A fine lady, alone in her oasis. A laugh snorted out of me. *I'll never be a fine lady.* I'd spent too much time with dirt under my fingernails.

What about now? Did I look like the daughter of a wealthy house? If Father's men saw me, would they spot me more easily? With a gasp, I tugged the robe off over my head and hurled it into the shadows of the room.

Don't be silly. No one can see. I folded the robe and stacked it with the others, fumbled around until I found the plain robe I'd rejected earlier and slipped into it. Out by the kitchen area, Thief yelped.

Balaam returned? No, Thief would growl, not yip. I edged to the tent entrance and peered into the night. Once my eyes adjusted to the dimness, I caught a flurry of movement over by my kitchen area near the fire. Thief was whining and digging at the base of one of the big storage urns.

What the—? Oh. That urn held dried meat. "Thief, stop that."

At my approach, Thief dug harder, sand fountaining behind him. The urn toppled and he scooted to scrabble at the stopper.

"Thief, leave it." I tugged him away from the urn. "I. Said. Leave. It."

Though I hadn't pulled him hard enough to hurt him, Thief yelped and cringed.

"What's wrong with—you're bored, aren't you. You miss all the people, the activity." Dropping beside him, I hugged as much of him onto my lap as I could, pushed my face into his fur. "I do, too, Thief. I do, too."

CHAPTER THIRTY-FOUR

L ATE ON THE THIRD DAY AFTER THE CARAVAN LEFT, a woman's voice called my name. Thief stiffened beside me on the rug in the tent's front room. "Easy, Thief." My fingers knotted in his ruff to keep him still. I raised my voice. "Who's there?"

"Good, you're home." An old woman shuffled through the tent entrance. "I didn't walk all this way for nothing. You're Sarah, the healer?"

"Yes." *Sarah the healer.* "How may I help you?"

She limped closer. "My joints ache. Tobiath's caravan said you're a gifted healer. Can you help me?"

When I released Thief he moved over to her, every muscle tensed. "Thief. Friend." Then I gestured toward the cushions my caravan friends had left me. "Please, sit."

"Would that I could." She winced.

Thief looked between us, seemed to notice my smile of welcome, and dropped to the ground, head on his forepaws.

I prepared some peppermint tea, with some dried leaves for her to take home as well. "Did you walk all the way here? Where do you live?"

She leaned on the walking stick that was nearly as thin as she was. "I started after breakfast, took it in easy stages." Pause. "My son knows I'm here, of course."

"What?" My pestle slowed in my mortar. Another gift from Hycania.

"Don't want you to think my menfolk don't know where I am. What I'm doing. They know and approve." She sipped tea. "Should reach home in time to prepare the evening meal."

"That's good." I sifted the crumbled herb into a small pot. "Make a tea with these leaves. Drink it as often as you can, and alternate hot and cold compresses on your sore joints."

"Thank you, I will." She dropped a coin in my hand and left the oasis.

OVER THE NEXT WEEK, more people came to me for help. A married couple with a child who had a skin rash. A man with an infected thumb. A mother who'd left her son at home with a fever. In the second week, I had two or three patients a day. Most mentioned Tobiath, a few of the women said Hycania had sent them, and one gruff man told me Ehud recommended me.

At first Thief whined or growled at every newcomer. Soon he ignored them, only perking his ears at the sound of the coins healed patients dropped into the big bowl by the entrance.

As I watched the mother of the sick child hurry away, I sighed and dropped to my knees to hug Thief. Once Midnight was all the company I had. Why weren't Rock and Thief enough for me now? Why did it only make me lonelier to watch my patients walk away?

I crossed to a salt bush the other side of the spring. On the far side, I nestled to dig. When I dropped the coin into my hidden treasure sack, it startled me to see how much fuller the sack was than on the day I'd taken it from my captors' tent.

My fingers chilled and closed around the mouth of the sack. I could never grow so callous again, kill when I—perhaps—didn't need to kill. Why had I never considered giving the men something in their food that would send them to sleep, so I could escape?

Because of me, Arseen could never consider his own choices, make better ones. Because of me, Sanipu would never know how wrong he was. Because of me—Balaam lived. He lived, and maybe, just maybe, lived more aware of the possibilities in life.

Now I tugged open my sack for a better look. Fingers trembling, I counted my earnings, then plopped to the ground. *I'm a healer in a way Aunt Kupo never achieved.*

The next day no one came to me for help. As the sun set, air cooling toward nightfall, Rock crashed out of a patch of brush, ears rigid, while Thief launched out from under a tree, barking.

"What is it?" I paused from grinding chickpeas to stroke his neck. Then I saw the long stream of riders approaching. *Good, another caravan*—No camels? Rock's shoulder twitched under my suddenly cold palm.

The lead rider booted his mount into a slice of fading sunlight. My father.

CHAPTER THIRTY-FIVE

THE MEN SWEPT INTO THE OASIS. *Mount Rock. Gallop off. Escape.* But I couldn't uproot from the sand, couldn't draw breath to call my horse. Thief crouched flat and whimpered.

Beard jutted, Father yanked Desert to a jagged halt right in front of me. Sand sprayed up to sting my face and hands. "Seize the girl's horse." His voice reached every edge of the oasis.

One of the men dismounted and grasped Rock's forelock, dragged him away. Thief clicked his jaws at the man, then slunk behind me with a yip when my father's man lashed out at him.

My father laughed.

Curse you. Curse you all. Should I order my dog to attack? How? Which man? How I longed to see Thief rip out my father's throat. Then I sagged. They'd cut my dog down before he got his teeth in an ankle, never mind a throat.

Father sat high above me on Desert. "Bind her hands and legs for the trip home."

Home? This was my home. A half dozen men gathered around me, rope at the ready.

My father swung down from his stallion and stalked closer.

"You'll marry as soon as your bridegroom wishes it. He will no doubt punish you for the delay, for the trouble you've caused us, but—" The blow split my lip. Blood poured down my chin.

Snarling, Thief leapt out from behind my skirts to launch straight for Father's throat. *Yes.* Father cuffed him out of the air, then kicked him aside. Thief yelped. Father kicked him again, and he crawled away.

"Thief! No!" I stumbled toward my dog, but before I took more than a step a half dozen hands gripped my arms, my shoulders. One especially raspy pair grabbed me by the throat.

I twisted out of the men's hold. "Stop it, he's only trying to protect me."

"Protect. You." My father halted in mid-pursuit of my dog to study me, brows low. "It is the job of your family's men to protect you, not some scroungy cur."

Behind me I heard Thief whimpering. Would he follow us all the way to my father's house? Whine for me outside the walls? How long before he gave up, wandered away? Became feral once more.

Off to one side I glimpsed Rock touching muzzles with one of the men's mares. She tossed her head, squealed, skipped back to touch nostrils with Rock again. Would my father's men sling me on my own horse for the return, or leave him here?

"I told you to bind her. Secure her." Father flicked a hand at me, and one of the men stepped forward.

Useless to fight, even if I knew how. But I could speak. "Wait."

Father's nostrils pinched. "And gag her."

I dodged back. "You want the income a bridegroom would bring into the family."

"Income?" Father's jaw hardened enough to grind chickpeas against. "A dowry costs me money, insolent girl."

One of his men tried to stuff a wad of cloth into my mouth. I jerked my head aside. "A bridegroom would bring money to our family over the years. Wouldn't you rather have that money now?"

The words burst from me.

"That makes no sense. Bind her, I said." He chopped a hand at the men surrounding me.

I veered away. "You want the money my bridegroom would bring over the years. The business his relatives and associates would give you. I'm offering you that money now, in one lump."

"Hush, you shameless—" Father lost momentum. "How could a mere girl get enough money to pay me? Me?"

Balaam, Sanipu and Arseen will pay it. Have already paid. If I said so, Father might realize I'd lost all value as a bride and have his men cut my throat at once. "Healers earn money. Aunt Kupo taught me well."

"Kupo." A derisive noise in his throat. "She died soon after you ran off."

The oasis vanished, and the waste beyond. Everything disappeared except Father's face. From the tilt of his lips, the slant of his brows, I knew. He'd killed her. Beaten her to death, or—

"She died in her sleep." He turned aside for a moment, but not before I glimpsed his scowl of frustration, as if her escape upset him as much as mine.

My legs melted beneath me. Calloused hands gripped my elbows.

I stiffened my knees. Took a deep breath. "Release me."

The men drew back automatically.

Father glared. "Don't obey her. Throw her on a horse."

Now I did what I'd never done. Took one long step toward Father, head high so he could see my eyes. "It's not like you to fail to take an opportunity to make money."

"There's no treasure here." He gestured around the oasis, at my tent.

"Leave your riches out for everyone to steal, do you?"

He scowled but didn't answer as I knelt on trembling legs for my treasure. To one side of us Rock was still making friends with the other horse. How I longed to fling my arms around his neck. Howl. *Aunt Kupo, Aunt Kupo.*

Later. Later I'd grieve for my beloved aunt. Would I grieve here in my oasis, or locked in my childhood room? I lugged up the heavy sack.

Father's voice whipped out. "What's in there, dirt? Grubbing in the dirt. My sister's legacy to you."

Your only legacy is hatred, Father. Pity flooded me. How sad he must be. How lonely. And he didn't even realize it.

A snap of his fingers. "Get on with it, girl."

Girl.

Father. My captors. The same. Broken creatures. Bullying others in an attempt to make themselves feel whole. Attempts that would never succeed.

"Here." I flung the sack at his feet. "This is Aunt Kupo's legacy to me." A few jewels fell at his feet. "Take it and ride away."

"So much?" His mouth gaped. Bent over the treasure, he darted a look up at me. "Why would you give it to me?"

"It's not a gift. It's my price. My bride price."

All the men in the oasis stirred, like trees shaken by the wind. Father took a coin in one hand. A jewel winked red in the other.

"Take it and ride away. Leave. Me. Alone." My tongue wanted to stick to the roof of my mouth, but I managed to shape the words. To stand tall and keep my eyes leveled on him.

Father straightened, jaw clamped. Over his shoulder, one of the men put a hand to his mouth. Not at the sight of so much wealth. No—the thought leapt from his mind to mine. What if Father took the treasure, and still forced me to go with him? Forced me to marry, enduring the attentions of a man older than his own father had been?

My shoulders drooped. Did I dare retreat into my tent? No, he might take that as insolence, burst into his usual rage, then beat me to death.

The silence stretched into mid-winter, or seemed to. Then the treasure sack clinked as my father hefted it. "Mount up, men."

One of them shuffled toward me, rope in hand, but Father whirled to hack the air with one hand. "No. Leave this worthless baggage to her fate. I said mount up."

Feet and hooves scuffled in sand, moved away. Rock whinnied shrilly, and I hurried to hold him still before he followed the other horses. Only my fingers in his rough mane kept me upright. In the distance, I heard the clash of my treasure as it banged against Father's thigh. Every coin I'd earned—one way or the other.

Well, thanks to Hycania and Tobiath, I had food, shelter, the means to care for myself while I earned more. Thanks to Aunt Kupo, I had the knowledge—

Aunt Kupo, Aunt Kupo. My hand sagged from Rock's mane. I crawled inside to curl on the healing room rug. *She's dead. Dead. I'll never see her again.* While sobs shook me, Thief crawled against me, belly and throat up. *I deserted you. I'm sorry.*

"Thief. Thief." I hugged him tight, tears spattering his fur.

My dog wriggled until he could bump my hand with his cold nose. When I didn't pat him, only hugged him tighter, he whined and craned to lick my face as warm air gusted over my back.

What? Warm air? I hunched around to find Rock had edged into the tent and stood beside the rug. I knelt up to loop one arm around his neck. My horse lowered his head and pressed it the length of my body.

"We're together." I pushed my wet face against his cheek. "Together and free."

CHAPTER THIRTY-SIX

WITH **T**HIEF **CUDDLED CLOSE,** and Rock's soft breath coasting over me, I drifted into sleep. Normally I would've huddled into my cloak against the night-time chill, but I slept until a night bird's cries sent me flailing upright. Was my father returning? Had he decided he might as well take me, and my treasure as well?

No way to dismantle my tent and gather all my household goods. Nowhere to run away and hide. Thief sprang up at my sharp movement, only to curl beside me again a moment later. Behind me, Rock shifted his weight, dozing on his feet.

My animals are at peace. There's no one here.

Footsteps crunching sand woke me soon before dawn. This time Thief bounced toward the tent entrance, yapping.

Father?

I longed to cover my face, to huddle as small as possible on the rug. Instead I forced myself to my feet, smoothed my crumpled robe, and stalked outside. A man I'd never seen before hesitated by the fire pit, roughly bandaged hand held out to me.

"Are you the healer?"

"That's right." Thief's ruff rippled in time with his growls. I caught him, made him sit. "Quiet, Thief. Friend. Who sent you? Tobiath?" No, this man looked too rough to know the merchant, much less his demure wife. "Ehud?"

The man shook his head. "Balaam told me about you. After I—I hurt myself."

Well, at least I knew what kind of wound to expect. "Take off that bandage and let's see what you've done to yourself." *And I hope you take that hint and don't tell me what you and Balaam were doing. Who you robbed.*

I cleaned, salved, and re-bandaged the sword cut without asking the outlaw's name. Without speaking to him beyond quiet instructions. After I finished, he tossed me a coin. Walked away with mumbled thanks.

Only after he was gone did I feel the trembling that shook me to my bones. Did I dare stay in the oasis? Father could choose to return at any time and seize me. Force me to return to his house. Force me to marry. Or one of Balaam's acquaintances might take issue with my treatment of him, or realize I lived alone. Molest me. Kill me.

But if I left the oasis, how would I earn my living? I stood to pace, robe threshing about my knees. I'd have to leave my tent. My urns of food. The herbs Hycania had insisted Tobiath give me. I couldn't carry all of it alone.

Thief whined. I dropped to clutch him tight. "I can't, Thief. I can't go back to that rootless life again."

FOR THE TENTH TIME since breakfast, I caught myself watching the horizon for my father and his men. I hadn't managed a single bite.

Now Rock bustled up beside me, ears hard forward, nostrils flared. *Someone's coming.*

Squinting at the horizon, I saw a dust cloud spiraling up at the skyline. Father and his men? A gang of Balaam's associates, on the way to me for healing—or to abuse the woman alone in an oasis?

Could be someone ordinary in need of healing. Or strangers who didn't even know of me, on their way to someplace else.

None of my patients had ridden horses or camels since the caravan had left, except Balaam.

Rock skittered in a tight circle and grunted out a whinny. One hip jostled me. I dodged aside, but couldn't make myself retreat to the tent. From inside I couldn't see who came for me. If anyone did. *Maybe they have nothing to do with me. Maybe they'll ride past.*

But the dust cloud drew ever nearer, aimed straight for my oasis. I glimpsed multiple horses at its source. Four—no, three riders. I dodged to my well-stocked kitchen and grabbed a knife. My father would never take me—

What did I expect to do, kill them? Kill myself? No. I shuddered and dropped the knife from nerveless fingers. *No. Wait. Wait and see who it is.* Thief joined me, tail rigid. Something flashed red around the neck of one of the riders. A moment later, blue sparkled on a second rider's breast.

Women. Two women and a man.

I stooped for the knife. Returned it to my kitchen. By the time I re-joined Rock and Thief, the riders had drawn close enough for me to see details. Two well-dressed women draped with jewelry, accompanied by a man in a simple brown cloak, mounted on a horse with the same delicate head and slender legs as theirs. A husband? A guard? He must be their guard, since he kept behind them a couple of strides.

As they rode closer, the guard's thickset figure and heavy features grew clearer. The women slowed their horses, a dainty chestnut with a blaze and a dun with mane and tail shades darker than his coat, to walk into the oasis.

"You are Sarah." The woman on the chestnut didn't ask so much as tell me.

I longed to contradict her, but just nodded.

The guard slid off his brown mount to take the reins of the other horses. The women dismounted and started for my tent in the same motion. Hycania told us of you," said the speaker as she strode away from her dun. "Let us see if you can help my mother. She suffers unbearable fluctuations of hot and cold, no matter the weather."

Now I could see the similar curling line of hair on their foreheads, the firm set to their chins and lips. "You can tie the horses to the trees—"

"My husband will see to the beasts." The mother passed me without glancing back at him.

Her husband? I turned to study the man I'd taken for a guard. His mouth wobbled into a shaky smile.

I returned the smile. "Surely you don't want to stand in the wind holding the horses? Even with the sun it's chilly today—"

"Healer, we're waiting." The daughter's voice lashed out of my tent.

"Please join us in the healing room, out of the wind—

"Healer." Mother and daughter yelled together.

I'd already run two steps when I realized their tone echoed my captors'. I stopped. Tucked my hands in the ends of the opposite sleeves. Paced forward. When I entered the tent, mother and daughter stood shoulder to shoulder, with identical sour expressions.

Just inside the entrance, I halted. "That's correct. I'm the healer. Not yours to command." *Like your husband.* "You want my help. The relief I can provide. Please treat me with respect."

The daughter took one hard step toward me. "Or what?"

"Or you can leave right now."

The daughter's mouth squared. "No one talks to me like that. No one." She spun in a circle, hands flapping the air, halted facing me. "No one ever has."

I stayed silent.

"Come, mother, we're leaving." She stomped past me.

But the mother studied me a moment. Shook her head. "No. I want what she has to give."

The daughter's robes whipped against my legs when she whirled. "Nonsense, we'll find another healer. Come."

Still the mother shook her head. "When? Where? I want help today. There's not another healer anywhere. We've searched." She sank to the rug.

"Very well." I joined her. "When you feel these fluctuations, you can use sage—"

The daughter's chin thrust out. "They aren't fluctuations, they're unbearable. What can you do for severe symptoms?"

Severe. "In that case, I'd recommend lavender or marigold—" Then I paused. She had yelled at me. Someone had shouted at me, ordered me about—or tried. And I'd stood up to her without a thought. Without hesitation.

Without fear.

While I quietly described what the mother could do to ease her agony, inside I skipped and sang.

EPILOGUE

THE FULL MOON CAME AND WENT. Often visitors to my camp approached without my knowing anything about it until they arrived. Thief grew used to strangers, though he never let anyone touch him but me. Since none of my patients owned, much less rode, a horse, Rock ignored them. Occasionally someone jogged in on a donkey or mule, but my gelding didn't acknowledge such creatures.

So the evening he whirled to face the dusk with a high-pitched whinny, I froze over the dirty dinner dishes. "What is it, Rock?" *Who is it?*

Now I heard the drum of hooves gallop closer. Father? No—only one set of hooves, not the horde my father would bring. But why would a patient approach at such a pace? Ah—one of Balaam's associates, perhaps?

Only when the horse swept into the oasis and the rider flung himself off in a whirl of robes did I recognize Ehud. All his teeth showed in a grin.

"Tobiath let me borrow a horse that I might reach you sooner with the good news. He wants you to ride with the caravan for the next season, maybe more."

"But why—?" Ah. "Hycania's with child?"

His grin gleamed in the dusk. "Yes."

"But—my patients. How will they find me?"

He held out his hands to me. For an instant, I thought of what Tamar would say if a camel puller dared to touch her. Thought of what my father would do if he saw. *I am no longer a fine lady. I'm a healer.* I laughed aloud, then stopped. "But I thought Tobiath didn't approve of dogs in the caravan?"

Ehud laughed too. "Not now that Hycania persuaded him to let her get a puppy, and the little creature is thriving."

He stepped closer to me, and held out both hands to wait for me to take hold of. "I worried about your patients finding you, too. Then I realized. Travel with us and word will spread. You can help people in need where ever we stop, people who could never travel to see you else. And your regular patients can find you easily enough when we're in their area." A short, sharp burst of laughter. "A caravan is always greeted with joy. How more so if we bring a healer with us? A good healer." His hands tightened. "The best."

My hands went lax in his. *I can help those I'd never see otherwise. People sick unto death. People who might die without me.*

He glanced around the oasis, and his hands squeezed mine again. "And visions of you here alone would no longer haunt me."

Our laughter mingled. "I'll start to pack."

Reluctantly, he released me. "What first?" He looked at my tent. "That's too big for us by ourselves."

He meant to help me? A man meant to help me? "You don't have to help me, Ehud."

"I know." This time his smile came slow and gentle as the dawn. "Let's begin." As he headed for my firepit, Thief came out of the brush at the edge of the spring. My dog's tail flickered.

Ehud bent to pat both thighs. "There's my friend. Come, Thief."

My dog leapt to greet him. So did I.

Acknowledgments

Thanks to Rita Cammarano for the seed of the idea for this novel; to Clint Ackerman for assistance with language use, as well as cover ideas; to Mike Pasley for his excellent feedback; to Cate Peace for beta reading and sharp editing; to Bridget MaryMartha Simpson for her enthusiastic support; to Nancy Moise Haws for several suggestions that strengthened the story; and to JJ Haws for his good humor.

ABOUT THE AUTHOR

LESLIE MOÏSE EARNED HER PH.D. in 19th Century British Literature at the University of Louisiana at Lafayette. Pearlsong Press has published her knitting memoir, *Love is the Thread*, and her prize-winning historical novel, *Judith*. R. C. Linnell Publishing published her poetry chapbook, *Linked by the Joy of Words*.

DR. MOÏSE IS PROGRAM POET for Bench Talk, a weekly radio show about new discoveries in science aired on Forward Radio. She is currently drafting an historical novel about 14th Century anchorite Julian of Norwich, the first woman to write a book in English. Dr. Moise is also revising *Selkie Song*, a young adult fantasy novel.

About Pearlsong Press

P**EARLSONG** P**RESS** is an independent publishing company dedicated to providing books and resources that entertain while expanding perspectives on the self and the world. The company was founded by psychologist Peggy Elam, Ph.D.

FICTION

If We Were Snowflakes—YA novel by Barbara D'Souza
Heretics: A Love Story & *The Singing of Swans*—
novels about the divine feminine by Mary Saracino
Judith—an historical novel by Leslie Moïse
Fatropolis—paranormal adventure by Tracey L. Thompson
The Falstaff Vampire Files, Bride of the Living Dead, Larger Than Death, Large Target, At Large & *A Ton of Trouble*—paranormal adventure, romantic comedy & Josephine Fuller mysteries by Lynne Murray
The Season of Lost Children—a novel by Karen Blomain
Fallen Embers & *Blowing Embers*—Books 1 & 2 of The Embers Series, paranormal romance by Lauri J Owen
The Program & *The Fat Lady Sings*—suspense & YA novels by Charlie Lovett
Syd Arthur—a novel by Ellen Frankel
Measure By Measure—a romantic romp with the fabulously fat by Rebecca Fox & William Sherman
FatLand & *FatLand: The Early Days*—Books 1 & 2 of The FatLand Trilogy by Frannie Zellman

ROMANCE NOVELS & SHORT STORIES FEATURING BIG BEAUTIFUL HEROINES

by Pat Ballard, the Queen of Rubenesque Romances:
Once Upon Another Time | *Adam & Evelyn* | *ASAP Nanny* | *Dangerous Love* | *The Best Man* | *Abigail's Revenge* | *Dangerous Curves Ahead: Short Stories* | *Wanted: One Groom* | *Nobody's Perfect* | *His Brother's Child*
A Worthy Heir
by Rebecca Brock—*The Giving Season*